D0037696

WITHDRAWN

WOLF PACK

TITLES BY C. J. BOX

THE JOE PICKETT NOVELS

The Disappeared
Vicious Circle
Off the Grid
Endangered
Stone Cold
Breaking Point
Force of Nature
Cold Wind
Nowhere to Run
Below Zero
Blood Trail
Free Fire
In Plain Sight
Out of Range
Trophy Hunt
Winterkill
Savage Run
Open Season

THE STAND-ALONE NOVELS

Paradise Valley
Badlands
The Highway
Back of Beyond
Three Weeks to Say Goodbye
Blue Heaven

SHORT FICTION

Shots Fired: Stories from Joe Pickett Country

WOLF PACK

A JOE PICKETT NOVEL

C.J.BOX

G. P. PUTNAM'S SONS
New York

PUTNAM

G. P. PUTNAM'S SONS
Publishers Since 1838
An imprint of Penguin Random House LLC
penguinrandomhouse.com

Copyright © 2019 by C. J. Box
Penguin supports copyright. Copyright fuels creativity, encourages diverse
voices, promotes free speech, and creates a vibrant culture. Thank you for
buying an authorized edition of this book and for complying with copyright
laws by not reproducing, scanning, or distributing any part of it in any form
without permission. You are supporting writers and allowing Penguin to
continue to publish books for every reader.

Library of Congress Cataloging-in-Publication Data

Names: Box, C. J., author.
Title: Wolf Pack: a Joe Pickett novel / C. J. Box.
Description: New York: G. P. Putnam's Sons, 2019. | Series: Joe Pickett
Identifiers: LCCN 2018049554 | ISBN 9780525538196 (hardcover) |
ISBN 9780525538202 (epub)
Subjects: | GSAFD: Suspense fiction.
Classification: LCC PS3552.O87658 W65 2019 | DDC 813/.54—dc23
LC record available at https://lccn.loc.gov/2018049554
p.   cm.

Printed in the United States of America
1 3 5 7 9 10 8 6 4 2

BOOK DESIGN BY KATY RIEGEL

For Jeremy Barnes,
a true hero

And to Laurie,
always

WOLF PACK

THURSDAY, APRIL 26

There's a whining at the threshold—
There's a scratching at the floor—
To work! To work! In Heaven's name!
The wolf is at the door!

CHARLOTTE PERKINS GILMAN,
"THE WOLF AT THE DOOR"

CHAPTER ONE

FOR WYOMING GAME WARDEN Katelyn Hamm, April really was the cruelest month. And this year was turning out to be the worst one of all.

And that was even before she got her pickup stuck eight miles from the highway.

It was the last week of the month and she was in the middle of what was known as shed war season. Bull elk and big mule deer shed their antlers throughout the winter, and now the war was heating up due to the low snowpack and the antlers' high price.

Shed war season was why she'd been grinding her green four-wheel-drive Ford F-150 through sagebrush, snowdrifts, and rock formations in the high foothills of the western slope of the Bighorn Mountains. Gnarled ancient cedars stood as sentinels among the granite formations towering on both sides, and she'd tried to keep her front tires in a set of untracked but snow-packed ruts meandering up and through the rough country toward the mountains.

Her destination had been a set of high, vast meadows just below the tree line of the mountains. Those meadows were designated as critical elk and deer winter range, and her aerial surveys two months earlier had revealed thousands of both. The elk liked to descend by the hundreds from the shadowed low timber to feed in the open on the meadows at night where the wind swept the benches clean of snow. Hundreds of mule deer moved up from draws and arroyos to do the same thing.

Now the meadows were littered with forty-pound elk antlers and heavy-beam deer antlers, the sharp tines and tips emerging from the snow as it melted, so new they glinted in the sun.

There were two ways to get to the winter range from the highway. One was a moderately developed gravel two-track five miles to the south. That route was officially closed during the winter months and marked by signs warning against entry. But antler poachers were resourceful. They drove around the gate closure and shot up the signs.

The other way to the high meadows was the rough, obscure two-track path that Katelyn had chosen to take. It wound up through the rock formations and cedars and ended on a high promontory that would give her a sweeping view of the meadows and anyone who might be in them.

For antler hunters, the western slope was a treasure trove.

For Katelyn Hamm, it was where she got her pickup stuck.

THE FRONT WHEELS had dropped into a deep but narrow erosion ditch that crossed the road. She hadn't seen the depth of the hazard because it had been covered by a long, narrow snowdrift that started in a copse of sagebrush and extended forty feet beyond in a crusty frozen wave. The impact was hard enough when the tires dropped that a cascade of ticket books and topo maps showered down on her from where they'd been secured by a rubber band around the sun visor. Her chin hurt because she'd smacked it on the steering wheel.

It happened, getting stuck in the middle of nowhere, and it occurred more frequently than any game warden would admit. The key was to figure out how they could free their vehicles without having to call for help, or worse, being photographed. Each year, the Wyoming Game Warden Foundation dinner featured a special PowerPoint presentation of game wardens stuck in their vehicles. It elicited lots of guffaws. Katelyn wanted to be one of the laughers, not the laughees.

She tried to rock the truck forward and back, hoping the tires would grind through the snow and grab a bite of dirt that would launch her out. But the more she rocked, the deeper the tires dug in.

Katelyn struggled into her parka inside the cab and jammed a green Stormy Kromer wool cap on her head, then tucked her auburn hair into the collar of her coat so the cold winter wind wouldn't whip her eyes with it. The hem of the parka gathered over the grip of her holstered .40 Glock.

She grimaced as she circled the vehicle, and not just from the wind. The tires were deep in the ditch and the front bumper was perched on the edge of it. The friction of her spinning front tires had glazed the snow and melted it down enough that they spun freely and could grip nothing.

In the gear box in the bed of her unit, she had two shovels, one with a sharp blade and the other squared off, and she could try to start digging, but the ground was still frozen solid. It might take her hours.

She could call dispatch and request a tow truck from town, eighteen miles away, but that would take hours as well, provided the driver could even find her in such a remote location, GPS coordinates or not. And would he have a phone or camera to document her situation? Of course he would.

"Well, damn," she said to herself. The wind whipped her words away.

SHE'D HEARD too many times that there weren't actually four seasons in the Rocky Mountains, but three: summer, winter, and mud. That was true enough, though there was the possibility of snow at elevation every month of the year. What that canard didn't account for was that no matter what the weather, the conditions, and snowpack, she still had hard calendar dates she had to consider in order to do her job.

There was a rhythm to it. Hunting season openers started with archery in the early fall through the last rifle seasons in December. Herd classification assessments of elk, deer, and pronghorn antelope took place in December and January. Checking up on local licensed trappers in the deep winter took her through late March, and checking fishing licenses lasted all summer. Interspersed throughout were mandated reports for headquarters in Cheyenne, regional training days in Cody, and various assistance requests not only from other game wardens but from local law enforcement, state troopers, and investigators.

Shed war season had become more exciting since the price for elk antlers had gone up to around fifteen dollars per pound, and mule deer antlers up to ten to twelve dollars. That meant a set from a mature bull could fetch up to six hundred dollars from the "antler man" when he came to town. Deer antlers fetched two hundred to four hundred dollars a set and were later sold to furniture makers, accessory manufacturers, and Asian buyers who ground up the material into powder and sold it as an aphrodisiac.

In a district where oil and gas activity was slowly coming back but still not out of the bust years, antler hunting could almost make a guy rich.

"Antler season" on the winter range opened on May 1, which meant antler hunters could legally spread out over the mountains and wintering grounds en masse to scoop up whatever they could find. It would be a free-for-all, filling flatbed trailers with sheds and overflowing pickup beds.

Unfortunately, some miscreants tried to beat the legal opening day and the other antler hunters. They'd try to sneak onto the meadows as soon as the snow receded enough that they could get there and back, despite the locked gate and the posted signs. Katelyn knew it had been happening for years, and she was determined to patrol the meadows by truck and catch the poachers.

Big-game animals were weak and stressed in the winter, especially in the last months before the grass pushed through the snow and the herds dispersed on their own. Antler hunters ran them off the meadows prematurely and sometimes spooked the herds away from their winter feed. It was cruel. Katelyn supported proper hunting ethics and was outraged at needless wildlife deaths.

SHE STUDIED the landscape around her and made a plan. Anything, she thought, to avoid calling for that tow truck.

A lone cedar tree twisted up from the shale about sixty feet from the front bumper of her pickup. Welded on that bumper was an electric winch with a tight spool of rusting cable and a hook on the end. She'd never used it and she hoped it worked.

The tree itself wasn't massive, but it was obvious it had been there a long time. Cedar trees didn't grow fast in Wyoming, but they had to be tough to withstand the wind, weather, and lack of rain. She'd pull out the cable, loop it around the trunk, and hope like hell that the winch motor worked and had enough torque.

Katelyn circled the tree and confirmed that it looked stout enough to serve as an anchor. Then, after a quick look around and with the wind at her back, she unbuckled her jeans and squatted to urinate. She hated going outside in the cold, but she had no choice. She'd drunk too much coffee that morning and there were no public restrooms for miles.

While she strained to finish quickly, she heard a hum in the sky. The sound was at a different frequency from the wind— lower and more steady. Then it was gone.

She rose and searched the sky while she fastened her trousers.

Empty landscape and wind sometimes combined to ferry far-away sounds over long distances. There'd been times when she'd clearly heard snippets of conversations from people too far away to see.

Maybe a low-flying plane or a piece of machinery?

Katelyn chalked it up to the quirkiness of her surroundings and got back to work.

SHE LOCATED the remote control for the winch in a grocery bag behind the seat of her pickup and plugged it into the outlet, then toggled the switch. The spool turned, spitting the hook out from the motor so it looked like it was sticking out its tongue.

It took ten minutes for her to feed out enough cable to reach the tree. The steel line coiled in front of her pickup and stained the snow orange from powdered rust.

Pushing aside stiff branches, she looped the cable around the lower trunk near the base of the cedar and secured the hook.

She moved to the side as far as the cord to the control would allow and gently activated the winch until the cable began to tighten. That way, if the line broke, it wouldn't whip back and injure her.

Then she heard the hum again and paused. This time, it emanated from somewhere over her shoulder—from the direction of the mountains.

She turned and the remote control slipped from her hands as she saw what was coming: a ragged column of sixty to eighty mule deer pouring over the summit of the hill. They were like molten gray lava, grouped closely together and flowing down the hillside in a wild panic.

Unlike elk, deer didn't bunch up in large herds unless they were migrating. This was more than unusual.

Their alarm was palpable as they scrambled down through the rocks and brush. A few lost their footing and fell. Others tumbled over the injured deer on the ground. But they kept coming. She couldn't tell the bucks from the large does because the males had dropped their antlers and they'd not yet regrown.

The animals didn't see her until they were a little more than a hundred yards away, but the sight of her didn't stop them. Instead, they started an arc to the right up the hillside and into heavier brush. She could hear branches snap and dislodged rocks tumble down the incline. She witnessed several more deer drop away and lay down, too exhausted to continue.

Then she saw the aircraft as it rose over the horizon. At first she thought it was a distant helicopter. But it wasn't distant. It was a drone, white against the pale blue sky.

The drone swung back and forth behind the fleeing deer, swooping down at times so close that it almost lit on their backs. It was remarkably quick as it shot through the air behind them.

The deer were being driven.

Katelyn was furious.

BY THE TIME she pulled the shotgun out from behind the seat and jacked a shell into the chamber—her intent was to blast the drone out of the sky—the aircraft had backed off and risen straight up out of range. The hum receded.

"Come back!" she shouted.

But the drone froze in place, high enough that the camera mounted on it could view the havoc it had created below and too far from her location either to identify or blow up.

She wondered if the operator was zooming the camera lens in on her standing there next to her disabled pickup. If so, Katelyn tossed her right glove to the side and gave it an emphatic middle finger.

The response of the drone was to swing from side to side as if laughing.

So she shot at it anyway, hoping that at least one of the buckshot pellets would fly high enough to do some damage. But the drone didn't waver. Instead, it slowly backed away and climbed higher.

It vanished out of her sight over the top of the hill. The hum receded until all she could hear was the wind.

She cursed the fact that she couldn't chase it until her pickup was freed.

AFTER WINCHING the truck out of the ditch and feeding the cable back onto the spool, Katelyn climbed into her vehicle and roared up the hill, hoping to get a visual on the drone operator before he fled. She almost got stuck again in a deep snowdrift, but she was able to downshift into four-wheel-drive low and grind through it. Thirty more yards and she'd be on top.

The view on the summit was what she remembered it to be. On top was a windswept flat pocked by burls of exposed granite. Beyond that was a steep descent—too steep to drive down. Fortunately, from her location she could see for miles along the western slope of the mountains.

But there was no other vehicle down there, or any tire tracks. Only a trail of injured and weakened deer, most of them fawns. And a pair of coyotes slinking out of the timber to finish them off.

She was flummoxed. Was it possible for someone to pilot a drone from so far away that they couldn't be seen?

Then, through the distant dark timber of the western slope, she saw a glimpse of a reflection of sun on metal. It vanished as quickly as it had appeared.

There was another quick flash as the vehicle ascended the mountainside, but the woods were too thick to make it out.

She knew there were old logging roads over there, and no doubt whoever had piloted the craft had retrieved it and was now getting away. There was no chance that she could get down the hillside and over the meadows in time.

SHE SPENT the next hour photographing the carnage and killing wounded animals that would never recover in their winter-weakened state. It was disgusting work, and she was enraged at whomever had piloted the drone.

What kind of sick mind would do such a thing? They'd been responsible for the deaths of dozens of animals.

She thought about what her next steps would be. She knew very little about drones except that they were illegal to hunt or scout with. Were they registered somewhere? Was there a way of figuring out who had them and when they flew?

All she knew was that the vehicle she'd spotted was headed away toward the top of the mountains and likely over the top, which was the demarcation line of her game warden district.

Katelyn's area of responsibility was nearly two thousand square miles on the western side of the Bighorn Mountains. Its name derived from the tiny mountain town of Shell, Wyoming.

The district to the east was the Saddlestring District.

It was managed by a game warden named Joe Pickett, who had recently gotten his job back.

CHAPTER TWO

AT THE SAME TIME, eighty miles to the east, Joe
leaned into the lens of a Bushnell spotting scope attached to the
open driver's-side window of his pickup. He carefully dialed the
focus knob until he could look at a big arroyo in sharp detail.
His new green pickup was parked in a pocket of aspen on the
hillside just below the county road that continued into the national forest. From that vantage point—one he had used countless times over the years—he could scope the lower ends of the
breaklands in his district and get a clear view of the deep red
draws that knifed through the foothills of the Bighorns.

These were the draws favored by local trappers hoping to
catch bobcats, red foxes, and raccoons. Occasionally, a mountain lion would stumble into the traps, and even more occasionally a coyote or deer. But bobcats were the primary target, and
they were surprisingly vulnerable. Stupid, even.

———————

IT WAS A CLEAR, cool day in mud season. Rivulets of snowmelt coursed down the hillside from big drifts still caught in the shade of the trees. The dirt roads he'd used that morning were slick with mud, and his tires were coated with a full inch of it all the way around. It was still a long way from summer, but he could almost see it from there.

Some of the species of wildlife Joe had encountered on his drive into the mountains were beginning to display springlike behavior. He'd noted three doe pronghorn antelope in different settings standing alone in the sagebrush as if they'd been expelled from their herds. Two froze in place and watched him go by with worried eyes, and the third ran away, looking back at him over her shoulder, as if imploring him to follow.

He knew that the lone does were likely scouting locations to give birth in a few weeks. If he came back later and approached them, he'd likely find a tiny fawn—or twins, which was common with pronghorn—curled up at the base of a brush. The mother pronghorns stood guard until their babies could keep up with them—and the instant family unit would rejoin the herd.

Pronghorn fawns fascinated Joe. When born, they were fully formed but miniature versions of the adult antelope. Within a week of birth, they could run just as fast—pronghorns were the second fastest land animal on earth, after cheetahs—and cover almost the same distance as mature animals.

He'd noted the sightings on his Wildlife Observation Form,

known by game wardens and biologists as a WOF, pronounced "woof."

A PRIME WESTERN bobcat pelt, unlike its eastern cousin, was fetching three hundred to five hundred dollars in the current fur market. In the last few winters, the bobcat population had boomed. Which meant the number of trappers had boomed as well.

Joe liked it better when the prices were down, not because he disapproved of legitimate trappers, or had an excess of affection for predators. But when fur prices were low, fewer amateur trappers ventured out into the foothills and mountains. There was nothing wrong with amateur trappers, either, but too many of them lost interest in their sets if they didn't produce quickly enough, and their traps went unchecked long after the seventy-two-hour requirement in the regulations. Or, worse, the traps were left out for months, and that meant many animals suffered cruel and unnecessary deaths: predators, deer, antelope, pets out for a walk.

So when he'd received a call the previous evening from a local trapper reporting that someone had littered an arroyo with leg-hold traps and left them unattended for a month after trapping season had ended, Joe had responded the next day.

"Failure to check" violations were serious and could result in ten days in jail, a thousand-dollar fine, and six years' revocation of a trapping permit if the judge chose to throw the book at the violator. And that didn't include the additional violations of trapping out of season and wanton destruction of wildlife if dead or maimed animals had been left in the traps.

GAME WARDENS PERFORMED an odd dance with local trappers during the season. Trappers needed to purchase a furbearing animal trapping permit and obey all the rules and regulations, but they weren't required to reveal where they set their traps. Therefore, in order to enforce the laws in their district, game wardens had to refrain from asking the trappers directly where they were set up and spend days trying to figure out each individual trapper's grounds by using their knowledge and skills and following clues.

As Joe scoped the arroyo, he noted irregularities that would likely be missed by casual observers. The weathered old log on the sloping wall of the draw looked out of place. Trappers wired their traps to branches or lengths of logs so they'd serve as drags if an animal tried to pull away.

A pile of vertical brush looking like a miniature tipi on the floor of the arroyo had an opening at its base. Joe recognized it as a "cubby set." Bobcats were preternaturally curious animals, and they were drawn to oddities and would check them out before proceeding on their way. Joe speculated that inside the cubby set he would find an open can of sardines or a dismembered rabbit, sure to lure a bobcat inside without it noticing the trap covered by loose dirt or sticks.

Farther up the draw, a slight movement caught Joe's eye and he adjusted the spotting scope. A single feather hung by a lanyard in the arroyo wall. It twisted slightly in the breeze. A passing bobcat would have to check it out and maybe even take a swat at it. Of course, the leg-hold trap was set in the gravel just below it.

It didn't appear that any animals had been caught and left to suffer and die. Joe was grateful for that.

"Yup," Joe said aloud.

Daisy, the yellow Labrador, lifted her head in response from where she was curled up on the truck seat. She stared at him with unblinking eyes.

"We've got us an illegal trapper," he explained.

After a beat, she lowered her muzzle back between her out-stretched front paws.

"You could pretend you're excited, you know."

She sighed. Daisy seemed to know that she'd be left inside the pickup while he went to work. Joe had no intention of seeing her get trapped, either.

HE UNCLAMPED the spotting scope and returned it to its case while he surveyed the landscape below. He could now pick out a set of ATV tracks through the sagebrush that he hadn't noticed earlier. That's how the trapper had accessed the mouth of the arroyo, and no doubt the route he'd use when he came back. Eventually.

So instead of taking his truck down there and leaving tracks of his own, Joe decided to walk in. He didn't want the violator to know he'd been there. Joe intended to photograph the sets, trigger and confiscate the traps, and set up a spare trail camera that would, he hoped, capture an image so he could identify the rogue trapper when he finally came back to retrieve his hardware.

Then Joe would throw the book at him.

HE SAT BACK and smiled to himself. He was inordinately happy to respond to such a mundane trapping complaint, even though the reporting party certainly wouldn't have thought it was routine or frivolous.

For Joe, he was simply pleased to get up in the morning, pull on his red uniform shirt with the pronghorn antelope patch on the sleeve, pin on his badge and nameplate, clamp on his worn gray Stetson, climb into his pickup, and drive into the mountains of his district.

Three and a half months of being on indefinite leave without pay from the Game and Fish Department had been a kind of nightmare for Joe, his wife Marybeth, and their three daughters.

His troubles had begun when Governor Colter Allen had sent him hundreds of miles south to Saratoga to investigate the disappearance of a well-known British woman executive after she'd departed from a high-end guest ranch. Everything about the case had gone sidewise, and Allen had ordered his chief of staff, Connor Hanlon, to fire Joe and announce it with a press release.

That's when ex-governor Spencer Rulon had stepped in and offered to serve as his lawyer. Joe could never have predicted that fourteen weeks later he'd have his job and district back, all of his back pay plus a substantial raise, his badge number restored, and a brand-new Ford F-150 pickup to replace the one he'd damaged.

Or that Governor Allen would be distracted while he fought for his political life in Cheyenne.

It felt good to be back to work again.

THE FOOTING ON the hill was loose and muddy and he didn't want to leave telltale boot prints, so he stepped from sagebrush to sagebrush on the way down. He'd pulled an empty daypack over his shoulders to use for confiscating the traps. As he reached the bottom, his cell phone vibrated in his breast pocket. Joe paused and fished it out. The screen showed that the call was from Katelyn Hamm, who managed the Shell district on the other side of the mountains.

Joe didn't know her well, but he'd talked with her over the phone a few times and had helped her out once when she had to enter a remote elk camp and arrest a belligerent for hunting under the influence. Katelyn was younger than Joe, married, with two children in elementary school. From what he could discern, she was serious, professional, and a hard worker. She was, he thought, a credit to the job. There were fifty game wardens in the entire state. Of those, only four were women.

He answered, "Joe Pickett."

"Joe . . ." The rest of her sentence faded away, except for the phrase "your side of the mountain."

Joe looked at his phone. Cell service was sometimes poor to nonexistent in certain places of his district and this appeared to be one of them.

He raised his phone and said, "I'll call you back when I get a signal." But he wasn't sure if she could even hear him.

JOE DISCOVERED HE'D been wrong about the violator not causing any damage. Around an elbow of the arroyo wall was the mutilated dead body of a big male bobcat. Clamped on its right rear leg was an exposed steel trap with its chain secured to a length of wood. The carcass had been there for at least a week, and ravens had plucked out its eyes and had begun feeding on its flesh.

Another violation had been added to the list.

He whispered a curse and photographed the violation before he bent down to remove the trap. Legitimate trappers were required to attach an identifying plate or sticker to each set, but Joe didn't expect to find one.

Surprisingly, he did.

It read:

> Tom Kinnison
> 2204 Elkhorn Dr.
> Winchester, WY

Joe was reminded once again that ninety-nine times out of a hundred, common criminals were not the brightest people. It was as if a burglar had left his business card on the kitchen table of the house he'd just looted.

He didn't know Kinnison and hadn't heard his name before, but now he knew where to find him. There would be no need to set up his trail cam or worry about not leaving tracks.

Of course, there was a very remote possibility that someone had stolen Kinnison's traps and set them out in the arroyo. That didn't seem credible, because Kinnison would have reported the missing property, and Joe would have been alerted through local law enforcement channels to keep an eye out for them.

No, he concluded, *I've got my illegal trapper.*

WEIGHTED DOWN BY ten steel traps in his daypack, Joe climbed the hillside back to his pickup, slipping once and falling and covering his left side with mud. He tossed the pack into the bed of his truck, wiped the worst of the mud off his clothing with an old towel from his gear box, and climbed into the cab.

Daisy wouldn't even turn her head to look at him.

"Don't worry," he said. "I'll let you out to run around when we find a cell signal."

As he started the engine and climbed on the two-track toward Hazelton Road, Joe keyed the microphone and raised the dispatcher in Cheyenne. The connection was poor, but it improved as he drove.

"This is GF-18. I need you to run a name for priors," he asked after the usual pleasantries. He spelled the name and cradled the mic in his lap while the dispatcher searched the law enforcement database.

Several minutes later, she came back.

"GF-18, we have no record of that individual."

That puzzled Joe. "Nothing?"

"Nothing. I tried Tom Kinnison, Thomas Kinnison, T. Kinnison, and just Kinnison in Winchester. No hits at all."

Which was unusual. Joe had learned over the years that game violations by an individual were usually just one rotten branch of a crime-filled tree. Men who flaunted wildlife regulations almost always had a rap sheet consisting of other crimes: DUI, moving violations, trespassing, breaking and entering, illegal drugs, on and on.

Plus, it was Joe's theory that committing wildlife violations signaled a general disregard for law in particular and civilization in general. The theory had been borne out time after time in his career. *Show me a poacher*, he'd once told Marybeth, *and I'll show you a career criminal.*

"Maybe he bought a trapping permit?" Joe asked.

That search concluded much more quickly.

"Affirmative," she said. "Tom Kinnison of Winchester purchased a trapping permit online January 10 of this year. There's no record of any other hunting or fishing licenses."

Also curious. He couldn't recall ever encountering a trapper who wasn't also a hunter or a fisher, and Joe had met nearly all of them in the area multiple times. Because a bobcat pelt fell under a federal regulation intended to combat the international market for illegal fur trading, it was necessary for local authorities to verify that the pelt was legally obtained by issuing a CITES (Convention on International Trade in Endangered Species) tag for each properly harvested animal.

"How many years does he say he's been a resident?"

"Fourteen."

Joe was puzzled. Winchester was a small mountain town twenty miles west of Saddlestring. He'd been there many times since he'd taken over his district, and he'd never heard of a long-time resident?

"Can you please email me his trapping permit?" Joe asked. The application would include Kinnison's age, height, weight, driver's license number, and hair and eye color.

If the man had lied on his application about being a Wyoming resident for fourteen years, there would be additional criminal charges to add to his rapidly growing list of violations.

So who was this guy?

THREE BARS OF cell service appeared on Joe's phone screen at the top of the mountain as he neared the paved highway. His intention was to return Hamm's call first, then check in with Marybeth. Marybeth was the director of the Twelve Sleep County Library, and as such she knew more about her patrons in Saddlestring and Winchester than anyone else Joe could think of. Perhaps she knew something about Tom Kinnison. And if she didn't, she probably knew someone who did.

Then Joe would pay a visit to the man.

But before he could proceed, his phone lit up with an incoming call. It was from Herman Klein, a third-generation rancher with a cow/calf operation on Spring Creek. It was strange that Klein had called Joe directly because Joe couldn't remember ever giving him his private number. In the past, when elk had been in Klein's hay meadow and needed shooing, or hunters had trespassed on his land, the rancher had called dispatch in Cheyenne.

"Joe Pickett."

"Joe," Klein said, "I got your number from the Forest Service fella in Bozeman."

Joe could only think of one U.S. Forest Service "fella" in Bozeman.

Courtney Lockwood administered the Federal Task Force on Wolf Reintroduction (FTFWR) for the tristate region—Idaho, Montana, and Wyoming. His area of responsibility included more than 328,000 miles and spread over two time zones, so you'd assume that Lockwood would be out of his office quite a lot. But he'd never known the man to leave his desk.

Lockwood was frequently quoted in the press on questions regarding the controversies of wolf management and their conflict with livestock and wild game. In Lockwood's view, the wolves that had been placed by the federal government into Yellowstone Park rarely ventured outside the park boundaries, and concerns about the predators roaming into other parts of the state were overblown and hysterical.

Although the wolves had been officially "de-listed" from federal control outside Yellowstone and the management of them had been turned over to the state in recent years, confusion reigned in the minds of hunters and ranchers over who had jurisdiction of which wolf packs and whether there would be fines and jail terms associated with killing the animals.

"What's up, Herman? How can I help you?"

"Well, I'll tell you," Klein said. "I know these wolves are federal and not a state deal. I know that. But I'm sick and tired of calling Courtney up there to tell him that there are wolves on my ranch, and a couple of them have killed my heifers."

"They have?"

"Well, not according to Courtney," Klein groused. "According to Courtney, there are no wolves around here."

Joe nodded. He'd heard of sightings as well and could vouch for the fact that on more than one occasion he himself had seen a lone black wolf. He couldn't swear that it had been the same alpha male each time, but it had *seemed* like the same one. That the wolf had appeared to him when Joe was injured, lost, or confused was something he couldn't logically explain to anyone.

Klein continued. "Courtney tells me they can't be wolves that harassed and killed my cows. He says it had to have been coyotes, mountain lions, or bears. He says none of them damned Yellowstone wolves have wandered off into this part of the state. To which I say bullshit."

In the background, Joe heard Klein's wife hiss, "Herman! Watch your language."

"Change that to 'bullcrap,'" Klein said.

"Gotcha. So what can I do for you, Herman?" Joe asked.

"Come right away and bring your camera."

"Do you see wolves right now?"

"Not only do I see one," Klein said, "I roped the son of a bitch and put it in my stock trailer. I need you to come here and verify it's a damned wolf. Courtney doesn't believe me, but maybe he'll believe *you*."

Joe raised his eyebrows. "There's a wolf in your stock trailer?"

"Goddamn right."

Klein's wife warned him about his language again.

Joe didn't want to tell Klein that new wolf management rules meant that the rancher had the right to "shoot on sight" outside of the specially designated wolf habitat area the state had negotiated with the feds.

"I'll be there within the hour," Joe said, and disconnected the call.

Herman Klein's ranch was en route to Winchester and he could stop along the way.

KATELYN HAMM ANSWERED on the second ring.

"Sorry about earlier," Joe said.

"Don't worry about it. It happens to me all the time. Just a sec—I need to pull over. There's a dead spot on the highway ahead and I don't want to lose you again."

Joe waited.

When she came back on the line, she asked, "Are you aware of anyone who likes to fly drones over in your district? We're talking big drones, expensive ones."

He said, "I've seen a couple of hipsters in the city park flying them around, but they looked more like toys than serious hardware. Why?"

"Somebody from over your direction used a drone to spook a big herd of mule deer off the winter pasture today. There's seven or eight mule deer that got panicked and injured and I had to put them down. I couldn't get a visual on the vehicle the drone guys used, but they were headed your direction when I saw it last."

"Antler hunters?"

"I don't think so. I think they were harassing mulies for kicks. It really makes me mad. Our deer numbers are down and I hate to see someone stress the ones that are here by air that way. Have you ever heard of such a thing?"

"Nope."

Joe had limited experience with drones apart from a military drone that had once been unleashed in the mountains by a rogue operator. Hunting or scouting with the aircraft was illegal, but he'd heard stories about their use in other states.

Katelyn said, "I got my shotgun out and I wanted to blast that thing right out of the sky, but it didn't get close enough. Don't tell anyone, though."

"I won't."

"Do you think it's your hipsters?"

"I kind of doubt it," Joe said. "The guys I saw looked like they were pretty small-time. Don't drone pilots have to register with someone like the FAA?"

"Hell if I know," she said. "I think so, but I've got to research it. I'll let you know what I find out—especially if there are some registered drone pilots over in Saddlestring."

"I'd be curious to find out if there are."

"Well," she said, "in the meantime, you might want to keep your eyes out. If you run across anyone playing around with big commercial drones, please let me know."

"I'll do that."

There was a pause. She said, "I'm sorry, I didn't even say welcome back."

"Thank you."

"I won't even pretend to understand everything that went down in Cheyenne," she said, "but I'm glad you're back where you belong. You're kind of a legend to a lot of us, you know. We look up to you."

Joe blushed and he was glad she couldn't see him driving his pickup while caked with mud.

MARYBETH SAID, "Tom Kinnison. How do you spell that?"

"K-I-N-N-I-S-O-N."

"Never heard of him, but I'll ask around."

Joe pictured her sitting in her chair in the office behind the checkout counter of the old brick Carnegie structure. She had blond hair, green eyes, and was using the businesslike tone she employed when her staff was close enough to overhear her on the phone.

Joe said, "Maybe you could check to see if he's one of your customers. Maybe he checked out a *Fur Trapping for Dummies* book."

She sighed with faux annoyance. "I'm sorry, we don't divulge what books our patrons check out to law enforcement or anyone else. If you want to know that kind of information, you need to show up with a warrant from Judge Hewitt."

Joe smiled. That *definitely* meant she was being overheard.

"Maybe I will," he lied.

"It wouldn't hurt if you spent a little more time in the library, you know."

She was being playful and he liked it.

Her voice hushed. "You are going to be home for dinner tonight, right? It's kind of a big deal for Lucy."

Lucy was their youngest daughter, and her eighteenth birthday was the next day. She was a senior at Saddlestring High School, a reluctant prom queen, lead actress in the last musical, and in many ways the wisest of all of his daughters because she'd spent years observing her older sisters, twenty-year-old April and twenty-two-year-old Sheridan. She'd learned from their mistakes.

Lucy was keenly aware of what went on around her and she was especially mindful of the intricacies and nuances of relationships—even Joe and Marybeth's. When the subject of a birthday dinner had been broached, Lucy had said she didn't want to hurt their feelings, but with her going off to the University of Wyoming in the fall and her boyfriend, Justin, going into the navy soon, the two of them wanted to spend as much time as possible together while they still could. Justin, she said, had asked to take her to the new Italian restaurant in Saddlestring and it would cost him a fortune.

Joe liked Justin as much as he did any of the boys his girls had gone out with, which is to say he'd preferred they not go out with any of them.

So the plan was changed, and the birthday dinner with her parents would now take place the night before her actual birthday.

"I'll be home."

"Good."

"I've got to see a wolf in a trailer and roust a bad trapper in Winchester. *Then* I'll be home."

It didn't need to be said between them how many times he'd gotten wrapped up in a case and had been late.

"*A wolf in a trailer?*" Marybeth said.

"I'll explain later."

"Okay, but try to be on time. Lucy plans to go out with her friends later tonight. She's a popular kid."

"I won't be late."

"Who knows? Maybe you'll get lucky if you play your cards right."

Then she hung up before he could respond. Which was good, because he was speechless.

Joe shook his head and whistled. His first day back on the job was more exciting than he'd thought it would be.

CHAPTER THREE

HERMAN KLEIN and his wife, Paula, lived in an aging white single-story clapboard home four miles from Bighorn Road. The ranch headquarters was easily identified because it was located within a mature grove of cottonwood trees on the west bank of Spring Creek, which had started to swell and roar with early-spring runoff.

Farm equipment and old pickups were scattered throughout the property, and a half-dozen black angus cows stood in a corral adjacent to the barn.

The Kleins lived alone and operated their ranch by themselves, although during busy times Herman employed itinerant cowboys who drifted through. Joe knew the couple had two sons and a daughter who had left for more exciting pursuits in other places, and he wondered what would happen to the place when the Kleins could no longer run it.

Joe noted the rusted stock trailer parked alongside a big outbuilding that was sided with corrugated steel.

As he rolled into the ranch yard, the inevitable pack of mismatched dogs boiled out from where they'd been sleeping. They surrounded his pickup, jumping, barking, and braying—but stayed far enough away from the vehicle that there was no danger of him running any of them over.

Daisy leaped up and placed her front paws on the top of the dashboard and barked back at them until Joe told her to stop it.

When he parked and looked up, he saw Herman Klein step out onto his front porch and wave. He had white whiskers, clear blue eyes, and stooped shoulders. He was wearing knee-high Muck boots and pulling on a worn khaki Carhartt parka and a dented black cowboy hat.

Paula Klein looked on from the kitchen window while nervously drying her hands with a dish towel.

Klein chinned toward the stock trailer and Joe climbed out of his pickup and followed. The ranch dogs bounced around him, but parted so he could walk through.

"Bring your camera?" Klein called out.

Joe patted the phone in his pocket to indicate he had.

"This way," Klein said.

The old rancher had a pronounced limp and Joe caught up with him in a few strides. Klein had once been a champion calf roper and team roper and, like all old rodeo cowboys Joe had met, he still suffered from his injuries.

"There were four of them in the south pasture," Klein said. "May have been more up in the trees, but I didn't see them."

"How exactly did you do it?" Joe asked.

"With a rope."

Joe chuckled.

"I saddled up my old gelding and took off after them," Klein said. "I can hardly walk these days, but I can still ride. I got the last one of the pack—roped him around the neck. I was going for a heel, but I missed. Then I dragged him back here and put him in the trailer and called you."

Team ropers were either "headers"—ropers who threw their lassos around the heads of running cattle—or "heelers," who caught the back foot.

"Take a look," Klein said.

Joe stepped on the fender of the old stock trailer and pulled himself up to look through the opening.

A big gray wolf sat back on its haunches in the far corner of the trailer. Although "gray" was the species, this particular animal was mottled brown and pewter with a white muzzle. It still had its thick winter coat, which made it look even larger than it actually was.

The wolf stared straight back at Joe without flinching. Its eyes were piercing and he felt an involuntary chill roll down his back.

Like the eyes of raptors flown by his falconer friend Nate Romanowski, wolf eyes showed no fear of humans. In fact, they hinted at contempt.

"He's a big one," Joe said. "I'd guess a hundred and twenty pounds."

It wasn't until Joe fished his phone out to take a few photos that he noticed there was a big bowl of water on the trailer floor as well as a bucket of what looked like dry dog food.

When he climbed back down, he said to Klein, "Yup. You roped a wolf."

"Send those to Courtney, would you?" Klein asked.

"I will."

Joe hesitated for a moment before saying, "I'm surprised you didn't shoot it."

Klein shook his head. "I don't have anything against wolves except when they kill my cows. This pack was just passing through. Despite what Courtney and his ilk think, not all of us dumb ranchers just blast away at the sight of his precious wolves.

"I just want him and his pals to admit that their wolves range a lot farther than they'll admit. And now we've got proof, don't we?"

"Yup. So what are you going to do with it?"

Klein nodded toward the cloud-shrouded mountains that dominated the western horizon. "I'll drive him up there and let him loose. Maybe he'll be smart enough to hightail it back to the park. But if he decides to come back and chase my cows . . ." The rancher finished his sentence by forming a pistol with his gnarled right hand and dry-firing it into the side of the trailer.

"Gotcha," Joe said.

"I'M IMPRESSED," Joe said as they walked back toward the ranch house and Joe's pickup. "That was some pretty good roping."

"No one was more surprised than me that I could still do it,"

Klein said with a smile. "Do you have time for a cup of coffee or a beer?"

"Maybe next time," Joe said. "I appreciate the offer."

"Well, damn," Klein said as he stopped in his tracks. "You got a brand-new truck."

"Yup."

It was a sore subject with Joe, because he held the record within the department for destruction of state property, and by a large margin. And that didn't count his state-owned home that had burned down on Bighorn Road.

"I heard you got a new house, too," Klein said.

"Yup. Marybeth really likes it."

The week before, they'd moved from a temporary town house in Saddlestring to a ten-year-old, three-bedroom, two-bath house on the east bank of the Twelve Sleep River. It was five miles from town and came with five acres, a barn for Joe and Marybeth's horses, and a workshop and garage big enough to accommodate their vehicles as well as the equipment he'd been issued for his job: a snowmobile, an ATV, and a drift boat. Joe looked forward to assembling his fly rod and walking down to the river to fish for trout when the runoff calmed down and the water cleared up.

The home was larger and more modern than the one they'd left on Bighorn Road, which Marybeth found ironic. Two of their three daughters were gone and Lucy was only months away from going to college herself. They could have used the extra room while all their girls were growing up. Now, she said, they had a bigger empty nest.

Although she still said she had plans to go into another line of work, Sheridan had been promoted to head wrangler at the Silver Creek Ranch near Saratoga, and April was finishing up her last year of college at Northwest Community College in Powell.

"Well, we're glad to have you back," Klein said. "Some of us were worried they'd assign some knucklehead to the valley."

Joe paused at his truck and turned and leaned back against it. "Thank you."

"Hell of a mess in Cheyenne, isn't it?"

"Yup."

"I wish we could get Governor Rulon back instead of this yahoo. Even though he's a damned Democrat."

Joe didn't comment. In his experience, character wasn't relegated to any particular political party over the other. There were knuckleheads on both sides of the aisle, and he made it a point to keep his head down, do his job, and stay out of the fray.

DURING THE ADMINISTRATIVE hearing before the Game and Fish Commission on Joe's firing, ex-governor Rulon had served as his lawyer pro bono.

Colter Allen's chief of staff, Connor Hanlon, had led off the proceeding by reading statutory language that stated the governor was well within his purview to let go any state employee whom he wished to let go at any time that he chose. He accused Joe of insubordination, incompetence, and, of course, listed his long record of damaging state vehicles.

Lisa Greene-Dempsey, the director of the department, had chosen not to appear at the hearing, which was a statement in itself.

After stating the governor's position, Hanlon had sat on a chair in the corner of the room with hooded eyes and a smirk. He'd refused to look over at Joe.

Rulon spoke next and quickly acknowledged that the current chief executive had the right to fire any game warden he chose to fire, but he insinuated that the governor had sacked his client not because of malfeasance but to pay back a political favor he owed. As it happened, it was to Joe's own mother-in-law: Missy Vankueren Hand of Jackson Hole. There was no love lost there.

"Not only that," Rulon had said, "but as we travel down the path of Governor Allen's true motivations in this action, we just might turn up some facts and long-buried allegations that my successor might just as rather have remain buried."

Joe noted that Hanlon had begun furiously tapping a text message to someone on his phone.

What Joe didn't know was that an hour before the hearing, a post had appeared on Facebook from a thirty-two-year-old married woman claiming that Allen had sexually assaulted her fifteen years ago, when she was seventeen. She'd written that she was visiting her uncle and aunt who worked on his Big Piney ranch, and while she hadn't told her relatives about it or called the local authorities, she'd informed scores of friends about what had happened and they could vouch for her story. At the time, she'd been scared of what he might do to her and her family if she went public.

And she ended the post with three words and a hashtag:

There are others. #MeToo

Joe had been pleased and surprised when Hanlon suddenly stood up at the hearing and interrupted Rulon and stated that Governor Allen no longer wanted to pursue the matter.

Then Hanlon walked quickly out of the room, clutching his phone.

A lot had happened since that day:

- Governor Allen had strongly denied the allegations, but immediately bunkered himself in his office and refused to take questions from the media.
- The woman who'd written the post was identified and gave interviews to the *Casper Star-Tribune*, the local *Sublette Examiner*, and K2TV News providing more details about her story, but declining to name the "others."
- Several state senators went on record saying they would like the Division of Criminal Investigation (DCI) to investigate the charge and provide the legislature with their findings.
- A second woman, who had since moved to Montana, had written a similar post on Facebook, alleging that Allen had assaulted her in his law office after business hours and threatened her if she ever talked about it. Allen denied that charge as well.
- Connor Hanlon had resigned as chief of staff and flew to Washington, D.C., for a job in the new administration.
- Tatiana Allen, the governor's wife and known as First Lady Tatie, had vanished from the governor's mansion and was rumored to be living with her sister in Pennsylvania.

- Lisa Greene-Dempsey had stepped forward to defend the governor's reputation as a means of keeping her own job, but protests outside the headquarters had convinced her to resign.
- Missy Vankueren Hand had gone on a solo world cruise for the second time in her life and hadn't been heard from, which was apparently just fine with her sixth husband, Marcus Hand.
- Rick Ewig, the game warden of the Gillette district, had been named interim director of the agency and he'd immediately restored Joe's badge number and seniority. He'd also signed off on purchase orders for a new pickup and a new station on the bank of the Twelve Sleep River.
- When Joe had asked Rulon if he had known about the extremely well-timed allegation beforehand, Rulon had responded by saying, "As a lawyer, I never ask my client if he's guilty. As my client, you should never ask your lawyer what he knows."

JOE TOLD KLEIN, "Let me know if you need any help releasing that wolf."

"I figure I'll be okay," the rancher said. "Maybe I'll take Paula along and we'll make a day of it.

"Oh," Klein interjected as Joe opened the door to climb into his pickup, "and don't forget to send those photos to Courtney."

"I won't," Joe said with a smile.

HE TOOK a longer route back to Hazelton Road, one that took him across the pasture where Klein had roped the wolf.

Just below the tree line, he intersected with three distinct sets of tracks in the soft mud.

Joe parked his truck and got out. This time, Daisy followed.

Wolf tracks were unique—the stride of the running animal caused the back paws to fall directly into the impression made by the front paws. They looked as if they were made by a two-legged animal.

Daisy sniffed the tracks warily and jumped back, her eyes scanning the timber.

"Do you see one?" he asked. He followed her line of sight.

There, in a small clearing about a quarter of a mile up the timbered hillside, was the lone black wolf looking back at him. The others were not in sight.

Joe locked eyes with it.

Then the wolf turned its head and loped away.

Joe felt a tremor wash through him. He couldn't help but think the wolf was sending him a warning of some kind.

CHAPTER FOUR

‖‖

ELEVEN HUNDRED MILES to the south, in Scotts-
dale, Arizona, Tim Kelleher couldn't believe his good fortune
when the extremely attractive young woman he'd been eyeing
on the street stopped and turned to him and said, "I'm Abriella
and I think I'm lost."

Abriella had shimmering jet-black hair, large hazel eyes, and
a full mouth that turned down at the corners in a kind of pout.
She wore a loose-fitting white peasant top, tight khaki shorts,
and a pair of blue low-top Chuck Taylors. Her legs were brown
and shapely. He guessed she was Hispanic, but that wasn't a bit
unusual in Arizona, although Scottsdale itself ran a little whiter.

"What are you trying to find?"

"A bookstore called the Poisoned Pen," she said. "I got directions from the guy behind the desk at the hotel, but I must have
made a wrong turn. I'm terrible with directions."

"Sounds like my wife," he said, laughing. He nodded to the

northwest. "You're just a couple of blocks away. The store is on Goldwater."

"I thought *this* was Goldwater."

"This is First Street."

Every day, Tim Kelleher walked his dog in the neighborhood. Actually, it was his wife's dog—a jaunty little Pomeranian. He left his bungalow on First and went west to Goldwater, then north as far as Nordstrom's before returning via Sixty-eighth Street. After crossing Indian School Road, he usually deviated so he could walk down the length of sidewalk that bordered the hip retro Hotel Valley Ho. All kinds of interesting people stayed at the Ho. He'd recognized Hollywood actors there, and there were scores of hot women wearing little to nothing strolling down Main toward Old Town.

Abriella fit the mold.

"I'm nearly home," he said. "If you want, you can follow me and I'll draw you a map."

"Are you sure you don't mind?" she asked.

The only thing he minded was that his wife, Karen, was home. Although the probability of something happening with someone as young and good-looking as Abriella was slim to none, the presence of Karen totally screwed things up.

TIM KELLEHER WAS a hound dog of the old school. He was well aware that he was thirty years and fifty pounds away from getting a second look by a woman of Abriella's age and looks, but why not dream? He used to score women like that when they found out who he was. But that was back east, where he was a big deal. Now just being on the same street with Abriella made today more interesting than most days. He'd happily take that.

"Isn't it a little hot out to walk your dog?" she asked while she kept up with him on the sidewalk. He noticed that there were beads of perspiration on her upper lip. He fought an urge to dab them up.

"Yeah—we're just about to the point where our afternoon walks will have to become morning walks. It's in the low nineties now, but by June it'll get to a hundred and five at this time of day. That's too hot for either the dog or me."

"I'm not from here," she said, although it was obvious. "I don't think I could take this kind of heat on a day-to-day basis."

He refrained from saying, *But it's a dry heat*, and said instead, "I'm still getting used to it myself."

"So you haven't lived here long?"

"I'm on my second year. Moved from Jersey."

"I could tell by the way you talk."

"I'm Tim Kelleher."

"Thank you for your help, Tim."

"It's my pleasure, honey."

"What's your dog's name?"

"Angel. My wife named her."

Tim was slipping. He knew better than to call a good-looking single woman's attention to the fact that he had a wife, and here he'd done it twice in ten minutes.

"She's a cute little dog," Abriella said.

Which, to Tim, was one of the few redeeming qualities about Angel. She was a chick magnet.

"So you're staying at the Ho?"

"The Valley Ho, yes. It's pretty funky."

"Are you here on vacation?"

"Kind of," she said. She didn't elaborate.

"This is it," he said as he turned from the sidewalk onto the flagstone path that led to his front door. He could feel the hot stones penetrate through the soles of his shoes. The house was simple and unassuming and he liked that it was located just a few blocks away from all the Old Town restaurants, shops, and good-looking young people. There were few tall buildings in this part of Scottsdale and he liked looking at the palm trees and large cacti that were placed about.

From his backyard he could see Camelback Mountain in the distance. The landmark undulated in the rising heat.

It was *so* different from Jersey.

SHE FOLLOWED AS he pushed through the heavy door. Inside, it was dark and cool and the central air-conditioning hummed white noise. He'd learned how to survive in Arizona in the summer: bunker in all day in a chilled house, start the car and turn the air-conditioning on full for ten minutes before he climbed in so he wouldn't be broiled alive inside, and only go out at night.

"Hey, Swole, this is Abriella," he said to the middle-aged man sitting on the couch scrolling through his phone. Swole was visiting from up north and he looked it. He wore oversized cargo shorts, a baggy T-shirt, black socks, and sandals. His meaty hairless legs were so white they appeared light blue. He looked like a tourist, because he was.

"Hi, Abriella," Swole said. He looked her over from top to bottom and didn't even try to be discreet.

Swole was a heavy-bodied man who towered over Tim. He'd arrived two days ago and said he'd like to stay a week and "soak up some sun" before heading back to the north where it still felt like winter.

Abriella nodded to him, but didn't speak. Tim guessed that she hadn't approved of the ogling.

"Who's this?" Karen asked suspiciously as she entered the room.

"Abriella," Swole answered from the couch. He'd burred the *r* in a stupid way, Tim thought. Tim shook his head at Swole to implore him to shut up.

Karen was wearing soiled gardening gloves and had obviously been making another vain attempt to grow something in the backyard that wasn't a cactus. She'd made it clear to Tim that she missed her flower garden in Newark. Karen used to have one hell of a head of hair that had been poofed and coiffed at least once a week. It had been her most remarkable feature. But she'd literally shaved it off and now had a buzz cut the color of aluminum. Easier to take care of, she'd said.

"She's lost and I told her I'd draw her a map," Tim said to Karen. "She's trying to find the Poisoned Pen."

"The *bookstore*?" Karen asked with surprise. The insinuation was that Abriella didn't look like the kind of woman who read books. His wife had that edge about her, Tim thought.

He felt suddenly protective of Abriella, and he noticed she stayed very close to him while he crossed the living room for paper and a pen on the faux-marble breakfast bar that separated the kitchen from the living room. Swole had ogled her like a lech and Karen had insulted her.

He found a small pad on the breakfast bar. It was one of hundreds he'd collected over the years from hotel rooms. This one was from the Fontainebleau Miami Beach.

"This is our house," he said as he scratched an *X* on the paper and wrote *North First Street*. "This is the Ho," he said, drawing a circle and writing *HO* in block letters.

She was paying close attention, he noticed. She was so close to him as he sketched, he could feel her body heat and smell her perfume. It was a fresh scent and it stirred him and he hoped Karen wasn't observing him too closely or he'd hear about it.

He was so preoccupied that what came next took him completely by surprise. Abriella reached out, he thought for the map, but it wasn't. Instead, her hand gripped the handle of a long butcher knife from the block and she drew it out so quickly it went *zip*.

Before he could ask Abriella what she was doing, she crossed the room to where Swole was sitting on the couch with his back to her. To Tim's astonishment, she plunged the blade into the base of Swole's neck near his clavicle and shoved it downward to the hilt. Swole arched his back and grunted and his phone tumbled from his hands to the floor.

Abriella jerked the knife out and stepped to the side to avoid the spray of arterial blood that arced into the air and pattered to the tile.

Karen took a deep breath to load up a scream, but before she could shriek, Abriella glided across the floor to where she was in the doorway and grabbed Karen's left ear. She jerked Karen's neck back and poised the knife across her throat.

She said to Tim, "Don't move or I'll cut her head off and use it to go bowling."

Karen's eyes were white and wild and trained on Tim. Her mouth was twisted into a grimace.

"Do what she says," Karen said.

"What do you want?" Tim asked. His throat was suddenly dry and the words came out in a croak.

In his peripheral vision, he saw Swole slump forward from the couch to his knees. He clutched at the entrance wound on his neck and made a horrible gurgling sound.

To Karen, Abriella said, "Get down."

When Karen didn't move—she was obviously too scared to process what she'd been asked—Abriella kneed the older woman and forced her down. The bloody knife stayed at her throat. Tim noticed that drops of blood from the blade now stained Karen's blouse.

With Karen on her knees, Abriella reached behind her with her free hand and withdrew a cheap-looking cell phone from where she'd parked it in the waistband of her shorts. Her eyes remained locked on Tim as she raised the phone to her mouth. She punched a button, waited two seconds, and said, "I'm in."

Abriella punched off before any reply and wedged the phone back into her shorts.

"What do you want?" Tim asked again. "If it's money, I've got some cash in a safe in our bedroom. But we're not rich, as you can see."

Swole crashed to the floor and lay on his side. Tim cringed at the sight.

"Why did you do that?" he asked Abriella. "You didn't even know him."

She rolled her eyes and said, "Guess."

A MOMENT LATER, Tim heard the crunch of gravel from a vehicle's tires on his back driveway. Whoever was driving it, he thought, must have been observing them from just up the street and they'd come to his house via the alley. There was a reason for that.

There were always some neighbors around—half of his block was retired—but none of them would be able to look out their front windows and observe a strange car at his house.

Three car doors slammed shut almost simultaneously, followed by three men, who entered by the back kitchen door.

They were all dark and in their late twenties or early thirties. Clearly Hispanics as well, and dressed casually in jeans and loose short-sleeve shirts. The man in the lead wore cowboy boots and the two behind him wore running shoes.

"Tim," Abriella said, "I'd like to introduce you to some good friends of mine. Meet Peter, Adelmo, and Cesar."

Peter was the first man in. He was tall and had smoldering movie star looks. He also had a fistful of plastic zip ties in one hand and a semiautomatic handgun with a long hotdog-like suppressor in the other.

Angel barked at them in a stiff-legged stance and skittered backward across the floor. She wasn't a brave dog or a particularly good watchdog, Tim thought.

"Shut that dog up," Abriella said to Tim.

"If only I could." Tim sighed.

Angel continued to yap—her bark was particularly high-pitched—so Peter raised his weapon and fired once.

Despite the suppressor, the sound was loud, and Angel's body was thrown across the floor against the far wall.

Karen cried out and Abriella conked her on the top of her head with the butt of the knife.

ADELMO WAS LIGHTER, with sallow deep-set eyes and skinny hairless arms. He carried a dented red metal toolbox.

Cesar was short and overweight, with a mop of black hair. He had a bulging canvas duffel bag.

Cesar quickly passed the other two men and went about dutifully closing all of the blinds and drapes to the outside. The inside of the house was now shadowed and gloomy. He lifted the duffel bag to the counter and unzipped it and began to pull out two heavy rolls of plastic that he placed on the surface. Tim recognized what they were. They were body bags.

"I didn't bring enough," Cesar said with a nod toward Swole's body.

Karen began to sob big racking sobs.

"Shut up," Abriella told her. To emphasize her point she flicked the butcher knife and sliced off the very tip of Karen's ear. Karen gasped and covered the wound with her right hand. She looked wordlessly to Tim with terrified eyes.

"Honey," he said. "Please try not to make any more noise."

She'd never been any good at that, but maybe this time . . .

PEDRO "PETER" INFANTE approached Tim and spun him around. Tim felt the bite of zip ties on his wrists as they were cinched up behind his back. Then Peter guided Tim to a kitchen chair and made him sit. More zip ties were used on his ankles to secure them to the chair legs. It was all done in a businesslike way.

When Tim looked up, he saw that Adelmo had his toolbox open on the kitchen table. He pulled out a cordless DeWalt twenty-volt hand drill. He tested it twice to verify that it was fully charged.

Zzzzzzzzz. Zzzzzzzzz.

Adelmo asked Peter, "Her first or him?"

"Maybe neither," Peter said. There was just a hint of a Mexican accent in his voice, Tim thought.

Peter stood in front of Tim and leaned toward him with his hands resting on his thighs.

"We can do this without any more drama," he said.

"Okay."

"Where is Ernie Mecca?"

Tim knew he flinched. "Who?"

"Please don't do this."

"I don't know who you're talking about."

Peter looked over his shoulder and growled as if angrily resigned to what would come next. He said to Cesar, "Start with her."

Karen said, "Tim, tell him what he wants to know. You aren't going to let them hurt me, are you? *Tim?*"

TIM KELLEHER WAS no stranger to violence and he knew it came in two kinds. It was either desperate or it was deliberate. Abriella's actions were not just deliberate but measured and chilling. Every move she'd made since entering his house was purposeful.

The three men with her were the same way. This wasn't a robbery or a home invasion. This was a professional operation.

Tim recalled hearing about a crew that consisted of three men and a woman. He'd never heard of any names associated with them, but he knew they were sent only for the most high-level jobs.

They were known as the Wolf Pack.

Abriella and Cesar bound Karen and forced her to sit on the floor with her back to the wall. They gagged her with a dish towel that Abriella found in the kitchen and pulled it tight so she couldn't scream.

Adelmo bent her right knee up for a good drilling angle and poised the bit an inch from her kneecap and looked to Peter for the okay.

Karen was terrified. She looked over at Tim and their eyes locked.

He mouthed, *Stay strong.*

She didn't like that advice and tried to struggle away, but Abriella and Adelmo held her in place.

Before Adelmo triggered the DeWalt, he paused and turned his head toward Tim.

"Last chance," Peter said. "*Where is Ernie Mecca?*"

Chapter Five

JOE HAD TWO STOPS in the town of Saddlestring that evening on his way to his new home on the river, and he intended to make them quick. He'd promised Marybeth he wouldn't be late for Lucy's pre-birthday party that night and he didn't want to screw it up. Marybeth had already texted him twice to remind him.

Unlike Marybeth, Joe didn't keep a family calendar of milestones in his head. It hadn't occurred to him until she explained it that not only was this Lucy's last birthday dinner with them before going off to college, but it was the last birthday dinner of *any* of their girls living at home. The last chicken was leaving the nest.

Joe kind of wished she hadn't put it in such stark terms. But he was glad he'd decided to forgo the drive to Winchester to meet Tom Kinnison after the incident with the wolves. With his luck, confronting Kinnison would result in some kind of long and complicated affair—one never knew what would happen when a man was accused of a crime—that would result in him being late.

He had nothing on his agenda for the next day, so he'd drive to Winchester first thing in the morning.

JOE ALREADY KNEW how he was going to play it because he'd played it the same way before.

Once he located the home of Kinnison, he'd walk up to the front door and knock. If someone answering to that name opened the door, Joe would say, "I guess you know why I'm here."

The subject's immediate response would dictate how things would go from then on. Over the years, the tactic had produced on-the-spot confessions to crimes Joe hadn't known a thing about until the confession moment. Sometimes, the subjects implicated other guilty parties Joe had never suspected were involved or knew anything about. And sometimes subjects confessed to a non-wildlife crime that Joe would pass along to the local police or sheriff's department.

He'd been waiting over the years for a suspect to blurt out, "It was me. I killed that son of a bitch and I'd do it again."

But that had never happened.

He was also aware of other possibilities. Kinnison's wife might open the door and explain that Tom couldn't check his traps because her husband had left the state—or had died weeks ago. Kinnison could deny everything and claim that the traps were stolen out of his garage.

Or Kinnison could pull a weapon out of his holster and start blasting because he didn't want to be arrested.

Anything could happen. And because of that, Joe knew he couldn't risk lighting the fuse to an incident that might take hours to resolve.

Not tonight, anyway.

THEY HADN'T YET arranged for mail delivery to the new river location, so Marybeth had asked Joe to stop by the post office in town, where they had a box. He didn't dislike going there, but it almost always took three times as long as necessary whenever he did.

It seemed like whomever he encountered inside wanted to stop and chat and catch up. The post office had always been the center of all local gossip and communication within the valley— even more than social media or the power lunch of local politicians and merchants at the Burg-O-Pardner—and it was a way for locals to check up on each other for good or ill.

Hundreds of times over the years, he'd overheard residents say things like "I saw Stan at the post office and he wasn't looking too good . . ." or "I saw Mary at the post office and she looked like she'd been rode hard and put up wet."

Of course, when the game warden went inside, he was cornered by ranchers who wondered when he'd be by to inspect last winter's elk damage or hunters who wanted to share their stories from the fall—or report potential violations. Going inside the building with his post office box key seemed to be a signal to others to take him aside and talk. Joe was psychologically unsuited to being rude to locals in his job as a game warden. He felt obligated to hear them out and offer advice and counsel.

So he tried as best he could to avoid them when he could.

Another downside to picking up the mail was simply that local poachers and habitual violators had a bead on his location. If the game warden was at the post office in town, that meant he wasn't on patrol out in the district.

Since Marybeth had also asked him to stop by the grocery store to pick up an order from the meat department, he was happy he had an excuse to end any long conversations.

THE POST OFFICE counter closed at five sharp and he could see the postal workers behind the glass preparing to do just that. It was a good time to get mail, he'd found. Anyone who needed postage or who had found a slip in their box to retrieve a package at the counter was pressed for time, or they'd have to wait a day. They'd be in a hurry as well and less likely to take him aside for a chat.

He emptied his box and gathered the mail under his arm. It appeared to consist of local circulars and solicitations from non-profits, but there were also a few letters in there, including what looked like birthday cards addressed to Lucy.

As Joe turned to stride out of the post office, he noticed a stooped man with a pointed white beard and a stocking cap who stabbed at his box with a key and kept missing. Each time he did so, he made a ticking sound as the key bounced off the front plate of his post office box. The man bent forward so he could see the lock better and tried again. He missed.

Tick.

Joe hesitated for a moment, then went over to him.

"Can I help?"

"Can't see a damned thing," the old man said.

Joe recognized him as Rolf Schweiring, the longtime mayor of Winchester. Rolf had held the office for more than forty years, but he'd moved to the bigger community of Saddlestring after he'd retired. Joe had heard that Rolf didn't like the way the new mayor operated and felt forced to relocate out of disgust.

Joe opened Rolf's box for him and the old man gathered his mail.

"I appreciate it," he said.

"Actually, I've got a question for you," Joe said as he handed back Rolf's key. "Since you probably know everyone there, have you ever heard of a guy named Tom—or Thomas—Kinnison back in Winchester? Lives on Elkhorn Drive?"

Rolf straightened up and ran his fingers through his beard like a comb. He asked, "What was that name again?"

Joe repeated it.

"Can't say I have," Rolf said. "He must be real new to the area."

Claims to have been there for fourteen years, Joe thought.

"He's a trapper and not a good one," Joe said.

"Nope, I don't know him."

Joe thanked him and headed for the door to get to his pickup before anyone else came in.

As he pushed through the door, Rolf said, "Elkhorn Drive is

kind of sketchy, though. I heard some real oddballs moved up there."

"Oddballs?"

"City people, I should say," Rolf said. "The type that normally don't last."

"Ah," Joe said.

"I'M PRETTY SURE my wife ordered something that she asked me to pick up," Joe said to the butcher at the grocery store. The man was setting out Styrofoam containers of breakfast sausage that he ground and seasoned himself.

"Miz Pickett?"

"Yup."

"Just a sec. It's in the back."

Joe thrust his hands in his pockets and furtively looked around. Going to the grocery store in uniform was as dangerous as going to the post office. He was just waiting for someone to sidle by him with a cart and ask why his entire left side was covered with dried mud.

The butcher returned with a large rectangular bundle wrapped in waxed paper. It was nearly two feet long. He handed it over the display to Joe.

"Be careful carrying it," he said. "You don't want any of the claws to poke out. They're sharp—they might take your eye out."

"Claws?"

"Five pounds of the finest Alaskan snow crab legs I've seen in a while," the man said.

Joe gulped. This was going to be expensive. He knew Lucy liked crab legs and she must have requested them for her special dinner.

"I'd like some of that breakfast sausage as well," Joe said.

At the register, he handed over his credit card. The purchase amounted to well over a hundred dollars. He couldn't remember paying that much in that store . . . ever . . . but he rarely shopped for groceries.

Marybeth was frugal and a good money manager. Joe credited her entirely for keeping them afloat while he was fighting to get his job back and receiving no income. Somehow, she'd done it. He knew he'd be bankrupt and destitute without her, and he'd learned not to question her financial decisions, because she thought long and hard about all of them.

But . . .

"Can I come over for dinner?" the checkout clerk asked with a sly smile.

"Might as well," he said. "It looks like we'll have plenty."

Then he thought of his back pay and raise. For one of the few times he could remember in their entire marriage, Marybeth had some extra cash. And of course she'd spend it on their daughters.

That was fine by him.

HIS CELL PHONE lit up as he exited the grocery store parking lot onto the state highway that would lead him south toward his new home. It was Katelyn Hamm.

"Joe Pickett."

"Joe, I'm glad I caught you. I found out a little more about my drone pilot."

He could hear the excitement in her voice. She was working this thing. He felt guilty for not having made any inquiries about local drone operators since he'd last talked with her.

"I ran into one of my trappers out in the badlands west of here. He's one of the good ones—I never have any trouble with him. One of his traplines is about ten miles away from the winter range."

"Yes," Joe prompted.

"He's been out every day checking his traps for the last ten days. He said that he's seen that drone in the sky for the last six days in a row. It's been buzzing around the base of the mountain and chasing deer and elk."

"Why didn't he call you?" Joe asked.

"Because he thought it was *us*," she said. "He said he figured the agency was using drones to count wildlife or check up on the game herds. I didn't want to tell him we aren't quite that sophisticated, that we use helicopters and planes."

"Interesting," Joe said.

"Maybe we *should* use drones," she said. "I think you're just as scared as I am flying in those little planes we use."

"You've got that right."

"But that's not all. He said each time the drone flew home it was headed in your direction, just like what I saw today with my own eyes. And one time he saw it land in a clearing on the face of the mountain.

"He was a real long distance from where it landed, but he said he saw a white SUV in the vicinity. Either a Suburban or a Yukon. He said he assumed the pilot of the drone was driving it, but like I said—he thought it was us."

That narrowed it down, Joe thought. While nearly every resident of Twelve Sleep County had at least one four-wheel-drive vehicle, how many white Yukons or Suburbans could there be? Cross-reference white SUV owners with residents who registered or piloted drones? The list had to be small.

"We might be able to narrow it down with that information," Joe said. "Please thank your trapper for the intel."

"I did. Are you going to have some time in the next couple of weeks to work this?" she asked.

"Not a problem," Joe said. "I'll let you know what I find out."

"I've got a favor to ask."

"Shoot."

"If you find him, please give me a call. I want to drive over and be there when we roust the son of a bitch. Not only was he responsible for stressing and killing my herd, he probably has video of me squatting in the brush with my pants down."

Joe said, "Yikes."

HE TURNED EAST off County Road 212 toward a wall of cottonwoods and stands of willow that bordered the meandering river as the sun flared over the mountains before its final descent. The last blast of the day threw a spotlight on the river valley that brought out the crimson of the brush and the light green of spring buds on the branches of the trees.

The gravel road led past a sign that read GAME WARDEN STATION. It was so new it looked like the lacquer on it hadn't dried yet. The department must have sent out some trainees to place the sign while Joe was in the field.

He liked it that passersby couldn't see his house from the county road, although at night they might be able to make out the lights through the trees. He wasn't used to privacy, and he knew it wouldn't take long for locals to realize he'd moved. In the meanwhile, though, it was pleasant.

A small herd of ragged-looking mule deer grazed just inside the cottonwoods and they looked up as he went by. They had the mottled look of animals that had endured a tough winter and were waiting to shed their winter fur so they'd be sleek again.

A cow moose stuck her head out of the willows in his direction, her nose like a black six-by-six beam. Despite her size, which he estimated as six feet tall at the shoulders and nine hundred pounds, she was wily in her movements and could vanish into the brush like she'd never been there at all. He'd seen her the last couple of nights when he came home and he noted her location and species as *Shiras cow moose* on his WOF pad.

He got a thrill out of seeing a moose so close to his new home, but he knew to be wary of her and to warn Marybeth and Lucy to be cautious as well. Although moose appeared lumbering and slow and their eyesight was notoriously poor—they could also pose a threat.

He'd recently heard of an incident near Dubois where a ranch hand named Ernesto Morales had been greeted every morning by a friendly cow moose outside his cabin that would still be there at night when he returned. Morales had named her Cow-winkle, in homage to the Bullwinkle cartoons of his youth.

Morales had enjoyed seeing her every day until the cow inexplicably cut him off one morning when he was on his way to the corral. Without warning, Cow-winkle rose up on her hind feet and struck down at him with her sharp front hooves, instantly breaking his right clavicle. When Morales was on the ground, she struck again and broke his ribs and pelvis.

Somehow, Morales had had the presence of mind to roll away from the attack until he was beneath his pickup, where he called 911 on his cell phone. Cow-winkle was still there circling the pickup when the local sheriff and game warden arrived to shoot her.

Morales and the local game warden had had no explanation for why Cow-winkle had suddenly turned on him like that. They'd speculated that perhaps she had lost her calf and gone crazy, but no one knew.

DAISY PERKED UP when Joe cleared the trees toward his house. So did Joe, because he saw the reason for the large quantity of king crab legs.

Dulcie Schalk's Jeep was parked out in front of the house. Schalk was the county attorney and Marybeth's best friend. They rode horses and drank wine together.

And Nate Romanowski's large panel van was next to it. Stenciled on the side of the vehicle were the words YARAK, INC., followed by a website address and a telephone number.

A slogan in script, *We Make Your Problems Go Away*, was a new addition.

Joe wasn't sure that was the best line for Nate to add, but it was certainly accurate in more ways than one.

JOE ENTERED THROUGH the garage instead of the front door to access the mudroom first. Daisy bounded past him to greet all of the guests. Nothing made her happier than a houseful. Labradors were like that.

It was slightly raucous inside. Before peeling off his muddy jacket, he stuck his head around the corner of the doorjamb. Through the kitchen, he could see everyone seated at the dining room table.

"Hey, there," he said. To Lucy: "Happy birthday."

Lucy grinned at him in a way that showed she was a little embarrassed by the dinner party. He understood.

Marybeth gestured to the guests and said to Joe, "Look who showed up."

"Welcome," he said to them all.

Marybeth, Dulcie, and Nate's partner, Liv Brannon, sat next to one another at the table. Lucy sat on the other side next to Nate. There was a nearly empty bottle of red wine and a fifth of Wyoming Whiskey on the table as well as a German chocolate cake with eighteen unlit pink candles.

Nate looked up and toasted a glass of whiskey on the rocks to Joe. He was tall and angular when standing, with his blond hair in a ponytail and hawklike blue eyes. He wore a button-down long-sleeve shirt with *Yarak, Inc.* embroidered over the breast pocket, plus jeans and desert combat boots. Compared to what he used to wear—cargo pants, combat boots, and a shoulder holster for his .454 Casull handgun—he looked absolutely civilized, which made Joe smile.

NATE HAD BEEN a de facto member of the family for more than fifteen years, ever since Joe had stuck his neck out to prove Nate's innocence in a murder he hadn't committed. Nate had vowed to look out for and protect Joe and the Pickett family, and that is what he'd done. He was a falconer with a Special Forces background and an eventful history: in and out of federal lockup, implicated in the demise of more men than Joe wanted to think about, and he was now the co-owner of a commercial falconry service. Yarak, Inc. was hired by farmers, ranchers, business owners, and commercial enterprises to deploy several species of highly trained raptors to chase off problem birds. It was known as "pest control or mitigation." He took on jobs with refineries to help rid them of invasive nesting birds, and with amusement parks to chase away pigeons.

Yarak, Inc. had been the brainchild of Liv Brannon, who managed the business side of the enterprise. Liv was a light-skinned African American and Louisiana native who had once been the executive assistant to an elite rancher/assassin in northeastern

Wyoming. She'd taken to the Mountain West—and to Nate—
with a palpable passion.

Joe liked her because she'd made it her life's mission to
keep Nate from serving up his own particular brand of justice
whenever he saw fit. Nate's methods ranged from tearing the
ears off of victims to blowing holes in them with his five-shot
revolver.

Marybeth saw that Joe was still peering around the doorjamb. "Why don't you join us? Did you forget the crab legs and
now you're hiding?"

"No. I'm covered with mud."

Nate laughed.

Marybeth said, "Well, go take a shower and get that uniform
off. I'll get the water boiling while you do."

"I'll help," Dulcie said, pushing back from the table. "I want
to open another bottle anyway."

After he handed off the package of crab legs to Marybeth, he
gestured toward the bourbon bottle on the table and said to
Nate, "Save some of that for me."

"I make no promises," Nate said.

Joe noticed that Lucy had a glass of wine in front of her even
though she was underage to drink legally. She smiled at Joe and
nodded to her mother.

HE SHOWERED QUICKLY and pulled on a clean
Cinch shirt. The salt smell of the sea from the crab in the pot
greeted him when he joined the gathering and sat down.

"Nice digs," Nate said, indicating the new house. "You must have friends in high places."

"Apparently, I do," he said. "It's a nice change."

"And it couldn't happen to a better guy," Nate said.

Joe looked up to check whether his friend was being sarcastic or sincere. Nate nodded to emphasize his sincerity.

"Thank you," Joe said.

"But it's still out of town," Lucy said. She'd always wanted to live closer to her friends and social activities and was the only one in the family who'd actually liked their temporary stay in the town house.

Nate said to her, "Someday, you'll look back on all of this and treasure what it was like to grow up in the country—in nature. People you meet will envy your upbringing in more ways than one."

Lucy looked from Nate to Joe as if to say, *Who is this guy?* Joe was thinking the same thing. He looked to Liv for an explanation.

"He's getting soft and sentimental these days," she said.

Joe said, "He sure is. I wonder what brought this change about?"

"He's happy and he lives with a great woman who keeps him on the straight and narrow," she said.

"Which is a good thing for everyone concerned," Joe said. "Left to his own devices, he tends to hurt people or sit naked in trees."

"Hey, you two," Nate said. "I'm right here."

He poured Joe a stiff bourbon and freshened his own.

Joe looked over at Lucy and smiled. She was a good sport, he thought. Having dinner with her parents and their friends was probably not the number one activity on her wish list.

AFTER DINNER, CLEANUP, and Lucy blowing out the candles on her cake, Marybeth, Liv, and Dulcie went outside to feed the horses and inspect the new barn. Lucy took her empty wineglass to the sink and went to her room to answer texts from her sisters and her friends. None of Lucy's circle used their phones to actually make a call.

Nate said to Joe, "She's a sweetheart, you know."

"Lucy?"

"Who else?"

"Yes, she is."

"Three daughters. You're a lucky man."

Joe shook his head and asked, "*Who are you?*"

"I'm a lucky man as well."

They clinked glasses and sipped.

Joe said, "Have you ever run across a guy from Winchester named Tom Kinnison?"

"I was going to tell you something profound, but instead I'll just answer your question. I've never heard of him."

"No one has," Joe said. Then: "In your travels around the county, have you seen anyone piloting a big drone? Maybe chasing wildlife with it?"

"Do you ever stop working?" Nate asked.

"No."

"To answer your question, yes. And it really pissed me off."

Nate told Joe that several weeks ago he'd been rappelling down a cliff face to check out prairie falcon nests on a scouting mission. He'd been looking for young birds that he could later add to his "Air Force." While Nate had paused at a falcon nest, he'd sensed another presence and spun around to see a large white drone hovering in place thirty feet away. The aircraft had been close enough that he could clearly observe the lens of a sophisticated video camera mounted on the frame.

"It was just suspended there taking my picture," Nate said. "It really made me mad because a stupid drone like that could scare away nesting birds or stress them so they don't have viable eggs. And it didn't fly away until I opened my falconry bag for my weapon."

"Did you shoot at it?"

"It was too far away and too fast to take a shot. But if I see it again: *Boom*."

"Any markings on it?"

"Not that I could see."

"Did you see a vehicle down below that might belong to the pilot?"

Nate narrowed his eyes. "I looked. I did hear an engine in the distance about ten minutes later. But I couldn't see the vehicle."

Joe said, "It sounds a lot like the drone Katelyn saw today."

"I've got a solution to both of our problems."

Nate's earlier sanguine persona morphed into a demeanor more familiar to Joe. His friend's eyes narrowed and he suddenly looked like the old Nate.

"I've been working with my peregrines on a new tactic," Nate said. "You know I train my birds to kill by releasing pigeons, right?"

"Right," Joe said.

"Well, in the last couple of weeks I've been tying a few loops of wire to the top of the pigeons and sending them up."

Joe shook his head. He wasn't getting it.

Nate explained: "If my peregrine smacks that pigeon from above in the usual way, its talons get tangled up in the wire, and both the falcon and the pigeon have to make a really clumsy landing."

"Is there a point to this?" Joe asked.

Nate rolled his eyes and spoke to Joe very slowly as if talking to a child. "Rather than strike from above, the peregrines are learning to fly past the target in the air and then double back to hit it from below."

It took Joe a moment to realize what Nate was telling him. "That's so they avoid the wire on top," he said. "Or the propellers on the drone."

"Exactly. They can take out a drone from underneath and knock it the hell out of the sky."

Joe sat back and rubbed his jaw. He said, "With my friends in high places, I could probably get the okay to hire you and your Air Force for a couple of days of drone hunting."

"Forget that," Nate said. "I'll do it for free."

They clinked glasses again, to a brand-new scheme.

Then Nate said, "Back to what I was about to tell you before. Look at the table. Tell me what you see."

Joe sighed. Nate liked to make his point—whatever it was—in circular ways that often left Joe frustrated.

"Do we have to do this?" he asked.

"Tell me what you see."

Before Joe could answer, Lucy came back into the dining room. Joe registered that she was hanging back and observing them.

Joe said, "I see a bottle of Wyoming Whiskey, two bourbon glasses, Lucy's birthday cake, a stack of plates and some forks, and wineglasses that will no doubt be full again the minute the ladies come back in."

He looked up to see Nate urging him on.

"What?"

"Think," Nate said.

"How much have you had to drink?" Joe asked sourly.

"How many wineglasses do you see?"

"Two."

"What does that tell you?"

"I have no idea."

Joe glanced over to Lucy. She was staring at the things on the table as well and she suddenly stepped back and raised her hand to her mouth.

"What?" Joe asked the both of them.

Nate said, "Marybeth and Dulcie left their glasses and Lucy took hers to wash out in the sink."

Joe shrugged, not getting it.

"Have you ever known Liv not to enjoy a glass of wine?"

"Dad, *she's pregnant*," Lucy blurted out.

Joe stared across the table at Nate.

"I'm a happy and lucky man," Nate said, beaming. "I'm also scared as hell. You'll be my best man."

It wasn't a question. It was a statement.

"You're going to get married and have a kid?" Joe asked. He was astonished.

"In that order," Nate said.

"Does Marybeth know?"

"Liv is probably telling her now."

Joe tried not to think about the terrible fates of Nate's earlier lovers. But he was sure it was something Nate himself had come to terms with.

The back door burst open and Marybeth ran in and yelled, *"Oh my God!"*

THE NEXT MORNING, on her actual birthday, a hung-over Joe drove Lucy to high school before proceeding to Winchester. Lucy had very reluctantly inherited Marybeth's minivan to use as her own just in time for the transmission to go out. While Lucy didn't regret not showing up at school driving an embarrassing *Mom-Car*, as she called the vehicle, it meant that until the repair was complete she needed to be ferried back and forth.

Joe pulled through the drop-off area and stopped his pickup. He could see Justin Hill standing near the flagpole, waiting for her to get out. He waved at Joe, and Joe warily waved back.

"Happy birthday," Joe said to her.

He was puzzled when she didn't immediately open the door and join her boyfriend.

She said, "I know you and Mom think I can't wait to get out of the house."

"Isn't that the case?"

She said, "Sheridan and April are kind of . . . big personalities. They've filled up the house my entire life, if you think about it."

Joe nodded.

Lucy turned to him and said, "It's kind of nice to have the two of you to myself for a while."

Then she leaned across the seat and gave him a kiss on the cheek.

Before he could respond, she was out the door.

Joe held it in until no one could see him before he let a tear roll out of his left eye.

Chapter Six

||||||||||||||||||||||||||||||||||||||||||||||||||||||||||||||||||||||||

ELKHORN DRIVE WASN'T a street, but a gravel road four miles outside of Winchester that followed the S-curve contours of the North Fork of the Tongue River. The winter had been hard on the road and had left it punctuated with football-sized potholes that were filled with brown rainwater from the overnight rain. Long straight sections of Elkhorn Drive were washboarded from frost heaves, and Joe drove slowly as his tires bounced over them to guard against the steering wheel wrenching out of his hands.

Twenty-two-oh-four was apparently more of a location than an actual address, and the navigation system mounted on his dashboard had given up and reverted to displaying his position as a red arrow moving down a path along the river.

At the place Joe stopped, there was a little-used two-track pathway cutting off from the county road through a stand of trees. He could see that it led to an ancient single-wide trailer in a small clearing about a hundred and fifty yards into the timber.

A fading hand-painted sign nailed to a tree trunk indicated the residence belonged to someone named Behrman.

Joe found it curious that his device had failed him, but chalked up the misdirection to the vagaries of technology applied to very rural locations.

The North Fork was angry and swollen with khaki-colored runoff that rocketed down from the Bighorns over boulders and large river rocks. The stream had jumped the banks, and water pooled within stands of willows and around the trunks of pine trees. Large branches and even entire trees had come down from above and were wedged into hazardous deadwood dams that diverted the flow and changed the banks of the river even in low-water years. The North Fork eventually flowed into the Twelve Sleep River past Joe's new house.

He knew it to be a superior trout stream once the flows dropped and the water cleared to reveal miles of pocket water and deep long pools. Most of the river was private, though, and fly-fishers he saw there in the summer months were either guests of the landowners—or trespassers. There was public access for fishing downstream and that's where most of the local meat fishermen went. The road he was on got steeper and rockier as it rose into the mouth of the mountain canyon and eventually faded away in a jumble of boulders.

Joe knew that between where he was on the river's edge and somewhere at the end of the road in the boulder field was where Tom Kinnison had listed his physical address.

He thought: *What a great place to live if you didn't want anyone to find you.*

JOE POWERED DOWN the front windows as the road parted from the bank of the North Fork and took a slight northern turn into heavier timber. The scent of wet loam, pine, and the slightly metallic smell of the roaring river filled the cab. Mist from the tumbling stream hung in the air and beaded on his windshield. The bright April sky darkened as tree branches closed over the cab of the truck and blocked out the direct sun. As the roar of the river faded into the background, Joe's senses rose to skin level.

There was no doubt that the road was no longer maintained by the county but was probably private.

He assumed he was closing in on Kinnison's residence and he wanted to be alert. Some suspects were known to hide out at the first glimpse of a Game and Fish Department vehicle.

He also assumed he would find another dilapidated trailer tucked up somewhere in the trees. Trappers—and especially incompetent trappers—weren't exactly known for their palatial estates.

INSTEAD, WALKING TOWARD him in the middle of the muddy road was a figure who appeared to have been transported from a villa in early twentieth-century Sicily.

The man was old, stooped, thin, and armed. He wore a dark short-brimmed fedora with a wide band and his trousers were tucked into a pair of tall rubber boots. His white shirt was buttoned at the collar and there was a glimpse of a black fabric vest under his bulky jacket. A cloud of white cigarette smoke hung around his head. A stubby double-barreled shotgun hung by a strap over one of his shoulders and pointed muzzle-down toward the road.

Joe stopped his truck and waved. In return, the old man squinted back at him and twin columns of smoke plumed from his nostrils.

"Hello there," Joe called out. He kept his truck running, and when he climbed out, he stood near enough to the open door that he could retreat behind it if the old man raised the shotgun.

"What do you want?" the man asked. "This is a private road."

He had a leathery face, a large nose, and deep inset dark eyes. Late seventies, early eighties maybe. He looked like he'd lived a rough life. His voice was high-pitched and raspy. Joe caught a flat Old-Country-by-way-of-New-York-or-New-Jersey accent in his cadence.

"I'm the Saddlestring game warden. I'm looking for a trapper who listed his address as being on this road."

"A *trapper*?" the man asked. There was a hint of amusement in the question. "What's his name?"

"Tom Kinnison."

"Tom? I don't know nobody . . ." And then the man paused. Joe noted that something passed over his face, but it was barely discernible.

Then: "He ain't here right now."

"So you do know him?"

The old man shrugged, but didn't answer.

"What are you hunting?" Joe asked, and gestured toward the shotgun.

"Nothing. It's for protection."

"Protection against what?"

"Bears. There's bears around here coming out of their dens. They're hungry. Oh—and wolves. I heard there were wolves around."

"There are some wolves around," Joe confirmed.

A twelve-gauge shotgun was a devastating close-in defense weapon for either species.

"You might consider picking up a can of bear spray," Joe said. "Spray is actually more effective on charging bears than a load of buckshot."

The old man waved the advice away. "I suppose there's also wolf spray."

"Not really."

He patted his shotgun. "*This* is my wolf spray."

"Is your place up the road?" Joe asked.

The old man said, "I live there, but it belongs to my son."

"So you and Kinnison both live there?"

The man nodded warily.

"Tell me," Joe asked, "is Kinnison a trapper?"

"How would I know? I stay outa his business and he stays outa mine." *Rat-a-tat-tat.*

"Do you know when he'll be back? I'd like to talk to him."

"Naw, I don't know when he'll be back."

Joe approached the old man and noted that he tensed up the closer he got. Joe made sure to keep his movements slow and deliberate. The last thing he wanted to do was get into a gun battle. Joe was a notoriously poor shot with his sidearm and he'd be no match against a shotgun blast.

He said, "If I give you my card, would you make sure he gets it? He can call or email me when he gets back."

"I ain't no errand boy," the old man said.

"What's your name?" Joe asked while he drew a business card out of his breast pocket and handed it toward the man. He was close enough he could smell the cigarette smoke from the man's clothing.

"Ernesto, but they call me Papa."

Reluctantly, Papa took the card from Joe and dropped it into his coat pocket without looking at it.

"Is your son around? Maybe he knows when Kinnison will be back."

"Naw, he took my grandson to school. I don't know when he'll be back."

"So I'm batting oh-for-two," Joe said. "What's your son's name?"

Ernesto/Papa glared at Joe an uncomfortable length of time. Joe got the impression that this wasn't the first time the old man had been questioned by law enforcement—and he knew he didn't have to say what he didn't want to say.

"His name is Bill," the old man finally said.

"Thank you. Well, please ask Bill to give me a call if he knows when Kinnison is going to be around. My cell number is written on the back of that card I gave you."

Ernesto/Papa nodded his head, but his eyes never left Joe's face.

"So," Joe asked, "have you encountered any bears on your walk?"

"No."

"If you do, please let me know. We like to try and keep track of them."

Papa looked at Joe suspiciously.

"I guess I'll head back," Joe said. He peered over the old man's shoulder. "Is there a place I can turn around up ahead? This road is too narrow for me to do a U-turn."

"Go about a quarter of a mile to the gate," Papa said. "You can turn around there."

"Nice to meet you, sir," Joe said while extending his hand.

Papa simply stared at it for a moment, then stepped back to clear the road.

JOE CLIMBED INTO his truck and put it into gear. As he rolled past Papa, he tipped his hat to him. The old man glared at him with dead black eyes.

"That was strange," he whispered to Daisy, who was curled up in the passenger seat.

Joe was a close study of people he encountered in the field. Almost all of them were armed, so Papa and his old-time shotgun wasn't unusual in itself.

The large majority of hunters and fishers Joe met were helpful, polite, and law-abiding. He usually had a good sense of them within a few seconds.

The remainder fell into two camps—they were either over-friendly or sullen. The overfriendly types were either on the up-and-up but nervous to encounter law enforcement—a feeling Joe completely understood—or they were guilty of a violation and they used their gregariousness as an attempt at distraction.

The sullen ones were harder to read. Sometimes they were that way because they figured they'd been caught red-handed and they were in the process of dealing with their inevitable citation or arrest. But sometimes they were that way because they disliked authority of any kind and they were just putting up with Joe in the hope that he'd soon go away.

Papa, it seemed to Joe, fit into the latter category.

Plus, he thought, former urbanites from the East Coast, which is where Joe assumed Papa had come from, generally had no experience seeing a game warden in the field.

TREES HAD BEEN removed at the entrance of the closed gate so that people like Joe had room to stop and turn around and go back the way they'd come. He noted the thick concrete columns that emerged from the loam on either side of a heavy steel gate. There was a keypad mounted in the right column for entry as well as an intercom and button.

The gate was formidable, and to Joe it stood out like a glass-and-steel high-rise in a mountain meadow.

As he did a three-point turn, he could see the layout of the compound beyond the gate. There was a large two-story home with a green metal roof flanked by smaller cottages on each side.

Two on the right, three on the left. The construction looked recent because the varnished logs on the structures shined bronze in the muted sunlight.

There was an attractive footbridge over a small stream that flowed through the property, and young cottonwood trees that looked recently planted.

A large open outbuilding on the other side of the ranch yard housed a collection of tractors, plows, and ATVs. Joe paused when he caught a glimpse of the back end of a white Ford Expedition parked in the building.

He flipped the caps off a pair of binoculars and raised them to his eyes. The license plate was covered with a coat of mud, but he could make out the numbers. It was Wyoming license plate 2-8948. Next to the bucking horse logo was the *2* that designated Laramie County, which was where the state capital of Cheyenne was located—and was four and a half hours and four hundred and forty miles away. Joe thought that was odd because locals usually got their plates in Saddlestring. He wrote down the plate number in his notepad.

And he wondered if inside the white SUV he would find the controls for piloting a drone.

He'd call dispatch to run the plate as soon as he hit the Winchester Highway. Then he'd call Katelyn and exchange the number with her.

Joe knew that Dulcie wouldn't approach Judge Hewitt for a search warrant of the property until they had more than a long-distance glimpse of a white SUV for probable cause. But if Katelyn could get a plate number from the vehicle driven by the drone pilot . . .

PAPA STILL STOOD where Joe had left him on the side of the road. Joe assumed he'd stayed there to make sure he came back.

As he approached the old man, Joe slowed his pickup to a halt and leaned toward the open passenger window.

"Do you mind if I ask you another question?"

The old man plucked the cigarette out of his mouth with nicotine-stained fingers and waited.

"Does anyone fly a drone around here?"

"So what if they do?"

Not exactly a denial, Joe thought.

"I'm just curious. We've been having some trouble with a drone from around here chasing game off the winter range. You wouldn't know anything about that, would you?"

Papa lifted his chin in a haughty way. "Are drones illegal, Game Warden?"

"Nope. Not if they're registered with the FAA. But chasing wildlife is a violation of state law."

Papa seemed to consider what he would say. Finally, he looked away. "I don't know nothing about drones."

Joe thought he was lying, but he said, "Well, if something comes to mind, you have my card."

Papa leveled his gaze again, but said nothing.

Joe watched the man recede in his rearview mirror as he drove away. He still hadn't moved from his spot.

———————

PAPA WATCHED AS the pickup burbled away and vanished out of sight.

Bill stepped out from behind an eight-foot stand of brush and joined him on the side of the road. Bill was a dark man who stood a head taller than his father. His short-cropped beard sparkled with silver, and he wore an embroidered cowboy shirt, a wide-brimmed black hat with a feather in it, and two-thousand-dollar ostrich-skin boots. His canvas rancher coat sagged on the left side due to the large caliber handgun in a special concealed-carry pocket inside the lining.

"What did he want?" Bill asked.

"He wanted to talk to Swole," Papa said.

"What did you tell him?"

"I told him he wasn't here. Which is true."

"Good."

"He said Swole was a trapper."

"Did he actually call him Swole?" Bill asked suspiciously.

"Nah. He asked for Tom Kinnison. It took me a second to realize who he meant."

Bill sighed heavily. "I told that guy not to mess around with those damn traps he bought. He must have done something stupid."

"Swole's a stupid guy," Papa said. "Then the game warden asked me if I knew anyone around here with a drone."

Bill rolled his eyes and grinned.

Papa reached into his coat pocket and handed the card to Bill. Bill read it and said, "Uh-oh."

ON THE WAY back to Winchester, Joe slowed near a bank of rural mailboxes mounted on a fence next to the turnoff to Elkhorn Drive. He hadn't paid them any attention when he'd made the turn to find Kinnison.

The third box from the left was the newest, and there were stick-on stencils pasted to the front opening.

It read: 2204, followed by HILL.

Bill Hill, Joe thought.

Then he moaned when he realized he knew that name.

Papa had said, *Naw, he took my grandson to school. I don't know when he'll be back.*

Bill had taken his son, Justin, to school, where the boy had waited out front for Lucy to arrive with *her* dad that morning.

BEFORE CALLING EITHER dispatch or Katelyn, Joe tried Marybeth's cell phone. It went straight to message.

He asked, "What do we know about Justin's family?"

SUNDAY, APRIL 29

We have the wolf by the ear, and we can
neither hold him, nor safely let him go.
Justice is in one scale, and self-preservation
in the other.

THOMAS JEFFERSON,
LETTER TO JOHN HOLMES

Chapter Seven

TWO DAYS LATER, on an unseasonably warm and cloudless morning on the sun-drenched western slope of the Bighorns, Katelyn Hamm observed closely as Nate Romanowski got prepared. The falconer had met her before dawn on the highway and followed her to the ridge where she'd seen the drone harassing the deer on the winter range. They'd parked their vehicles below the summit of the ridge so they couldn't be seen from below on the valley floor.

She hadn't met Nate before that morning and she was both wary of him and fascinated by him at the same time. She'd heard some of the stories, but it was impossible to know what was true and what was legend. Several of the falconers she knew in her district spoke of Nate with awe and in hushed tones. But an FBI agent she'd worked a case with said Romanowski should be rotting in federal prison and that "vigilantes" like him were a thing of the past and a threat to the future.

Joe claimed his friend Nate was talkative, but the only exchange she'd had with him in the last two hours was when he'd pulled up beside her pickup on the road.

"You're Katelyn, I presume."

"Yes."

"Lead on."

HE WAS TALL and rangy and there was a calm about him that was unnerving, she thought. He didn't waste movement, and everything he did had a purpose. His broad back was to her as he leaned inside his vehicle and spoke in a low tone to the three or four birds he'd brought, as if prepping them for their assignments. She'd been a little concerned when he strapped on a leather shoulder holster with a large revolver under his left arm, but she'd heard about that, too.

He carried a five-shot .454 Casull revolver manufactured by Freedom Arms in Freedom, Wyoming. It was a hand cannon that could fire high-velocity rounds through all of the walls in a house and come out the other side, or disable an oncoming car. Supposedly, he was lethal with it.

The Yarak, Inc. van had been retrofitted. The back seats had been removed and replaced by several stiff rows of horizontal dowel rods mounted on the floor. Plastic sheeting had been placed over the carpeting and was splashed with white excrement. Behind the rods, or "stoops," were square wire cages that appeared empty.

She guessed the van had the capacity to transport fifteen to twenty birds.

Four falcons stood erect on the first two stoops. Their heads were covered with tooled leather hoods, and long rawhide jesses hung from the talons that gripped the rods. The birds were so preternaturally serene that she had to watch them for several minutes to confirm that they were living, breathing creatures and not products of taxidermy.

Because she knew her voice would carry on such a still day, she spoke softly to Nate's back.

"There's no guarantee that drone will be up this morning, but a reliable trapper I know told me he's seen it nearly every day in this area. That's what I told Joe, anyway."

Nate grunted that he understood, but he didn't turn around.

"Thank you for coming," she said. Then she felt embarrassed for saying it.

"This is a whole new concept," she said, as if to explain herself. "I've never dealt with a drone before. Nobody has. It's as new to me as it is to Joe. We're in uncharted waters."

He straightened up and turned around. His eyes were pale icy blue. He pulled a thick welder's glove on his right hand. "I'd like to get that guy as much as you do."

She nodded toward the falcons inside the van. "So do you let them fly up to get into position?"

He shook his head. "We wait until we've got a target."

"How do you control them when they're in the air?"

He looked at her for such a long time that she felt an urge to turn away. She felt chastened for her lack of falconry knowledge.

Then he said, "I don't."

JOE WAS four and a half miles away in the timber on the other side of the winter range. He'd used a forgotten logging road to get to the bottom third of the mountain, and he'd parked in an alcove where he could scope the meadow and get a few clear views of the sky above through openings in the pine trees.

He'd left his house at four-thirty that morning so he could get into position. Daisy had roused herself enough to jump into the cab, and she snored softly while curled up in the passenger seat.

Before the sun rose, he used his dome light to page through agency statutes to assure himself they were on firm legal footing.

According to section 12, "No person shall use any aircraft with the intent to spot, locate, and aid in the taking of any game animal from August 1 through January 31 of the following calendar year. Nothing in this Section shall apply to the operation of an aircraft in a usual manner where there is no attempt or intent to locate any game animal, such as aircraft used for the sole purpose of passenger transport."

And: "(B) 'Aircraft' means any machine or device (including but not limited to airplane, helicopter, glider, dirigible, or unmanned aerial vehicle [UAV]) capable of atmospheric flight."

He saw the problem: Whoever was piloting the drone had been doing so on April 26, when it was technically legal to do so. It would be hard to prove that the pilot wasn't scouting big game with the purpose of hunting them later.

But there were two statues Joe thought he could apply in

these circumstances, and he felt he could cite them without hesitation to the pilot, as well as to Dulcie to bring formal charges.

The first statute was under section 23-3-107—"Wanton destruction of big game animal."

It read: "(A) No person shall wantonly take or destroy any big or trophy game animal."

The key word in the statute for Joe was *destroy*. The pilot was destroying winter-weakened mule deer by running them until they collapsed. Katelyn could document that charge, and each dead deer was a first-degree misdemeanor.

The second statute was section 23-3-303—"Waste of edible portion of game bird, fish or animal."

It read: "(A) No person shall take and leave, abandon or allow any game bird, game fish, or game animal except trophy game animal, or edible portion, to intentionally or needlessly go to waste."

Obviously, Joe thought, the regulation was written to apply to violators who left what they killed or caught. But he thought it would apply to the pilot as well.

An angry judge could fine the pilot a thousand dollars for each wanton destruction and waste charge, confiscate the drone and controls, revoke hunting and fishing licenses from the pilot, and sentence the miscreant to months of jail time. Dulcie could choose to involve the feds in the case to further hammer the pilot for not registering his aircraft and for breaking other federal laws.

It would be new territory going after a drone pilot, Joe knew. But nothing made him angrier than someone who caused the needless death of wildlife.

He knew Katelyn felt the same way.

Nate had his own reasons for going after the drone.

"ANY SIGHT of it yet?" he asked Katelyn over his hand-held radio. They'd decided to communicate outside the departmental channel on the off chance that the pilot listened in.

"Nothing," she said. "But I can see about eighty deer and a half-dozen elk out on the meadows."

"I can see the elk," he said. Another ten to twelve cows and calves were still in the shadows of the timber below him and had not yet ventured out into the open. He'd noted that the forest smelled of their musky scent.

"Your friend Nate is here," she said.

"I thought he would be."

"We're ready for anything. I hope we picked the right day."

"It's a beautiful morning for a takedown," Joe said.

THE NIGHT BEFORE, Joe had done some rudimentary research on the Internet on drones and drone pilots. There were both federal rules administered by the Federal Aviation Administration and various state regulations.

For a $150 fee, pilots had to obtain a remote pilot certificate by passing a test at an FAA-approved Knowledge Testing Center. After passing, the pilot had to complete an Airman Certificate and Rating Application to receive a certificate to fly the aircraft. The drone itself had to be registered as either a "hobby-ist" or "non-hobbyist" item.

Joe wasn't surprised to learn that both of the requirements were routinely ignored. Anyone could buy a drone and put it in the air upon receipt, and enforcement of the federal rules was all but nonexistent.

There were less than one hundred and twenty registered drones in the entire state of Wyoming. According to the digital database, none of them were located in Twelve Sleep County. There were also no certified pilots in the area.

Which meant that whoever was flying the drone was doing it illegally, which also wasn't shocking.

What *was* a surprise was that dispatch in Cheyenne reported to him that the owner of Wyoming license plate 2-8948 could not be determined. In Joe's years on the job, that had never happened before. He assumed he'd misread the plate on the back of the white SUV, because he could think of no other explanation.

WHILE HE WAITED, he replayed a conversation he'd had with Marybeth the night before. They'd been in bed. It had been about Justin Hill and his family.

She'd confessed that she didn't know very much about them.

She said, "I know Justin lives outside of Winchester and ei-ther takes the bus to high school or gets a ride. What's strange is that I've seen several different guys drop him off in front of the school, which confused me. I thought maybe they were his uncles or something. For a long time, I didn't know which one was his dad."

Joe asked about the several different guys, and Marybeth described stout, serious men who could all be Justin's father because they seemed like the right age.

"I finally met his dad, Bill, at Senior Honors Night," she said. "I remember seeing him with those two other men who had dropped Justin off at school. The three of them were seated together by themselves in the back row of the auditorium, looking really bored.

"Bill walked up to Lucy and Justin after they'd both gotten awards. He wasn't super friendly."

Joe asked what she meant by that. He'd been at the event, but he recalled that he was talking with some fathers who were hunters in the lobby while Marybeth stayed inside the school auditorium after the ceremony.

She said, "Well, I mean, Lucy and Justin have been a couple for the entire school year. You'd think Bill would have a little bit of interest in us and our family. But he just walked up to remind Justin that they needed to get going home. Bill hardly looked at me or at Lucy. And Justin didn't really introduce us, which I found strange. He's such a nice, polite boy, but I got the impression he was uncomfortable when his dad showed up. Like he was embarrassed he was there."

Joe asked for a description.

"Kind of dark," she said. "Not from around here, I thought. But he was all decked out in cowboy clothes that . . . just didn't look right. He wore one of those fancy embroidered shirts with piping on it like country singers used to wear, a great big ten-gallon hat that was creased wrong, and boots that looked like they cost as much as your entire wardrobe. And one thing I noticed—he had a thick gold chain around his neck. I thought that was unusual."

Joe agreed. He asked what Bill Hill did for a living.

"He's retired, I guess," she said. "I asked Justin once, and he said his dad sold his company back east and moved here. He didn't say what kind of company it was. It was clear Justin didn't really want to talk about it, so I didn't press. Lucy was kind of glaring at me at the time—as you can imagine."

JOE WAS PUZZLING over what he'd learned about the Hill family when his handheld radio lit up and Katelyn said, "There it is."

DAISY HEARD IT first and raised her head from the seat. And from somewhere above in the sky, Joe could hear it as well—a low buzzing sound.

KATELYN PRESSED THE binoculars to her eyes and kept the drone in her field of vision while she spoke to Joe on the radio. She didn't dare lose sight of the aircraft.

Behind her, Nate was moving.

"Do you see it?" she called to him.

"I don't have to see it," Nate said. "These guys have to see it."

The drone moved quickly through the air from left to right against the dark green backdrop of the timber on the western slope. She guessed that it was fifty feet above the treetops, but as she focused in on it, the drone began to drop in elevation as it homed in on the grazing deer and elk.

She lowered the binoculars and looked over her shoulder.

Nate had emerged from his van with one of the peregrine falcons on his right fist, the jesses wrapped around through his fingers to keep the bird tight. He reached over with his free hand and gently removed the hood from the bird.

Its eyes were two cold black beads. The falcon displayed no emotional reaction other than opening and closing its hooked beak. Nate raised the bird shoulder height and pointed in the general direction of the streaking drone.

She watched as the falcon leaned forward and craned its neck out. She could tell by the slight movement of its head that it had locked in on the target and was tracking it through the air. She found it astounding since she could barely see the drone without magnification.

Nate let go of the jesses. She could feel a blast of air as the peregrine unfurled its wings and flew free with two short percussive flaps of its wings. The tips of the jesses brushed her cap as the falcon bit into the air and rose above her. She ducked as an afterthought.

He turned on his heel and retrieved a second peregrine and repeated the procedure and the release. Katelyn watched, mesmerized.

There were now two birds in the sky, but they were harder to see than the drone because they'd flown high above the valley in tight circles.

"They caught a thermal," Nate said to himself as much as to Katelyn. "They can gain a lot of altitude in a hurry."

She turned back toward the drone and could now make it out with her naked eye. It was hovering over the gathering of elk but not descending toward them. Nevertheless, the elk were nervously raising their heads while they shuffled around.

The large herd of deer wasn't yet in a panicked run, but they were starting to walk toward the edge of the meadow away from the aircraft.

She raised the radio. "Joe, do you see it?"

"No, but I can hear it."

"Do you have a visual on the pilot?"

"Nope."

Frustrated, she let the binoculars drop by their cord to her chest while she gestured toward the drone hanging over the winter range and then toward the falcons that were still rising into the light blue sky.

To Nate, she said, "The drone is right there, but your birds are going so high into the sky they might go into orbit."

He gave her that look again that chilled her and said, "Wait."

JOE SWUNG OUT of his pickup and eased the door closed behind him to keep Daisy in. He didn't want to slam it and alert the drone pilot, whom he thought might be close enough to hear the sound through the trees.

He walked from the pickup to the edge of a larger clearing and cocked his head. He could hear the hum of the drone but nothing from the pilot or the pilot's vehicle.

Then he thought of something. By trying to locate the pilot in the thick timber, he might give himself away. The pilot might hear him coming and possibly flee before Joe could find him.

Although it was tough to be patient while the aircraft was suspended somewhere above him, he had to be. And he had to stay hidden in the timber and not venture into the open where he could get a better view of the aircraft.

Because if he could see the drone in the sky, the drone could see *him*.

So he stepped back into the shadows, turned down the volume of the radio to a whisper, and held it up to his ear.

Wait.

KATELYN NOTICED THAT the deer were covering more ground and she quickly realized why. Although the drone wasn't herding them like it had done before, it was shifting its focus from the elk and moving in their direction. It was still high enough above them that they hadn't spooked, though. It was as if the pilot were toying with them, staying just far enough out of their bubble to alarm them but not set them into a panic.

Without warning, the drone rose quickly. She tracked it against the dark timber, but it didn't take long before the aircraft rose above the summit and vanished briefly in the blue.

"What's he doing?" she asked out loud.

"No idea," Nate responded.

"Where are your falcons?"

"Damned if I know."

Once it attained a very high altitude, the drone shot across the sky and descended again in a flash. It was now hovering in front of the deer herd, which caused them to spin and reverse course back to where they had started out. Then, in an airborne flanking maneuver, the aircraft flew around the herd and was in front of them again.

The pilot was keeping the deer in one spot, herding them as if the drone were a sheepdog. Katelyn could sense the panic level rising within the herd. Several deer raised up on their hind legs before settling back down to the ground.

"The son of a bitch is playing with them," she said to Joe over the radio.

"Yup."

From behind her, Nate whispered, "Here come the killer falcons."

She craned her head back and couldn't see them at first. A second later, two tiny dots appeared in the sky like flyspecks on a cloud.

The specks got larger as they dropped. It was as if two bullets had been fired.

Peregrines didn't flap their wings when they dropped. Instead, the birds pressed their wings against their bodies and descended like missiles, headfirst. Their talons weren't outstretched to grab the target in flight, but folded back to make the falcon more aerodynamic. An instant before intercepting its prey, the bird would unleash its balled talons and strike like a hammer.

She shifted her attention to the drone. It was in the process of circling the herd again. Below it, the deer milled and jumped, unsure where to go.

The falcons shot right by the drone on either side of it.

"They missed!" Katelyn yelped.

Nate said nothing, but his silence told her to remain calm.

She saw one of the falcons flare out its wings and roll and stop its descent just past the aircraft and reverse course so it was now flying *up*. It struck the drone from below so hard that Katelyn could hear a *smack* even at that distance.

The drone tilted sidewise in midair and the propellers whined as if straining. It dropped twenty feet before regaining its equilibrium, and stabilized for a beat just as the second peregrine delivered another strike into its underbelly.

With a sound she'd heard only in World War II movies, the aircraft whined and arced toward the valley floor and hit well away from the herd of deer in a high-speed crash that sent bits of white metal and plastic scattering across the new spring grass.

Three or four falcon feathers that had been dislodged by the hits floated down from the sky.

Katelyn was thrilled. She turned and grinned at Nate.

"That was magnificent," she said.

She was surprised to see that his eyes were moist and he could barely speak.

"I'm so proud of them," he whispered.

—————

JOE HAD A good angle on the crash in the meadow because it happened less than a hundred yards away from him. The drone had whistled through the air and then smashed into the ground with surprising force. Pieces of it were scattered through the spring grass. Afterward, it was utterly silent.

Joe no longer had to worry about walking into the open or being spotted from the sky. He picked his way down the rest of the hillside through the timber. The trees were too close together for him to consider driving his pickup down.

As he descended, he was filled with joy. Nate's Air Force had accomplished its mission and he was back at work on the best kind of day imaginable. It was sunny, almost warm, but not yet hot. Late April in Wyoming was pre-bug and post–snow and ice. He could almost hear the wildflowers in the meadow straining to grow and open.

Joe paused at the edge of the timber and raised his handheld.

"Now we see who comes to pick up the pieces," he said.

"Do you have eyes on anyone?"

"Not yet."

"Keep us updated."

"Will do."

He could hear Daisy whine from inside the cab of his pickup up on the hillside. She didn't like it when he left her there. He hissed at her to simmer down, and he wished he'd closed the driver's-side window after he'd left.

He hoped that the drone pilot wouldn't hear her crying and get spooked.

Although it was in pieces, the drone was bigger than Joe had guessed it would be. He counted four propellers—two still attached to the carcass and two others broken off in the dirt. There were no obvious markings on it.

The wreckage reminded him of when he'd been called out to collect a dead eagle that had been hit by a passing vehicle: magnificent, large, and full of life one moment, and a ragged and broken spent casing after impact.

To his right, maybe three hundred yards away, he heard an engine start up deep in the timber. That was followed by the popping of rocks under tires as the vehicle descended toward the meadow and the crash site.

Joe pressed tight to the trunk of the tree he was hiding behind.

The drone pilot was on his way to retrieve the carnage.

At that moment, Daisy leaped from the open pickup window and thundered down the hillside toward—and past—where Joe was standing. He called to her, but she was beside herself and on a mission of her own.

She ran out into the meadow to retrieve the drone that had fallen from the sky. Her hard-wiring overruled Joe's command to stop and come back. He did have to admit to himself that the drone fell to the earth the same way a shot pheasant or grouse did when he was bird hunting. And when she bolted out to retrieve a dead bird, he praised her effusively for it.

"*Daisy!*" he shouted.

But she didn't halt until she was on top of the wreckage and could see firsthand that it wasn't a dead bird. She looked back at Joe with a befuddled expression and her tail swiped back and forth like a metronome.

He heard the squeal of brakes from his right. The drone pilot had no doubt seen Daisy out there as well.

Before the driver was able to throw his vehicle into reverse, Joe craned around the tree and lifted his binoculars.

He could see the squared-off white nose of an SUV on an ancient two-track that emerged from the timber. But it was stopped and in shadow before coming out into the open. It retreated just as Joe focused his glasses on its snout.

But he recognized the license plate: 2-8948.

JOE, KATELYN, AND NATE circled the crash site in the meadow and shook their heads. Daisy had been banished back to Joe's truck.

Katelyn photographed the scene before approaching the main body of the drone and squatting down next to it.

"There's some writing on the side," she said. "It says this is a DJI Phantom 4 Pro. It looks expensive."

"Not expensive enough for the pilot to come get it back," Joe said sourly. "Thanks to my dog."

She said, "We can bag up the pieces and send them to the forensics lab in Laramie. Maybe they can pull a fingerprint or two. Maybe even some DNA. The camera on it looks like it's in good shape. I'll be interested to see if we can retrieve some of the images."

He nodded.

She said, "With that plate number and some forensics, I think we have enough for a search warrant of the Hill property."

"Even though the plate doesn't seem to be registered to anyone," Joe said.

"Have you ever run into that before?"

"Nope."

Nate told Katelyn and Joe that he needed to get back to his shop. He said that the second peregrine had wounded its wing on the propeller and he needed to assess whether stitches were necessary.

"Thank you," Katelyn told him.

"Ditto," Joe said. "I wasn't sure it would work."

"Neither did I," Nate said.

He neared Joe and said softly, "Call me if you need some help."

"I thought you were out of that business," Joe said.

"I'll always help a friend."

With that, Nate climbed into his vehicle and drove away.

WHEN NATE WAS GONE, Joe and Katelyn picked up bits of the drone and put them into evidence bags with gloved hands.

She said, "Your judge or mine?" Meaning, in which county should they pursue the search warrant and eventual charges. The crime had taken place in hers, but the likely suspect was in Twelve Sleep County.

"What's your judge like?" Joe asked.

Katelyn chose her words carefully. "Judge Caroline Hartsook-Carver is smart and very ambitious. She's got her eye on running for higher office. Some cops in my county say she chooses her cases by how they'll make her look, meaning how much press coverage they'll generate. I don't know whether she'd get excited about a drone or not."

"I'd say Judge Hewitt, then," he said. "He's cranky, but he's also a big hunter. I don't think he'll look very kindly on someone stressing out the winter herds."

"Sounds good," she said. "I'll leave that up to you. But I want to be there when we go to Bill Hill's place. This is personal to me."

"Deal," Joe said.

"This is shaping up to be a real unusual case," she said. "Who knows where it will go?"

He agreed. Joe could not yet draw straight lines between abandoned traps, drone activity, Papa Hill, a license plate that couldn't be accounted for, and a security gate that looked like it should be outside a military installation rather than a bunch of log homes in the Bighorn Mountains.

He tried not to think about what Lucy's reaction would be when she learned that he was going after her boyfriend's family.

CHAPTER EIGHT

INFANTE SAT AT a battered and sun-bleached picnic table in a deserted campground at Upper Tonto Creek in the Tonto National Forest two hundred and fifty miles east of Scottsdale. He had a dilemma.

On the table in front of him was a cheap cell phone, a bottle of Gran Patrón Platinum tequila, and a thin leather wallet. A slight breeze played through the tall trees surrounding the campground and the air smelled of pine and desert dust. It was much cooler in the mountains beneath the Mogollon Rim than it had been around Phoenix. The display inside the panel van had said it was seventy-nine degrees when they arrived. It would get much cooler as the sun dropped, because the campground was located at more than five thousand feet.

Their timing was fortunate. It was still too early for the summer throngs of day-trippers and campers to flee the desert heat for the mountains. They'd seen only two hard-side recreational trailers in the Ponderosa Campground on the way up, and there were none at Upper Tonto. There was no campground host, either.

The terrain was rough and complex. It was high desert with tall pine trees, spectacular cliffs and bluffs, and red-rock formations. Deeply eroded creeks flowed with rust-colored runoff. He could easily imagine Geronimo and his bloodthirsty Apache band moving through the area to pillage and harass white ranchers and hapless soldiers in the 1880s. Infante had once been enamored of Geronimo, until he'd read about him and found out that the war leader was actually distrusted and despised by his fellow Indians and that nearly every word he'd uttered was a lie, including to his own people. Still, though, he had a great name, and the tortures he devised—roasting white women alive and disemboweling captured male Mexicans or Americans and staking them to anthills—were certainly inventive.

But Infante had broken with Geronimo's methods the more he read about the Apache. Geronimo had tortured and killed for the fun of it, with no purpose in mind other than sadism. It wasn't to obtain information, gain territory, or terrorize, which in Infante's mind were pragmatic reasons. In fact, Geronimo was so savage he'd turned even his own people against him, and he'd given white soldiers motivation to pursue him to the ends of the earth.

THEY'D CHOSEN the most remote site in the campground to park. It was at the end of the gravel road on top of a rise that overlooked the creek. From that location, Infante would be able to see an approaching vehicle from below, and it would be very difficult for anyone to simply happen by without warning.

Cesar and Adelmo had recently returned to the campsite after scouting the rock formations on the mountainside. They'd both been sweating and covered with dust when they got back, but Cesar claimed he'd found a perfect location for what they were about to do. Infante trusted Cesar's judgment in these matters and he promised the both of them they could share the $180 bottle of tequila on the journey back to Payson.

As always, Cesar had borrowed Adelmo's tools to prep the work. He'd cut off the tips of the fingers of all three bodies with wire cutters and had broken up their dental work with a ball-peen hammer. Identifying marks on the skin were removed with a utility knife.

Then Cesar had sawed up the bodies so they'd be easier to carry. Cesar had located an additional body bag from his stash.

Infante pushed the bottle aside and once again opened the man's wallet on the table. He thumbed through the credit cards, the scraps of paper, the eight hundred dollars in cash, and the ID.

And he tried to decide what to do.

HE'D LEFT ABRIELLA in Payson that afternoon. She'd refused to stay at the chain hotel he'd picked out for her and instead had insisted on getting a suite at a casino resort that cost twice as much. He'd kept the other three reservations for himself, Cesar, and Adelmo.

It was standard operating procedure when they were on the road: four separate hotel properties, all individual rooms. They never stayed at expensive places. Only fools stayed in the same hotel and called attention to their arrival.

They'd traveled to the national forest for more than five hours via AZ-87 N and AZ-260 E in two vehicles: a Mercedes SUV driven by Abriella and the panel van with the three body bags on the back deck driven by him. At the resort, Adelmo had climbed out of Abriella's Mercedes and joined Infante and Cesar in the van.

"I don't do nature," she'd told him.

He didn't insist that she come along. He'd learned better.

Abriella Guzman scared even him. Compared to Abriella, Adelmo Cruz the torturer and Cesar Reyes the body-disposal expert were Boy Scouts.

Adelmo and Cesar looked like thugs all the time, despite what they wore or how much they tried to smile. They were blunt objects.

But he felt a chill when Abriella's sweet, childlike, heart-shaped face turned suddenly cold and ruthless. It was as if her eyes retracted into her skull, leaving two black holes. It happened so quickly, this transformation from charming and attractive to deadly and remorseless, that it took his breath away.

She never talked about her past, even during long rides in the car. Infante had heard that she was from Mazatlán in the state of Sinaloa, the daughter of a high-profile cartel lieutenant. As a teenager, she'd been kidnapped by her father's enemies in a home invasion, and raped and abused by her captors for months afterward. After she'd escaped, she'd hunted them down and killed them one by one over the next several years. She'd also killed their girlfriends, wives, and children.

Infante didn't know for sure if the story was true or apocryphal, and he never asked her about it. He was afraid if he did, her eyes would go cold, and who knew what would happen next. He'd seen her do things that would haunt the dreams of the hardest men.

If she hadn't possessed such skill with entrancing targets and luring them to their deaths, Infante would gladly cut her loose or kill her and never think about her again. But who else could have met up with Tim Kelleher on the street and quite literally been invited into his home? Infante knew that he himself could come off as handsome and smooth when he wanted to, but he could still sense innate caution from strangers when he talked to them. Kelleher would have gone to the other side of the street when he saw a lone man out on a walk in his neighborhood.

But Abriella was mercurial and high maintenance as well. Those traits always kept Infante on edge. He preferred careful and deliberate planning, and he was willing to be patient and even abort a lucrative operation if the risk was too high.

Not Abriella. She insisted on expensive rental cars and the best accommodations. And when she got close to a target, the target would end up dead no matter what other circumstances there were. His bosses absolutely loved her.

So if she said she "didn't do nature," he didn't argue with her.

To Infante, Abriella was a female version of Geronimo. And she'd probably warm to the comparison.

———————

CESAR AND ADELMO huffed through the rocks and trees after their fourth foray away from the campsite, and they sat down heavily at the picnic table.

"One more trip," Cesar said, catching his breath.

Adelmo cracked the seal of the tequila and took a long drink before handing the bottle to Cesar. Adelmo licked his lips and said it was really good.

"I don't have to tell you not to drink too much of it," Infante said. "We've still got a couple of hours before it's dark. Save the rest for the drive back. I'll even buy you both another bottle when we get to Payson."

"Why do we have to wait?" Adelmo asked.

Infante waved his hand toward the trees around them. "The people around here get really nervous about forest fires. If someone saw smoke, they'd call in a truck or a helicopter to put it out. We can't risk it. Right, Cesar?"

"Right," Cesar said.

Adelmo nodded, but it was obvious he'd rather finish up and go to the hotel.

Cesar said, "Let me catch my breath and we'll get everything ready. These bodies are fucking heavy, you know. From now on, we kill only skinny ones."

That struck Adelmo as funny and he brayed a laugh. Infante smiled to go along.

Cesar had described to Infante the large crack in the rocks he'd found above the campground. He said it was deep enough that they couldn't see the bottom, and he guessed that it went ten to twelve feet down. He'd tested the depth by dropping rocks into the opening and counting the seconds until he heard a thud. It took three seconds.

They'd kick the body parts into the crack, then douse them with gasoline from a five-gallon can stored in the van. Then they'd throw in the empty body bags to burn as well. No one would see the rising smoke in the dark, and the flames would be largely contained within the narrow cavern.

Someday, a hiker or hunter might discover the charred bones. Infante didn't worry too much about that. The bodies would be tough to identify, and the Wolf Pack would be long out of the state by then.

AS CESAR AND ADELMO prepared to leave with the last body bag and the can of gasoline, Infante took the cash and handed the wallet to Cesar. "Make sure it burns," he said.

Cesar chinned toward the cell phone on the table. "You want me to get rid of the burner, too?"

"Not yet."

FOR THE SAME REASON they used only cash and not credit cards to pay for everything—and getting more cash was never a problem—it was SOP for the four of them to use only inexpensive prepaid cell phones, which they bought at roadside convenience stores. The phones were replaced every three or four days. The only calls made on them were to each other. Unlike with smartphones, the burners they used did not allow for GPS tracking.

That way, there was no digital record of their movements, and transcripts of their calls couldn't be used against them by law enforcement or their enemies.

It was the stupid use of a smartphone that had led them to the man who had called himself Tim Kelleher. The man just couldn't play his role. He kept calling his old friends back in New Jersey without realizing that people could listen in and track him down.

It was a question Kelleher kept asking Infante in Kelleher's house that afternoon: "How did you find me? Did somebody rat me out?"

By that time, Infante had pretty much convinced the man that they'd let him live if he gave up Ernie Mecca.

Karen had passed out from pain at that point, both of her knees a mess. Infante was disgusted that Kelleher had done nothing to save her. He'd just sat and watched. He hadn't even offered his wife any words of encouragement as the drill went in.

"You killed the guy who knew," Kelleher said, nodding toward the body of the man on the living room floor. "That's where he came from. Swole was with Ernie until he couldn't stand the boredom and the cold up there, and he came down here to visit."

"Where did he come from?" Infante asked. He sensed Adelmo coming up behind him with the drill in his hand.

"I don't know," Kelleher said, his eyes big. "Montana. Wyoming. Colorado. One of those fucking square states up north."

"You can do better than that."

"Really—Swole knew how to keep his mouth shut, and I never asked because I don't care and I didn't want to know. As far as I'm concerned, Ernie is dead to me. We never talked. All I know is that Ernie always wanted to play cowboy. He always went to Western movies—shit like that. It was always a thing with him. So he went to someplace where he could do that."

Infante had nodded to Adelmo, and the drill whined. Then Adelmo moved in until the bit was an inch from Kelleher's shoulder.

"I'd tell you if I knew," Kelleher said in a panic. "I'd really tell you if I knew."

"Swole never mentioned where he lived? Come on, Tim: *Think*."

But it was obvious he really didn't know, and Abriella cut his throat from ear to ear. Infante and Adelmo jumped back so they wouldn't be painted with blood.

Then she walked across the room and did the same to Karen.

That was the thing with Abriella, Infante thought. A few more minutes and Kelleher might have recalled a place name, or come up with the name of a guy who knew a guy who knew where Ernie Mecca was living.

And if she hadn't taken this Swole character out within a minute of entering Kelleher's house, maybe he'd have sung.

But they'd never find out.

———————

THE PLACE WAS such a slaughterhouse after the bodies were zipped into bags and hauled out to the van that it took eighteen hours for Cesar to clean it up. They kept the drapes closed, and Cesar worked through the night, scrubbing down the walls and floors and ripping up blood-soaked carpeting to expose old linoleum. He went through three gallons of bleach.

Few people really understood how difficult it was to leave no trace—especially when three victims had bled to death in a house. Infante knew that if highly qualified forensics people followed up, they would find something—a hair, dried blood in between the cracks of the hardwood floor, *something*—that would confirm that murders had likely taken place there. But that didn't concern him. All he cared about was that there were no traces of the Wolf Pack left to be found.

Cesar wiped down every surface and even packed the Kelleher couple's clothing in suitcases and then took them along so it looked like they had gone on an extended vacation.

While Cesar did his job and cursed Abriella for the gore she'd left behind, Infante monitored the local television news and listened to a police scanner. There was plenty of violence in Phoenix—gang-related drive-bys, mainly—but no one called about two missing people in Scottsdale. Infante wasn't surprised that the Kellehers hadn't made friends close enough to them to be concerned about their comings and goings. Tim was a famous hard case, and Karen didn't seem to be much of a peach, either.

—————————

INFANTE KNEW IF the address on the driver's license panned out, they'd be headed northeast. That was the direction they were already going, so they wouldn't have to backtrack. They'd be out of Arizona and into New Mexico by the next day, then up into Colorado. Infante had skied at Aspen and Telluride, but both Wyoming and Montana were a mystery to him. They seemed like states that existed in cowboy movies but not in real life. That part of America was foreign to him.

He heard a distant *whump* when the fire was lit. Soon after, he heard shouting and several gunshots followed by hysterical laughter.

At the sound of the gunshots, he pulled his weapon from his waistband and placed it on the picnic table in front of him with the other items. He checked the road down below them, hoping no one else had heard the shots and decided to investigate.

He was furious with Adelmo and Cesar. Why would those idiots fire a weapon and risk discovery? He cursed them in Spanish and English.

Then it was nearly quiet: only the sound of the distant creek and the muffled crackling of the fire itself. Soon he could smell the burned gasoline and the roast-pork odor of burning flesh. Small bits of clothing from the burning suitcases rose into the dark and danced a slow dance until they extinguished and fell. He hoped none of them started a grass fire.

He took a long pull of the tequila and screwed the cap back on. It was smooth and tart at the same time.

When Adelmo and Cesar emerged from the darkness, they were still giggling.

"What happened?" he asked in a tightly controlled hiss.

"There was a bobcat down there." Adelmo laughed while doubling over. "That cave was its den! It came out on fire and it scared Cesar so bad he shot it."

"Fucking cat," Cesar growled. "I'm glad he didn't get far."

"I've never seen him so scared," Adelmo howled.

"Did any grass catch on fire?"

"No, sir," Adelmo wheezed. "And we stomped on that burning cat until it went out."

INFANTE STEPPED ASIDE and used the burner to place a call. Although he doubted that the name and address on the Wyoming driver's license were authentic, he needed research that he couldn't do on the road himself.

Calling his bosses was always an act of last resort. He hated to do it, and he prided himself on how rare it was necessary. But they had researchers and lawyers to do this kind of follow-through.

When the call was taken on the other end, he said simply, "Tom Kinnison. Winchester, Wyoming."

He disconnected and slid the phone into his pocket. He'd keep the burner until they called him back. Then he'd destroy it and replace it with another.

Infante walked to the van and slid behind the wheel and started it up. Cesar and Adelmo tumbled in. Adelmo was still laughing and Cesar clutched the bottle of tequila by the neck. They smelled of sweat, smoke, and liquor.

"*Son idiotes de mierda*," he said under his breath.

You're fucking idiots.

Which made Adelmo laugh even harder.

INFANTE WONDERED WHAT Abriella would think of going north into the Rocky Mountains. He figured that since she "didn't do nature," she'd probably hate it.

And if Abriella Guzman was in a foul mood, the scene at the Kelleher house would seem restful in retrospect.

MONDAY,
APRIL 30

Middle of the night grey wolf come
Take his wife and family some.

WOODY GUTHRIE,
"JIGGY JIGGY BUM"

CHAPTER NINE

THE NEXT MORNING, Katelyn Hamm made lunches in her kitchen for her two boys. Eight-year-old Tyler got a salami sandwich and ten-year-old Brody got his usual PB&J. Her hair was still wet from the shower and she was in uniform except for her holster and weapon, which was on the top of the refrigerator where she always placed it when she came home.

She could hear her sons arguing over something in their bedroom down the hall and she yelled at them to cool it and get dressed. An apple, a bag of chips, and two sleeves of string cheese went into each lunch box. Her boys were competitive and she knew they compared their lunches to see if either of them had gotten something the other hadn't. It was ridiculous.

Her husband, Ryle, had filled his thermos cup with coffee and left for his job at the welding shop just a few minutes before. He'd exited through the door that led to the one-car garage, and she realized she hadn't yet heard him start his truck outside. Maybe, she thought, he was scraping ice off the wind-shields of both of their vehicles, which was something he did during the winter while she made lunches and got the boys off to the bus stop.

The Shell game warden station where they lived was one of the oldest in the state. It was made of log construction and the rooms were tiny, but it was charming in its way, and they put up with it because they had no other options. There were mature trees around it, and there was a large shop outside to park her pickup and store gear and equipment. The barn was decent, and there was a corral for her two mules. Katelyn preferred riding mules over horses in the mountains. Mules were bombproof, and they rarely spooked.

She heard the sound of flesh-on-flesh from down the hall, and Tyler called out in pain. "He hit me."

"He started it," Brody said.

"Is there blood?" she asked.

"No."

"Boys, get dressed."

SHE LOOKED UP as Ryle came back into the house. She could tell immediately that something was wrong because he was pale and he looked shaken.

He said, "There are two men outside who would like to talk to you."

Ryle was a few years older than Katelyn and he'd had a string of hard luck. They'd lost the feed store he'd opened due to the economy and other difficulties after sinking their savings into it. Since then, he'd gone from job to job in Shell over the past few years. He even filled in as a substitute school bus driver from time to time. He was a competent welder, but it wasn't the profession he would have chosen. It had beaten him down.

He never discussed how disappointed he was not to be the top breadwinner in the family, but she knew it ate at him. It was her salary, insurance, and access to the game warden station that kept them afloat. It was obvious to both of them that if she had a different career and they lived in a bigger community, he'd have more job options. But they were in Shell because that's where her district was and she'd been turned down twice after applying for other districts in the state that had gone to game wardens with more seniority.

Often, when she returned to the house from the field, she'd catch him brooding. She appreciated the fact that he never complained and that he didn't show that side of himself to the boys.

"Who are they?" she asked. It wasn't unusual for hunters or landowners to simply show up at the station any day of the week or at all hours.

Ryle said, "They look like feds to me."

"Meaning?"

"Guys in overcoats and ties, black Ford Expedition."

Katelyn paused to try to think. She wasn't expecting anyone—especially feds.

She thought, *What have I done?*

"Tell them I'll be out in a minute as soon as I get the lunches done for the boys."

"You don't want me to invite them in?" Ryle asked.

"No."

He hesitated, not sure how to proceed.

She looked up and said, "If they're going to just show up at our house without warning like this, they can wait a few minutes. They should have called ahead."

"Okay, I'll tell them."

She slid each sandwich into a ziplock bag and sealed it.

"Let me know what they want," Ryle said as he went back outside.

KATELYN TOOK a sidewise glance at the two men as she shooed Tyler and Brody out the front door.

Tyler had green eyes, straw-colored hair, and a wide face. He'd always been pudgy, but he was growing into a tall and strapping boy. Brody was a miniature version of Ryle, with dark features and a furtive nature.

"Who are those guys?" Tyler asked her. It was a good question. She thought that neither of her boys had probably ever seen men wearing anything but jeans and open-collar shirts in their little mountain town of eighty-five people. Except on television.

"Don't worry about them," she said. "Probably something to do with my work."

"Do you want us to stick around?" Tyler asked, narrowing his eyes at them and giving them a glare.

She grinned at her son. She liked it that he was protective of her.

"No, it'll be fine," she said. "Now get going or you'll miss the bus."

SHE HUGGED HERSELF as she approached the two men because she hadn't pulled on a coat against the early-morning chill. To their credit, she thought, they'd hung back until the boys were on their way.

The two men were outside their big SUV, leaning against it and waiting. They were both in their midthirties, she thought. The one against the front quarter panel had short-cropped brown hair, rimless glasses, and a thin face. The man with his back to the closed back door was a head shorter. He had ginger hair and mustache and a doughy, expressionless look. His hands were jammed into the pockets of his overcoat.

"Can I help you?" she asked.

"You're Game Warden Katelyn Hamm?" the tall man said.

"Yes."

He reached inside his knee-length dress coat and withdrew a wallet badge.

"I'm Special Agent Jeremiah Sandburg of the FBI," he said. "This is Special Agent Don Pollock. We're here hoping we can take about a half hour of your time on a special matter as it pertains to the Department of Justice."

She looked them over. "Two special agents with a special matter. That sounds really . . . special."

They didn't return her grin.

"Can we come inside and talk?" Sandburg asked.

"I've got two boys and the place isn't really good for meetings," she said. "What do you want to know? We can talk here."

Katelyn wasn't sure why she took that stand other than it just didn't feel right. The house was a mess like it always was, but it wasn't *that* bad. She just didn't want the two men inside. There was something imperious about them and she didn't want to be judged.

"Is there someplace private we can talk?" Pollock asked. "It's cold out here."

"You should have been here two months ago," she said. Then she gestured toward the road. "There's a restaurant in town called the Hitching Post. Vern's got a private room in the back they use for Lions Club meetings. I'm sure we could use that."

Sandburg and Pollock looked at each other and apparently agreed.

"We'll meet you there in five," Sandburg said. He didn't ask if she had the time or if she had other duties she had to attend to. She wished she did.

Again, she thought, *What have I done?*

The two of them climbed into their vehicle with Sandburg at the wheel. They looked straight ahead as they pulled away.

Katelyn watched as the Expedition went down the road, its exhaust burbling out a small cloud of white.

She was trembling, and she knew it was not entirely from the cold.

_____

VERN LOOKED OUT at her from the kitchen over the batwing doors.

"They're in the back," he said.

She passed by two tables of local ranchers who were finishing up their morning coffee, having already had breakfast and gossiped. It was an everyday thing at the restaurant, and they all acknowledged her as she went by.

Katelyn had always been treated well by the locals and she attributed it to the fact that she was professional and did her job. She responded to calls when she could have begged off and she didn't issue superfluous tickets to flaunt her authority. The locals treated her with respect and she treated them with respect. She didn't talk down to anyone.

It was a quality the two FBI agents could use, she thought.

It bolstered her confidence that she was now in full uniform and the meeting with the FBI was as public as it could possibly be in Shell. Most federal employees weren't held in very high regard in the area, and the ranchers would be on her side if things went haywire, she surmised.

Sandburg and Pollock sat at a table beneath a Lions Club banner. Each had a heavy white mug of coffee in front of him.

"You found it," she said.

"It's not very hard to find, considering it's the only restaurant here," Sandburg said with a chuckle. "This is an interesting part of the world where you are. Neither of us have ever been here before."

She nodded. She wasn't surprised. But she was still annoyed at that tone she detected from Sandburg. It was paternalistic and superior. He seemed to be willing himself to speak slowly and deliberately so she would understand.

"First off," Sandburg said, "I have to ask you if you'd like to have your lawyer present."

"My lawyer? Why?"

He waved it away. "Don't worry, I didn't mean to alarm you. I make it my practice to say that line every time I talk with someone."

"Am I in some kind of trouble?"

"I wouldn't say that at all."

"Then why would I need a lawyer here?"

"Like I said, it's just procedure to make sure we ask."

She flinched. "I don't need a lawyer. I don't even *have* one."

"Of course not," he said with a laugh. "Life is simpler out here."

Sandburg continued. "I really envy you, you know. I get up every morning and sit in traffic for an hour to get to work. You wake up every morning and see mountains and blue sky and send your kids off to school and then spend the rest of the day outside. What a wonderful life you have here."

"There's a little more to it than that, but I do like it here," she said, still a little shaken from the lawyer talk.

"You have a wonderful family and a happy marriage, right?"

"Right."

"Good clean living in the mountains. What more could anyone ask for? It's the American dream."

"I guess," she said. She wondered where this was leading.

"So," she said, pulling out a chair and sitting across from them, "what are we here to talk about?"

This time, the agents didn't look at each other. They were still, and she recognized the tactic for what it was: an effort to intimidate her. She resented them for it.

While Pollock got up and closed the door to the main dining room, Sandburg said, "We have a favor to ask of you, but first I need to set the stage a little, if you don't mind."

She reluctantly nodded for him to go on.

He said, "I assume you have to deal with the same layers of bureaucracy that we deal with on the federal level, and if possible we'd like to avoid that. So instead of us going through our protocols and having the U.S. Attorney for Wyoming reach out to your governor and wait for him to talk to your director, we'd prefer to do this on a back channel. You know, LEO to LEO." Law enforcement officer to law enforcement officer.

"Do what?"

"We need you to kill an inquiry," Pollock said.

She just looked at him.

"My colleague is sometimes a little too blunt," Sandburg said. "What we need is to make sure that you want to do the right thing."

"Which is what?"

Sandburg placed both of his elbows on the table and steepled his fingers. "I'm sure that in your duties you have the discretion to make judgments and that not every minute of your day is by the book. We all make decisions like that if we're good at our jobs and we think about the greater good.

"If a good cop is chasing a bank robber who shot a teller and ran away, he doesn't stop his pursuit because he sees a motorist run a red light, right? Technically, the motorist broke the letter of the law, but it's much more important to catch that bank robber."

She nodded.

He continued. "So sometimes it's best to look the other way and concentrate on higher-priority items for the sake of the greater good, right?"

"It depends on the circumstances," she said.

"Of course it does," Sandburg said. "But wouldn't you agree that those of us in law enforcement are at our best when we use our best judgment?"

"Yes," she said with hesitation.

"So if Agent Pollock and I were to tell you that a case you're pursuing might actually endanger thousands of lives if it results in a trial and conviction, would you consider dropping that inquiry?"

Katelyn said, "Thousands of lives?"

"Maybe tens of thousands," Pollock answered. "Maybe millions."

She said, "You boys must have me confused with someone else. I'm a Wyoming game warden. I enforce our regulations. What could I possibly be involved in that would be such a big deal to the FBI and the Justice Department?"

Sandburg paused long enough to make her squirm before he said, "It's our understanding that you're intending to bring charges against a local drone pilot."

"For taking pretty videos of wild animals," Pollock added.

Katelyn sat back. "I didn't see that one coming." Then heatedly to Pollock: "He wasn't taking *pretty videos*. He was harassing weakened big-game herds to the point that they panicked and ran to their death."

Sandburg said, "So you destroyed his fifteen-hundred-dollar drone in retaliation. Isn't that enough?"

"No. It's not enough. He really pissed me off."

"Hardly a reason to bring charges against him."

Pollock snorted a chuckle.

She leaned toward Sandburg. "You need to explain to me how letting a violator off the hook saves millions of lives. It doesn't make any sense to me."

Sandburg raised his eyebrows. "I wish I could, but I'm prohibited by law from revealing that to you. Not only that, but my superiors would go batshit. You'll just have to trust two special agents from the FBI who traveled thousands of miles on taxpayer money to have this conversation with you. If that doesn't show you the gravity of our request—I'm not sure what could."

Pollock added, "If you go after him, you're trading a big-eared Bambi or two for the deaths of innocent human beings. We're talking about American citizens here."

He sat back and rolled his eyes and said, "That seems like a no-brainer decision to me."

She asked, "Who are these millions of Americans whose lives I can supposedly save by not doing my job?"

Sandburg swept his hand through the room as if it were filled by a crowd. "They're all around you," he said. "Everywhere you look."

She looked from one agent to the other. Her mouth had gone dry and she felt a steady pain in her stomach. "Why should I trust that you're being straight with me?" she asked. "I understand the part about doing a back channel around the bureaucracy, but if this was really just about a few dead deer versus thousands of people, like you say, I'd think the bureau would make its case to people much higher than my pay grade.

"What's so damned special about this drone pilot?" she asked.

"Again," Sandburg said, "we can't reveal that information to you."

Pollock glared at her. "Just drop the fucking case, sister. Pretend it never happened. Just go about your day saving mooses and squirrels and fish, or whatever else the hell it is you do. You do *not* want to make the wrong choice here."

"Are you threatening me?" she asked. She said it calmly, but it felt like a shout.

"We don't threaten," Pollock said. "We don't need to."

"We're the FBI," Sandburg said unnecessarily.

"And you have no authority over me," she said. "I don't work for you."

The two agents looked quickly at each other as if agreeing to take the next step, whatever it was.

Sandburg asked, "Have you ever heard of a federal statute called 18 U.S.C. 1001, also known as 'False Statements and Concealment'?"

She warily looked on.

The agent reached into his jacket and produced a document, which he unfolded. He slipped on a pair of reading glasses.

"'Whoever, in any matter within the jurisdiction of any department or agency of the United States knowingly and willfully falsifies, conceals or covers up by any trick, scheme or device a material fact, or makes any false, fictitious or fraudulent statements or representations, or makes or uses any false writing or document knowing the same to contain any false, fictitious or fraudulent statement or entry shall be fined under this title, imprisoned not more than five years or, if the offense involves international or domestic terrorism (as defined in section 2331), imprisoned not more than eight years, or both. If the matter relates to an offense under chapter 109A, 109B, 110, or 117, or section 1591, then the term of imprisonment imposed under this section shall be not more than eight years.'"

He looked up from his paperwork to Katelyn. "Shall I interpret that for you in common language?"

She gulped and nodded.

He said, "If you lie to us about anything, we can put you in federal prison."

Pollock grinned. He said, "Have you heard of Martha Stewart? Scooter Libby? Bernie Madoff? Michael Flynn? All of them went down for lying to FBI agents."

"I haven't lied to you," she said. "This has nothing to do with me."

Sandburg said, "Remember when I asked you about your wonderful family and happy marriage?"

She crossed her arms over her breasts. "Yes."

He said, "You neglected to tell us that your husband, Ryle Hamm, is a substance abuser who spent so much money on illegal drugs that he lost his business."

Pollock flipped open a notebook he'd slipped from his pocket and perused his notes. He said, "And you neglected to tell us that he moved into an apartment in town for two months before you reconciled and let him come back."

"That couldn't have been a very happy time for you," Sandburg said.

She felt like she'd had the wind kicked out of her.

"I don't think I said what you accuse me of," she stammered. "That's personal and it was between Ryle and me. It's no business of yours. I was just making conversation when you asked."

Ryle was a good father and a good man. Unlike too many men she knew of, men who were dissatisfied and thought only of themselves, he hadn't voted with his feet and left. And after struggling with alcoholism and drug abuse for a period of years, he'd joined Alcoholics Anonymous and had cleaned himself up. He never missed a meeting. She was proud of him for that.

"There's no such thing as 'just making conversation' when it comes to 18 U.S.C. 1001," Pollock said. "The act of omission is treated the same as lying. Can you imagine using that as a defense? That you were 'just making conversation' when you lied to us?"

"You could have asked to have a lawyer present," Sandburg continued. "You waived that right and then proceeded to make false statements."

"I can't believe this," she said. "This is insane. Go ahead, play back your tape. We'll listen to what I said."

Sandburg said, "There is no tape. We don't need a recording when we've got two agents who will testify that you told us a falsehood."

"You didn't even take notes . . ."

"We don't have to," Sandburg said. "We heard you. If need be, we'll write up what's known as an FD-302. What is that, you ask? An FD-302 is a form that summarizes our conversation here and what our impressions are of this exchange. We'll write up the fact that you lied to us. The 302 will be the basis when we testify in court that you willfully withheld information from us that is easily verifiable.

"Think about your boys," he added. "What would they do if you lost your job and were sent away? Would your addict husband take care of them?"

Her eyes flashed with anger. "He's not an addict. He had a problem once and now he's clean."

Sandburg shrugged as if to say, *Not my concern*.

"This is just so ridiculous and unfair," she said. "You two set out to trap me. It's insane."

Again the shrug from Sandburg. Pollock sat back in his chair and looked at his fingernails.

"This is just a bad dream," she said to them. "How did you even find me? We haven't even filed any charges against the drone pilot."

"Good," Pollock responded.

"There's something else you need to see," Sandburg said. He withdrew an iPad from a briefcase that was at his feet. As he scrolled through it, Katelyn stared dully ahead. She couldn't believe what was happening to her. Twenty minutes earlier, she was making lunches for her boys.

Sandburg found what he was looking for and rotated the device so she could see the screen.

She gasped.

The photo was of Katelyn squatting near the cedar tree looking over her shoulder at the airborne camera with an angry expression. Her white buttocks were exposed and her pants were gathered around her ankles.

"How did you get that?" she asked, but she already knew the answer.

"That isn't the question," Sandburg said. "The question is how many people will see it when it's online? Will your boys see it? Will your fellow game wardens see it? One can only imagine the comments."

"He sent it to you," Katelyn said. "The drone pilot."

"It doesn't matter where we got it," Sandburg said. "I can promise you *we* won't circulate it in any way. But I can't speak for others."

Pollock sighed and said to her, "All you need to do is drop the case and you'll never have to worry about any of this. We'll go away and you'll never have to see us again. What could possibly be easier?"

KATELYN WALKED STUNNED through the dining room. If anyone greeted her she didn't hear them. She walked out through the front door and placed both of her hands on the hood of her truck and lowered her head.

She could hardly breathe, and she was grateful that the tears that came from her eyes and pattered on the sheet metal of the vehicle hadn't come earlier while she was talking to Sandburg and Pollock.

She thought, *What would Joe Pickett do?*

And were Special Agents Sandburg and Pollock going to visit him?

CHAPTER TEN

AS HE WALKED across the parking lot of the Twelve Sleep County Building, Joe idly swung by its chain one of the bobcat traps that he'd confiscated from the breaklands. He pushed through the front doors and waved at Stovepipe, who manned the metal detector that was the first stop en route to the courthouse and the sheriff's department.

"I don't think that thing will pass through," Stovepipe said, pointing to the steel-jawed leg-hold device.

"Probably not. Is the machine actually working?" Joe asked about the metal detector. It was usually out of commission and was more ornamental than effective.

"It should be," Stovepipe said. "We had some guys up from Denver to calibrate the settings. Judge Hewitt got pretty pissy when he found out it wasn't working again."

Judge Hewitt was known for packing a 9mm semiauto under his robes, and he'd never been shy about pulling it out if the situation warranted it within his courtroom. But he didn't like the idea of others with concealed weapons who might shoot back.

Stovepipe wore a black Gus McCrae–style cowboy hat and a purple silk scarf around his neck. He always looked like he'd just dismounted from delivering a herd of longhorns to Belle Fourche. He'd been stationed at the metal detector for longer than Joe had been coming to the building.

Joe placed the trap, his gear belt and holster, and all of the metal he had in his pockets into a plastic tub and sent it through the machine on the moving belt.

"Where are you headed?" Stovepipe asked.

"I'm gonna talk to Mike and Dulcie," Joe said, meaning Sheriff Mike Reed and County Attorney Dulcie Schalk.

"Damn," Stovepipe said as Joe walked through without setting off the device. "Maybe it works."

Joe gathered the trap and his phone and he realized he'd forgotten to remove his belt with its metal Wyoming Game Warden Foundation buckle.

"Nope," he said to Stovepipe. "It's still not right."

"Don't tell the judge when he gets back," Stovepipe said.

Joe paused. "He's not around?"

"Negative. He was invited to the Kansas Governor's One Shot Turkey Hunt in El Dorado. Then he goes straight from there on a spring brown bear hunt in Alaska."

"When will he be back?" Joe said.

"After he kills his turkeys and then his bear, I reckon."

Joe snatched the trap out of the tub, but left the rest of his hardware for Stovepipe to keep an eye on. When Stovepipe started to object to the trap, Joe said, "Evidence," and continued on.

SHERIFF MIKE REED rolled his wheelchair from his desk to his credenza, where his computer was located. "The names don't ring a bell," he said. "Bill Hill and, what was the second name?"

"Tom Kinnison."

Reed's movements weren't as fluid as they'd once been, Joe noted. His friend's physical deterioration had come rapidly. Reed had announced recently in the Saddlestring *Roundup* that he had no intention of running for reelection when his term ended the next year. Rumors were swirling about who might run to take his place. Joe had heard that two of Reed's deputies— Justin Woods and Ryan Steck—were interested in the job and were already bad-mouthing each other.

Reed's condition made Joe morose. His friend had been ambushed by gunmen a few years ago, but he'd had the determination and strength not only to continue his run for sheriff, but to administrate the department better than it had been run by previous occupants. Sheriff Reed's wheelchair-accessible van delivered him quickly to crime scenes and situations, and the sheriff was rarely impaired from doing his job by his lack of mobility.

But a long bout of pneumonia had laid Reed up over the

winter and sapped his strength more than Joe had previously realized.

"How are you feeling, Mike?" Joe asked as Reed brought up his monitor and tapped on the keyboard.

"A little better," Reed said. "I thought I was a goner in January. It must be my good looks and clean living that got me through."

"No doubt," Joe said with a smile. He knew Mike still liked his bourbon every night.

Joe had been plagued throughout his career by corrupt, venal, and small-minded sheriffs. Previous to Reed, Joe had clashed with two of them in a row: Sheriff Vern Dunnegan and his henchman replacement Kyle McLanahan. Mike Reed was such a welcome exception that Joe hated to see him go. Sheriff Reed had restored faith in the department throughout the county.

"Too many people think they can't be replaced," the sheriff said, as if reading Joe's mind. "Fact is, everyone can be replaced."

"That doesn't mean I have to be happy about it," Joe said. "After all, Governor Rulon got replaced."

"Good point," Reed said with a chuckle. Then: "It looks like your Bill Hill and Tom Kinnison are clean-living individuals as well. No arrests, no complaints, no callouts."

"And you've never run across either one?" Joe asked.

"No. But I'll be happy to ask my guys," Reed said. Then: "It's pretty difficult to live in this county and absolutely not make a mark. Especially if you're living behind a great big security gate like you described."

Joe agreed. "Marybeth has been doing some research on those two men as well and she's not finding much. It's kind of a strange situation."

"More than strange," Reed said. "Most folks have digital footprints a mile long. These two seem to have somehow avoided that. By the way, you might caution your wife that the new sheriff may not give her the same access to our law enforcement databases."

Joe nodded. "I'll let her know."

From her desk at the Twelve Sleep County Library, Marybeth could get into several state, regional, and national criminal databases, courtesy of Sheriff Reed. Her ability to do research had aided Joe countless times.

"Let me know what you find out," Reed said. "And don't hesitate to give me a call if you need some help."

Joe stood up with his hat in his hands. "Thank you."

"I'm glad to see you're doing so well after what happened," Reed said as he pushed back from his computer. The look on his face was gentle and sincere. "You got your job back, plus a new house. Even a dandy new pickup. It's about time you found yourself on the right side of fortune."

"I agree."

The sheriff smiled slyly. "But you know what that means, don't you?"

"It could all come crashing down on my head just as quick."

"Let's hope it doesn't. You deserve a break after all these years of putting up with that crap and all those people."

Joe flushed and shuffled out into the hallway.

———————

DULCIE WAS AT her desk scrolling through emails on her computer when Joe leaned in and knocked on her open door.

"Got a minute?"

"For you, always," she said with only a hint of sarcasm. Her eyes shifted to the leg-hold trap he had dangling by the chain. "I see that you brought me a lovely gift."

"It's an earring," he said. "I'll bring you one for your other ear the next time I stop by."

She grinned and rolled her eyes. "I really am here on business," he said.

"Then shut the door and sit down."

SHE LISTENED CLOSELY while Joe outlined the parameters of the case he was building against Bill Hill and Tom Kinnison. As always, she took notes on a legal pad while he talked.

Dulcie was a careful and thorough prosecutor and her track record for convictions was impressive. If anything, Joe thought, she was *too* cautious at times.

When he was through, she asked, "When will you get the forensics results back on the drone?"

"Soon, I think," Joe said. "Katelyn's handling that. I'm kind of surprised I haven't heard from her today. She's eager to be there when we talk to Hill."

"Which is premature at this point," Dulcie said.

"What about the partial plate number?" Joe asked. "Isn't that probable cause? Judge Hewitt's granted search warrants in the past for less than that."

"He isn't here," Dulcie said. "I'd have to make the case to Judge Hartsook-Carver. She's filling in until Judge Hewitt gets back from shooting bears. In fact, I think she's scheduled to be on the bench here tomorrow for a preliminary hearing."

Joe winced. He recalled what Katelyn Hamm had said about her.

"Right now, I think we both know you could be accused of going on a fishing expedition," Dulcie said. "I'm not sure Judge Hartsook-Carver will go for that, and I don't really want to present it to her as is. I haven't worked with her enough to know if she'd approve a search warrant based on what you've got, but I doubt it.

"Bring me more to make this a better case," Dulcie continued. "Either the forensics, or a witness, or something bombproof. Then I'll go to her. All we've got at this point are some traps left in the woods, an old man walking around legally with a shotgun, and a smashed-up drone. Oh, and a white SUV with muddy license plates from Cheyenne."

Joe said, "When you put it that way, it does sound a little lame."

She said, "Even *you* have to admit that right now you're probably more curious about what's behind that big security gate than just bobcat traps and drones."

"That's not entirely true. Guys who break game laws don't

stop there. I think of it as a Wyoming version of the broken-windows method of policing."

Dulcie considered what Joe had said. "That's an interesting take."

"And it's legitimate. There's something wrong with a guy who deliberately harms wildlife. It's an indicator of a disturbed mind-set. It's kind of like finding out that a kid enjoys torturing animals—you aren't that shocked when he becomes a school shooter later on."

"That's a bit much," she said cautiously.

"Maybe. Maybe not. A man who leaves steel-jawed traps unattended has a cruel streak. And a guy who chases deer for kicks with a toy airplane until they die from stress is capable of much worse. If someone deliberately hurts innocent wildlife, it isn't much of a leap to think he'd do the same to human beings."

She nodded while she thought it over. "The fact that Bill Hill is the father of the boy dating Lucy has absolutely nothing to do with this, I know."

"Maybe a little," Joe confessed.

"Marybeth shares your concern," Dulcie said. "It drives her crazy that she knows so little about Justin's family or where his dad comes from. This thing about the traps is just something that makes the whole thing even odder."

"True."

"Come back with more, Joe."

"I will."

"In the meantime, I'll start writing up the search warrant

request for Judge Hartsook-Carver. That way, we can just plug in whatever additional evidence you get and we'll be good to go."

"Thank you."

As he pushed his chair back to stand up, she mused, "I may just put in a call to the FAA."

He nodded for her to continue.

"You said drone pilots are supposed to register their drones and get some kind of license, right?"

"Right."

"Maybe they'll be interested in talking to Hill as well," she said.

"I doubt it. This is pretty small potatoes."

"Maybe not to Judge Hartsook-Carver," Dulcie said while arching her eyebrows. "If this case brings in the feds, it might be much higher profile. It might interest the media, if you know what I mean."

Joe said, "That's kind of brilliant. Bringing in the feds would normally be the last thing I'd want to do. But I see your point. Judge Hartsook-Carver might really like the exposure."

"That's why I make the big bucks," Dulcie said. "I'll make a couple of calls and let you know what they say."

He clamped on his hat and held up the trap. "Do you want to keep this in evidence?"

"Not until you bring the other one." She laughed.

As he opened the door, she said, "Big news about Nate and Liv, isn't it?"

"Yup."

"I bet you didn't see that one coming."

"Nope."

"Neither did I. I guess Liv is taming him after all."

"Maybe."

"Nice talking with you, Joe," she said with a dismissive wave of her hand.

He left the building as quickly as he could after he gathered up his possessions from the security area. Joe knew that Dulcie had once been attracted to Nate because she'd asked him several times about the falconer. Marybeth had hinted to Joe that maybe he could introduce them when Nate was unattached, and he surmised the idea had come from her close friend.

No doubt Dulcie was speculating that if Joe had followed through with the introduction when he'd been asked about it, the story might have turned out differently.

WHEN KATELYN DIDN'T pick up, Joe left a message filling her in on his meetings and asking her to call him back.

SINCE HE WAS in town, he stopped for lunch at the Burg-O-Pardner and sat at the counter and ordered a cheeseburger and a side of Rocky Mountain oysters. Behind him at a large table, the usual lunch crowd of present and former city fathers ate and gossiped and critiqued stories in that morning's *Roundup*. They seemed to agree that the high school sports coverage was decent, but that the editorial advocating for a pause in the new grizzly bear hunting season was stupid and revealed the true liberal bias of the new editor.

When he was through eating, Joe spun on his stool and asked the men if any of them had heard of Bill Hill or Tom Kinnison. They looked back at him with blank faces. Then the former sanitation plant manager spoke up and asked Joe if Hill lived outside of Winchester.

"He does," Joe said.

"I thought I remembered that name. He called about garbage pickup."

Which made the other men chuckle. There was no curbside trash pickup in Saddlestring, much less in rural Twelve Sleep County.

"He was kind of rude when I told him we couldn't offer it," the man said. "You know how those types are sometimes. They move out here to be in the middle of nowhere, but they expect the same big-city services they left."

After a beat, Joe asked, "Is that all?"

The man nodded. "I just talked with him that one time and he left a bad taste in my mouth. That might not be fair to him, but that's what happened."

JOE WAS OPENING his pickup door outside the Burg-O-Pardner when the fry cook came out of the restaurant and chased him down.

"Mr. Joe?"

Norman Fast Horse was a Northern Arapaho who was also on the business council for the Wind River Indian Reservation. Joe had met him several times because Norman had a son in April's class at high school. Norman always called him *Mr. Joe*.

"How are you doing, Norman?"

"Decently."

Joe waited. He knew Fast Horse was extremely deliberate in conversation and it didn't help to rush him.

"I heard what you asked the fellows," he said.

"Yes?"

"I don't know either of them guys."

"Okay."

"But I talked to Hill's father a couple of times. He comes in early for breakfast before the fellows show up."

Joe recalled the old man outside the compound with his shotgun.

"He's a strange bird," Fast Horse said. "I call him Vito, like in Vito Corleone. That's because he reminds me of the old man in the movie. He mumbles like that, and he sure doesn't act like he's from around here. He looks more out of place than the rest of you illegal aliens."

Joe smiled. He admired how Fast Horse had kind of slipped in that "you illegal aliens" shot. He'd often seen Fast Horse wearing a T-shirt with a vintage photo of four armed natives and the lines HOMELAND SECURITY—FIGHTING TERRORISM SINCE 1492 printed beneath it.

"I met old man Hill," Joe said. "I got that same impression."

Fast Horse said, "He asked me what Rocky Mountain oysters were and I told him. When he found out it was bull testicles, I thought his eyes were going to bug out. I laughed so hard I thought I was gonna cry. So every time he comes in I say, 'How about some scrambled eggs and oysters, Mr. Vito?'"

"What's his reaction?"

"Ah, he just kind of smiles. Then he does this," Fast Horse said as he formed a pistol out of the fingers of his right hand and pointed it at Joe's chest.

"*Bang*," Fast Horse said.

JOE WAS THINKING about that *Bang* when he checked his phone as he drove out of town toward the breaklands to check more traps. Katelyn had yet to return his call, but there was a *Call me* text from Marybeth.

"I've been going through the databases all day," she said with obvious agitation. She recounted that she'd run both names through NIBRS (National Incident-Based Reporting System), NCIC (National Crime Information Center), ViCAP (Violent Criminal Apprehension Program), and RMIN—the Rocky Mountain Information Network that included Arizona, Colorado, Idaho, Montana, Nevada, New Mexico, Utah, and Wyoming.

"Nothing," she said. "Nada. These guys are as clean as fresh snow."

"Huh," Joe said.

"Then I did a couple of conventional searches. Finally, something about Bill Hill came up."

Joe listened carefully.

"He received an award from the Newark Chamber of Commerce for businessman of the year. There wasn't much else except his name. He was also the guest of honor for the New Jersey State Policemen's Benevolent Association. Good, right?"

"I guess."

"But that's not the interesting thing. Both of the hits were within the last two years. There is absolutely nothing before that."

Joe asked, "How can that be?"

"You tell me," she said. "Do you realize how impossible it is to not come up in a Google search? *Everybody's* on there for something. And if this guy ran a corporation important enough to win a big award and he's so charitable that the state police honor him . . . I don't know. It's baffling. It's like he just showed up on earth for the first time to receive two awards. Then apparently he picked up lock, stock, and barrel and moved to Wyoming."

"Nothing about his business at all?"

"Not that I can find. I'll keep looking, but this is really strange."

"What about Kinnison?"

"He doesn't exist on the Internet," she said. "He's a ghost."

Joe shook his head. It kept getting stranger.

"There is one thing," Marybeth said. "I just got a text from Lucy, and her play practice got canceled after school. She asked me if I could pick up Justin and her."

"I'll do it," Joe said. "I assume Justin needs a ride to his house?"

"Apparently."

"I'm all over that."

"I thought you would be," she said. "But be careful. You're not going out there to snoop around."

"Of course not," he said with a grin.

Chapter Eleven

LUCY WAS WARY when she opened the passenger door and looked in at Joe behind the wheel.

"Mom couldn't make it?"

"Nope. You're stuck with me."

"No problem, Dad. Do you mind giving Justin a ride home?"

"Not at all."

She turned to the back seat and grimaced. The floor and bench seat were covered with gear bags, winter clothing, an M4 semiauto rifle chambered in .308, a necropsy kit, and other day-to-day detritus. Daisy was excited to see her and she did a little dance on the front seat.

"You'll have to sit up front with me," Joe said.

"Obviously." She sighed.

She shinnied in first and Justin climbed in behind her and thanked Joe for the lift. Daisy took a position on the floorboard facing them with her head wedged between Lucy's and Justin's thighs.

"Kind of crowded in here," Joe said. "On to Winchester."

WHILE LUCY AND JUSTIN talked about mutual friends and their last year in high school in a comfortable rapport, Joe observed the boy with furtive side-eyes as he drove. Justin was tall, good-looking, and easygoing. He was quick to smile, and he treated Lucy with respect and with not just a little awe.

"Don't you usually get a ride home?" Joe asked Justin. He'd heard about the large SUV that delivered Justin and picked him up.

"Yeah, well, I do," Justin said. "I was going to get picked up after play practice, but it got canceled, so I'd have to wait around for a couple of hours with nothing to do. Lucy said it was okay to come along with you."

"It's okay," Joe said. "I don't mind at all. Who usually picks you up? Your dad?"

"Sometimes," the boy said with a barely discernible eye roll. "Usually, it's one of the guys."

"One of the guys?" Joe asked.

He felt a nudge on his rib cage from Lucy, although she continued to look straight ahead.

"Yeah," Justin said. "One of my dad's friends."

Before Joe could ask about Bill Hill's friends, Lucy jabbed him sharper with her elbow.

"I met your grandfather the other day," Joe said. "He seems like an interesting character."

Another sharp jab.

"That's one way to put it," Justin said with what Joe read as disapproval.

"You know, Mr. Pickett," the boy said, "I've always wanted to ride along in one of these trucks. What's that thing do?" he asked, pointing toward a radio mounted under the dashboard.

"It's a commercial scanner. Lots of guys out in the woods talk to each other on walkie-talkies," Joe said. "Sometimes they say things to each other that they probably shouldn't. The scanner will pick up that back and forth."

Justin leaned forward, obviously interested. Lucy sat back between her boyfriend and her dad and closed her eyes as if sleeping.

"Like what?" Justin asked Joe.

"Like, 'I think that game warden is gone and he didn't see a thing. Drag that deer out of the bushes and I'll meet you on the road.'"

"Has that ever happened?" Justin asked.

"Yup."

"That's so cool."

For the next ten minutes, Justin asked questions and Joe gave him a personal tour of the inside of the cab. He'd spent so much time in this new truck and a multitude of old—and mostly destroyed—Game and Fish pickups over the years that he'd forgotten how interesting it might be for a first-timer to observe all of the gear, electronics, and tools of his trade.

Lucy turned her head back and forth from Joe to Justin as if watching a tennis match.

Justin was especially interested in the toggle switch that turned on the "sneak lights" mounted under the front bumper. The muted lights allowed Joe to drive ahead in the dark without alerting others who might be on the lookout for him.

He twisted around and his eyes got big when he saw the M4. "What's *that* for?"

"I'm guessing you don't see a lot of rifles," Joe said.

Justin started to respond, but seemed to catch himself. Then he said, "Well, I don't see a lot of *hunting* rifles."

Joe waited for more that didn't come.

Lucy said, "Tell him about the rifle, Dad." Obviously, she'd sensed the tension.

Joe said, "Unfortunately, we get called out quite a lot to dispatch big-game animals that get hit on the highway. I use that to put the animal out of its misery so it won't suffer."

"What do you do with the meat?"

So they were on to a different topic. But Joe had noted Justin's earlier hesitation.

Joe said, "We take it to the homeless shelter in Saddlestring or Winchester, usually. I also know a couple of social workers who know about families down on their luck."

"That's really great," Justin said. "But isn't wild meat kind of, you know, *crappy*?"

"Not at all," Joe said.

"He's right," Lucy interjected. "Elk steaks are a big treat around our house."

"I thought you were a vegetarian?" Justin asked her.

"I usually am," she said.

Joe said, "Justin, a Wyoming vegetarian is someone who only eats meat once a day."

Justin laughed at that, then said, "My mom was a vegetarian. I don't think that helped her when she got sick, but I'm not sure."

Joe was momentarily flummoxed. He realized he'd never heard a mention of Justin's mother from either Lucy or Marybeth. Or maybe they had talked about her and he hadn't paid any attention.

Lucy sensed her dad's confusion and said, "Justin's mom died a few years ago before they moved."

"Oh, I'm sorry," Joe said.

"Yeah. It's okay. She wouldn't have liked it out here. She was a city girl, you know? She hated the idea of camping or anything like that. All of this space would have just weirded her out."

AS THEY NEARED the highway exit to Winchester and sizzled across the bridge over the Twelve Sleep River, Justin said, "I'd really like to learn how to fly-fish one of these days because it seems like such a cool thing to do."

"He's watched *A River Runs Through It* a thousand times," Lucy said, laughing.

"Not that many," Justin said. "Maybe just a hundred."

"I'd be happy to teach you," Joe offered, surprising even himself. "Don't worry—you won't have to cast like they do in the movie to catch fish. Presenting the right fly to a fish in the right circumstances is more important than making forty-yard casts. It's more about learning what bugs are hatching and about what trout like to eat."

Justin said he'd been watching videos on YouTube about casting and tying flies. He asked Joe about streamers, nymphs, and effective dry flies.

While he answered, Joe could sense Lucy's unease with the topic. While she no doubt wanted her parents to like Justin or at least not be hostile toward him, it was obvious to Joe that Lucy wasn't sure she wanted her dad and her boyfriend to become fishing buddies, either.

Then Joe asked, "So none of the guys at your place fish?"

Again, the hard nudge from Lucy. But Justin didn't indicate he'd seen it.

"I wish," Justin said. "But we're all from New Jersey. I guess there's some fly-fishing there, but nobody I ever knew did it."

Joe saw an opening. "Does your dad fish?"

Justin replied, "No, sir, not really. He went striper fishing in the ocean once, but he got seasick and he said it was a perfectly crappy experience. I would have liked to try it, though."

"What does he do?"

"Well," Justin said, "he's retired now."

"What did he *used* to do?"

"He was sort of a banker back in Jersey, but you'd have to ask him."

Joe found it an odd response, and it was obvious Justin didn't want to continue the conversation.

"What kind of banker?" Joe asked.

"I don't understand any of that stuff. He went to work in the morning and he came home at night, when he wasn't traveling. He was gone a lot. But he helped out the cops, I think. They gave him an award."

After a beat, Justin said, "He doesn't like to talk about it and I don't ask."

"How many people live on your property?" Joe asked. Then, to cover himself, he added, "Surely someone would take you fishing?"

"*Dad*," Lucy said, turning toward Joe with flashing eyes. "You're *interrogating* him."

"Sorry."

Justin grinned painfully. "My dad's really into cowboy stuff, but the guys are still kind of . . . settling in, I guess. My dad and I are two different people, I guess you could say. Same with his friends. I don't have a lot in common with any of them."

The way he said it, with utter sincerity, made Joe feel for the boy. And it made him almost sorry he'd pressed the issue.

The road morphed from the county road to the two-track that led to the Hill compound. Trees closed in on both sides of the road and soon they were passing under the pine branch canopy.

To change the subject and clear the air, Joe said, "The first time I came up this road my GPS froze right here. Look, it's doing it again."

He chinned toward the unit, which indicated they were stalled at 2204 Elkhorn Drive.

Neither Justin nor Lucy seemed to recognize the oddity and they exchanged glances.

"But I know I need to keep going," Joe said.

"Yes, sir."

"So who lives in that trailer back there where the GPS gave up?"

"An old couple," Justin said. "I've never met them."

"We're almost there," Lucy said. She was grateful.

JOE STOPPED the pickup in front of the massive gate. He assumed Justin would walk from there, but the boy left his backpack on the floorboard and stepped out of the truck.

"You're embarrassing me," Lucy whispered to her dad.

"I'm sorry for that. Have you ever been here before?"

"Once." Then Lucy, like Justin before, caught herself before she said any more.

Joe turned and looked at her.

"It was innocent," she said while her face flushed. "Please, Dad."

He was pretty sure he didn't want to hear any more, and he felt his own face flush hot as well.

Through the windshield, Justin flipped up the cover of a keypad attached to the stone arch and punched in a key code. Joe observed carefully. All of the buttons Justin pushed were on the top row of the keypad, and he made four distinct movements. That meant the sequence was a four-digit variation using only the numbers one, two, and three.

The gates swung inward toward the compound. Joe's and Lucy's eyes met.

"Just drop him off," she whispered. "And let's go home."

Joe nodded as if he meant it.

Justin slid back into the cab after Joe drove through the open gate.

"IT'S THAT BIG HOUSE," Justin said as Joe rolled into the compound.

"Gotcha."

As they neared the collection of buildings, Joe smelled smoke. In a clearing in the center of all of the outbuildings, three men were gathered around a large premium barbecue grill.

The white SUV he'd noted earlier was parked in one of the metal outbuildings. It was next to a dark silver Lincoln Navigator with smoked windows.

Ahead, Papa Hill sat slumped in a lounge chair smoking a cigarette and holding a bottle of beer in his lap. A huge man with a shaved head the size of a medicine ball stood with his wide back to them. A dark man wearing a brown cowboy hat with a tightly curled brim, a black long-sleeve shirt embroidered with white stitching, and snakeskin boots looked up as the pickup approached. He winced visibly at the sight of Joe's arrival.

"That's my dad," Justin said with a sigh. "This is good."

Joe stopped the pickup.

"Thank you again for the ride," Justin said to Joe.

"It was my pleasure," Joe said. "Let me know when you want to go fishing."

The boy grinned at that, then pecked Lucy on the cheek and opened the door.

"Let's go now," Lucy hissed to Joe.

Instead, he pulled on his hat and got out. He could feel Lucy's eyes burning holes in his back.

Justin skirted the three men and headed toward the house, but he paused on the landing to observe what would come next. He had a pained expression on his face as if anticipating that something awkward might happen. Joe guessed that Lucy was right with him on that.

"Howdy," he said to the assemblage. "I'm Joe Pickett. I'm the game warden around here."

The big man turned slightly and looked over his shoulder. His movement was stiff, as if he were too muscle-bound to pivot. He had close-set eyes that made his round face and head seem even bigger than it was. His expression was of benign hostility.

"I'm Bill, Justin's dad," the black-clad cowboy said. "How do you do?"

Papa Hill simply squinted at Joe through a haze of smoke.

"I'm fine, thanks," Joe said.

"Justin is smitten with your daughter," Hill said as he looked over Joe's shoulder at Lucy in the pickup.

Joe grunted.

"Thanks for giving the boy a ride. Jeff"—he gestured toward the big man—"was planning on picking him up like he does every night."

"I'm Jeff Wallace," the big man said in a surprisingly high voice. "I'm his *driver*." There was a hint of condescension in his tone, as if he considered the task beneath him.

"Nice to meet you," Joe said to the both of them.

Hill said, "When I was Justin's age I couldn't wait to get my learner's permit so I could drive. My boy shows absolutely no interest. Kids these days are different, I guess."

Joe knew that to be true. He had no explanation for it.

"This is my dad," Hill said.

Papa Hill grunted and looked away.

"We've met," Joe explained to Bill Hill.

"I heard."

Hill was pleasant without being friendly, Joe thought. He had a half smile on his lips, and his chin was elevated more than it needed to be when he spoke, as if Joe amused him now that he was there.

There was a picnic table next to the grill, Joe noted. On the table were two empty cartons for six-packs of beer next to a small Yeti cooler. There were four empty bottles next to it.

The grip of a semiautomatic pistol poked out from a shoulder holster that was coiled and placed on the corner of the table. The leather of the apparatus was slick and shiny and well used.

So when Justin said he didn't see many hunting rifles, he meant *as opposed to other guns*.

"This is my Big Green Egg," Hill said, tilting the mouth of a beer bottle toward the heavy round ceramic barbecue grill. It was the shape of a large football. "Ever seen one?"

"Nope."

"It's an amazing device," Hill said. "It's the Cadillac of barbe-cue grills. This baby will smoke meat long and slow, or you can set it to cook a steak at seven hundred degrees. This is my sec-ond one over the years. I couldn't live without it."

Joe nodded. The odor of cooking meat made his mouth water.

Hill said, "We got a special delivery of Portuguese linguica sausage today from Lopes Sausage Company in Newark. As you can guess, it's pretty hard to find around here. Do you want to stay and try it?"

It was an invitation, Joe thought, but it wasn't a real invitation.

"I'm sorry, but I've got to go."

"Want a beer for the road?"

"No, thank you."

Wallace smirked and turned his head back to the Big Green Egg, which was obviously more interesting to him than Joe.

"I was wondering if a guy named Tom Kinnison is around."

Joe noted that Hill's eyes fluttered slightly at the mention of the name, although his half smile never wavered. As if to bolster Joe's observation, Wallace cocked his head and slightly rotated it to hear better.

"Why do you want to speak with Tom?" Hill asked.

"It's about some traps I found with his name on them," Joe said. "They had this address."

"Traps?" Hill asked.

Wallace was obviously trying to suppress a chuckle, and Joe could see his huge shoulders bob up and down.

"Is he here?" Joe asked.

Hill raised his hands palms up and shrugged. "I told that guy he shouldn't be messing with things that he doesn't understand. Just because he watched *Jeremiah Johnson* a hundred times on TV. What does a Jersey guy know about animal traps, anyway? What does he even know about fucking wild animals? So what did he do?"

"He left them unattended."

"And that's a no-no?" Hill said, obviously not impressed.

Joe felt the back of his neck get warm. "It is."

"It must be a big no-no for this guy to come all the way out here," Wallace said with a derisive laugh.

"I'll tell Tom not to do that anymore," Hill said.

Joe gritted his teeth. "That's *my* job."

Wallace rotated slightly and said, "And it sounds like a really important job, too." Then he grinned. He had small, wide-spaced teeth.

As the tension rose, Joe wondered if Lucy could overhear everything from inside the truck. He hoped not, because Hill, Wallace, and Papa were clearly trying to humiliate him.

Not in front of my daughter, Joe thought.

He looked up to see Justin still standing on the porch, taking it all in. He looked mortified.

"Tom is out of the state," Hill said to Joe. "I'm not sure when to expect him back."

"I already told him that," Papa Hill said with a roll of his eyes. "I don't think he's the brightest bulb."

Meaning Joe.

Hill took a long pull of beer and said, "Papa, he's the father of Justin's girl. So be nice."

Papa Hill glared at the Big Green Egg, as if he were waiting for it to hatch.

Joe said, "I understand Wallace here is your son's *driver*, but what does Tom Kinnison do?"

Wallace narrowed his eyes at the word *driver*, as Joe presumed he would.

"Tom does a little of this, a little of that," Hill said. "Apparently now he's a mountain man as well, with all of his little traps. He thinks he's Jeremiah Johnson, I guess."

"Do you know where he is?" Joe asked Hill. "Does he have a cell phone number I could call?"

Hill said, "He probably does, but I don't know it. I wouldn't have any idea how to get in touch with him. Plus, this doesn't really sound like some kinda *emergency*."

Wallace chuckled again at that.

"Please tell him I need to talk with him," Joe said.

"We will convey that information," Hill said, as if reading it from a script.

"Thank you."

Hill said, "Sure you don't want to stay for a beer and a bite of linguica? When you cook it right and you bite into the casing it pops and fills your mouth with greasy Portuguese wonder."

To illustrate it, Hill raised his hand and loudly kissed the tips of his fingers with exaggerated aplomb. Wallace laughed dutifully.

Joe said, "I guess you know the other question I've got to ask. Then I'll be on my way."

Hill shrugged and said, "No idea."

"Do you fly your drone around here or just over the mountain on the winter range?"

"More over there than here," Hill said without hesitation. "I like to observe the wildlife up close."

No remorse, no defensive tone.

"Observing is one thing," Joe said. "Running elk and deer to their death is another."

Hill replaced his now-empty bottle with a full one from the cooler. As he twisted off the cap, he said, "I can't help it if they run. I don't make them panic. All I want to do is get good photos, and you should see some of them I've got in the house. Some people say I should enter some of those shots in the *Wyoming Wildlife* photography contest, they're so good."

Wyoming Wildlife was the official magazine of the Game and Fish Department. It was a shot at him, Joe knew.

Joe said, "You know what you've been doing is illegal, right?"

Hill rolled his eyes. "So arrest me and stop wasting my time here."

Joe didn't get it. He'd expected Hill to deny the allegation or obfuscate.

"Since you confessed, I'm not going to haul you in," Joe said. "But I am going to issue you a citation for multiple counts of wanton destruction of big-game animals. And I may follow that up with other charges at a later date."

"I confessed?" Hill asked with a gleam in his eye.

Joe patted the digital recorder in his uniform breast pocket he'd activated when he got out of the truck. "I've got it all here."

"Very wily," Hill said.

Jeff Wallace looked to Hill for an indication of what he should do next. If the big man came at him, he wasn't sure he could pull his handgun or bear spray fast enough to protect himself. He had a horrifying vision of Lucy watching while he was assaulted.

But Hill didn't look over to Wallace. He shook his head and smiled almost sadly.

He said, "You have no idea what you're doing here or what kind of shitstorm it might mean to you and your career."

"Maybe so," Joe said as he reached around and withdrew his citation book out of his back jeans pocket. While he wrote out the violation, he said, "I'd suggest you take a ride into Saddlestring tomorrow and visit with our county attorney. If you do that, it'll make it easier on everyone concerned."

"Will I get my aircraft replaced?" Hill asked. "You destroyed a DJI Phantom 4 Pro. We're talking about a fifteen-hundred-dollar unit with a one-inch twenty-megapixel camera on it and a six-camera navigation system. I need to be made whole."

"That's not going to happen," Joe said as he signed the ticket and tore it from the book. "Here."

Hill signaled Wallace with a nod of his head, and the big man stepped over and took the citation from Joe. Wallace stared into Joe's eyes as he crumpled it up in his fist and let it drop to the grass between them.

"That wasn't a good idea," Joe said. He took a step back to create more space between himself and Wallace. He hoped he wasn't visibly shaking.

"You know what also isn't a good idea?" Hill asked. "Me driving into Saddlestring and throwing myself on the mercy of the court. So I won't be doing that." He smiled with no humor.

"Maybe you'd best get in your truck and go home," Hill said to Joe. "Our sausages are just about ready and I want to eat them in peace."

Wallace returned to where he'd been and leaned back against the picnic table. He had a massive chest and his arms were as big as Joe's thighs. The weapon was within easy reach just behind him.

He said to Joe, "I don't get this at all. I thought you people were supposed to be all neighborly. Western hospitality and all that other bullshit. But here we are, minding our own business on our own property and you come rolling in here accusing my friend Tom and my boss of all kinds of stupid shit.

"Not only that," Wallace said, "you do it in front of his *son*. And you're too stupid to know that nothing at all is going to come from this."

Joe looked from Wallace to Hill. He had no idea what that meant.

"I think maybe the best idea," Wallace said, "is for you to get back in your truck and get the hell off our place."

Joe looked around. He flicked his eyes toward the house. Justin was still there and he looked upset. Joe regretted it.

"I think maybe you're right," Joe said.

"Spend a little time reflecting tonight," Hill said with sympathy in his voice. "Reflect on the fact that you can quite easily make all of this just go away. *That*, my friend, will make it easier on everyone concerned."

WHEN HE WAS back behind the wheel of his truck, Lucy said, "That was scary for a minute there, Dad."

"And I'm sorry for that. I didn't expect it to go there." His heart was still racing.

She sighed. "How did you expect it to go when you got out of the truck?"

"Not like that. He acts like he's untouchable."

"I'm glad you came back," she said. "Now I have to text Justin and make sure we're cool. I think we are, because we don't have a problem with each other. It's our fathers who are the problem."

The gates whirred and closed behind him as Joe drove out of the compound. He could see Bill Hill, Jeff Wallace, and Papa Hill all standing near the Big Green Egg watching him go. They were having an animated conversation. Justin was nowhere to be seen.

"I've got a job to do, Lucy," Joe said.

"There was more to it than that," she said. "Just keep Justin out of it, please. Me too."

WHILE LUCY TAPPED out a text to Justin on her phone, Joe speed-dialed Katelyn Hamm to fill her in on what had just happened.

Again, she didn't pick up.

CHAPTER TWELVE

||||||||||||||||||||||||||||||||||||||||||||||||||||||||||||||||||||||||||||||||||||||||||||||||||||||||

TWO HOURS LATER, Nate Romanowski watched as the Wolf Pack came into town, although at the time he didn't know who they were.

He stood on top of the buckled roof of the Saddlestring Trust building on Main Street between two pitted-stone gargoyles. In one hand was a burlap sack filled with cooing pigeons. In the other was a five-foot animal control pole.

The last of the sun was ballooning over the western horizon before sliding behind the mountains. It infused the light with a soft bronze glow that painted the street as well as the sides of the buildings.

What had distracted him enough to look down on the street below him wasn't the arrival of the two vehicles, but an altercation between two drinkers who'd stepped outside the Stockman's Bar to smoke cigarettes and argue about what flies were the most effective on the river: a stone fly and prince nymph combo *or* thin mint streamers cast close to the bank and stripped in.

The argument got heated and Nate anticipated a shoving match, until one of the participants angrily tossed his cigarette aside and went back to his barstool. The remaining combatant looked up and was startled to find Nate staring down at him.

"What are you doing up there?" he asked with a slur.

"Not arguing like an idiot," Nate said.

The lone drinker seemed to search for a snappy comeback as he looked up at Nate again, to see a much larger man than he was backlighted by the dusk sky. So he settled for "Well, shit," and turned and went back into the bar.

Nate tied off the end of the writhing sack with a leather jess and leaned it against the back end of one of the gargoyles before going back to work. He wondered why someone would have ordered stone gargoyles for a bank ninety years ago and he came up with no answers.

If it weren't for the drunks arguing about fishing flies, he never would have noticed the two vehicles cruise slowly down the street and swing into the parking lot of the Bighorn Motor Court, a 1950s-era motel. One was a white Chevrolet panel van. The other was a sleek black Mercedes GLE 350 SUV.

Both had Arizona license plates.

YARAK, INC. HAD ten working falcons, and falcons had to eat. No prey was better for both feeding them and flight training than wild pigeons.

During hunting and feeding seasons, with the raptors circling overhead in the stratosphere, Nate released the captured birds at random as if they were trap loads with wings. As the pigeons streaked and darted through the sky, the falcons would ball up their talons and drop like guided missiles until they smacked their targets in the air. There was an audible *pock* sound on impact and an explosion of feathers and flesh.

Bloody remains rained down from the sky and the raptors followed their meals to the surface, where they'd feed on their prey until their gullets swelled to the size of hen's eggs.

Wild targets kept his birds tuned in and sharp. The Air Force existed in various stages of *yarak*, which was a falconry term for absolute peak performance.

He could feed his falcons road-killed rabbits in their mews to keep the birds healthy, and sometimes Nate resorted to that when he couldn't stockpile pigeons. But high season for commercial falconry was fast approaching, and he wanted to make sure his birds were locked and loaded.

Because his pigeon coop was getting close to empty, it was time to restock. The best locations for capturing pigeons were either in the lofts of ranch barns or the rooftops of old buildings on Saddlestring's truncated Main Street.

The Saddlestring Trust building was the best hunting ground of all because there were two abandoned wood structures on top that had once been used as storage. There were enough broken slats of wood on the tops and in the walls for the birds to be able to come and go as they pleased, and the openings were high enough to prevent predators from invading. Inside, it was warm and dry, and the ancient shelving was perfect for nests and perches. The floors were coated with several inches of white pigeon excrement that had built up over the years.

The optimum time for going after them was in the early evening when the birds had returned for the day and were sleeping shoulder to shoulder on the wooden shelves inside the sheds. Nate inserted the loop pole, tightened the cord around the neck of bird after bird, and gently lifted them out and placed them into the sack. They let him do it, which had always been the case. It was as if, Joe Pickett had once observed with incredulity, the pigeons felt it was their duty to *offer themselves up* to Nate.

He didn't know why they submitted so easily. He knew only that he had that effect on various species and it was a gift for a master falconer. Like when pronghorn antelope walked up to him when he was archery hunting and stood broadside. Or when ducks paddled around in a pond so he could scoop them up and place them in a bag.

When Joe had accompanied Nate once on top of the building and had attempted to capture a pigeon inside the shack with the animal control pole, the birds had exploded into a panic and shot out of the openings like errant sparks.

Which was why Nate no longer invited his friend along.

AS NATE UNFURLED a second sack and approached the other shack, he wondered if his child would have the same effect on creatures. He hoped so, but if not, Nate wondered if he could teach his child a skill that he wasn't sure he fully understood himself.

He attributed his ability to spending so much of his life in the home environment of birds, fish, and animals. So much time, in fact, that he assimilated into their brutal and amoral world where every action boiled down to freeze, run, or attack. Eat or be eaten.

Nate observed fish by lying motionless in trout streams for hours, breathing through a tube and letting the current move his body downriver. He studied big-game animals by sitting naked in trees and watching them graze, sleep, and act out herd dynamics below his dangling feet. And he entered the world of birds of prey by practicing the ancient sport of kings—falconry.

Wildlife seemed to regard him as one of them. Would he be able to convey that to his little boy or girl?

His little boy or girl.

As the baby grew within Liv, the awesome responsibility of having a child grew within Nate's consciousness. It was both frightening and thrilling, but more of the former, because it was something he'd never contemplated.

Although Liv assured him otherwise, Nate wasn't sure it was a good idea to bring a tiny human being into his world. Granted, he'd made a deliberate decision since meeting Liv to come back onto the grid and reenter the modern world. To become a businessman and a proud capitalist. But his past was filled with brutality and violence that he could never fully reconcile. His presence seemed to attract bad actors and his sense of justice demanded retribution. And inside, it was still there like a poised wolverine.

Sometimes, he entertained thoughts of simply running away. He justified that train of thought by making an argument that the best way to keep his lover and child safe would be to remove himself from their orbit. That he would actually be doing them a favor by being a ghost.

Those thoughts went away when he watched Liv sleeping beside him, and when he felt the presence of their baby inside her.

Being a ghost was simply abandoning his family. Any mouth-breathing sperm donor could do *that*. It was the most shameful thing a man could do, and no amount of self-justification could wipe out the stain.

So despite moments of self-doubt and deluded justifications, he'd made the commitment to Liv, his child, and himself to become a stable and loving provider. To keep them safe, like he had for the Pickett family in the past.

One of the qualities he most admired about Joe Pickett—despite Joe's ridiculous sense of duty and Dudley Do-Right methods—was his devotion to Marybeth and his daughters. Joe was an anachronism of sorts, and despite his own rocky childhood and lack of role models to fashion himself after, his friend believed that the highest calling was to be a good husband and father and to do the right thing. There weren't enough men out there like him, Nate thought.

That he'd ever be thrust into the same role had never occurred to Nate before the last few months. And despite the many violent and dangerous situations he'd lived through, he knew this one might be the hardest yet.

NATE HAD DEPOSITED six pigeons into his sack when he heard a shout from the direction of the motel. He looked up to see four people—three men and a woman—emerge from their two vehicles and join together in the parking lot. Although he couldn't make out the words, he could tell from the tone of their conversation that they were having a dispute. And it wasn't about which flies to use on the river.

Something about the scene struck him as discordant. The occupants of the vehicles had not gone into the lobby of the motel to check in. The three men looked roughly the same age—late thirties, early forties—although the woman appeared slightly younger. Two of the men hung back while the driver of the van tried to huddle with the woman, who angrily waved him off.

They didn't look like a family, nor tourists. Both vehicles looked new and the Mercedes was very high-end, so it was unlikely the occupants were passing through looking for work. They came across as exotic and out of place. And although it would be very difficult to quantify if he was asked, Nate felt a distinct sense of menace from the four of them. It was a feeling he'd felt before, and he'd seldom been incorrect.

Nate lowered the sack, tied it off, leaned the animal control pole against the shack, and walked across the sticky tar surface of the roof toward the direction of the motel. At the end of the building, he climbed over the parapet and dropped down four feet to the roof of the Welton's Western Wear building, then onto the corner pharmacy. He bent over and kept low enough that he couldn't see the visitors, nor they him.

There was now a street between where he crouched down on the roof and the motel parking lot, but he could hear them easily because there was no traffic on the road.

Instinctively, Nate reached under his left arm for the reassuring grip of his weapon. It wasn't there. He realized with a start that he'd left his revolver and shoulder holster in his van before he climbed the ladder to the roof of the Trust building.

Going soft, he mouthed sourly to himself. *Losing my edge.*

"IF I HAVE to stay in this shithole town, I'm staying at the Eagle Mountain Club," the woman said.

"We don't want to attract attention," a man with a calm demeanor responded. "We'll only be here a couple of nights."

Nate raised his head slowly until he could see them. Because the setting sun was in his eyes, he knew he wasn't casting a telltale shadow on them below. But the intensity of the sun in his face made it tough to make out the individual features of the figures within the group.

The calm-speaking man was tall and dark, and he spoke and moved with an easy confidence.

"We have the address," he told the woman. "Adelmo and Cesar will scout it out tonight and confirm the location. We think it's right out there in the mountains. Once we're sure, we can hit it quickly and go home."

"Will you even need me?" the woman asked.

"We always need you, Abriella."

She laughed derisively.

She was a beauty, Nate could tell. She was athletic and slim, as well as fiery. She carried herself in a way reserved for females who knew every man in the room was stealing looks at her and every woman was cowed by her aura. She was also overdressed for the spring weather in a down coat and boots, as if she'd prepared for the Arctic.

Nate realized he'd initially misjudged the dynamics of the group. He'd assumed that the tall man was the leader and the other three were subordinates. But their body language suggested otherwise. The woman, although shorter and smaller than all of them, was at the top of the pack. The tall man was the conciliator. And the other two just wanted to be somewhere else.

She said, "Well, if you need me, I'll be at the Eagle Mountain Club up on the hill."

The Eagle Mountain Club was an exclusive golf and fishing resort with private residences as well as bungalows that could be rented on a nightly basis if the guest was sponsored by a member. It wouldn't open until June.

"It's closed until summer," the tall man said. "Getting in there will raise a lot of questions."

"That's your problem."

"What do you expect me to do about it?" he asked.

"Make a couple of calls. I bet you can find somebody who will make the arrangements."

The tall man turned and looked at his two companions, who had stayed out of the argument. Both men leaned back against the panel van with their arms crossed over their chests and their heads down. They offered the tall man no support.

"I made reservations for Adelmo and Cesar here," the tall man said, indicating the motel. "I got rooms for you and me at the Holiday Inn."

Abriella laughed. "Do I look like someone who stays at a fucking *Holiday Inn*?"

"I got you the Governor's Suite. That has to be better than a normal room."

"If this state even has a governor," she said. "Forget it. Cancel it or you can have it. But make some calls and get me into the Eagle Mountain Club, or let them know that I quit. Tell them that I'm on my own because you wouldn't bend your rules."

"They're *our* rules, Abriella."

She scoffed. "Also tell them I know where they live. Tell them that, Peter."

"Please . . ."

She turned to the two men, apparently named Adelmo and Cesar. "Get your shit out of my Mercedes, because I'm taking it."

The two men looked at each other, and one of them reluctantly pushed away from the van and walked toward the SUV with slumped shoulders.

The tall man said, "I'll make a call."

"Well, aren't you a sweetheart?" Abriella said to him in a younger, sweeter voice.

Then, as the tall man turned his back to her and raised a cell phone to his mouth, Nate raised his head a few inches more to get a better look at her. She was formidable.

She stepped aside to allow the third man to retrieve three large duffel bags out of the back of the Mercedes.

"Get it all," Abriella commanded. "Just don't touch my stuff."

What the man removed next Nate recognized immediately

as long gun cases. Four of them, even though hunting season was months away.

Nate considered his first impression of them, that they didn't logically fit. He added the phrase *We can hit it quickly and go home* to the formula and stirred it in with four gun cases.

He didn't know the result of the brew, but no part of it alleviated his suspicion of them. Joe, he knew, would be very interested in the visitors.

The fourth man helped load the gun cases into the back of the panel van.

The tall man concluded his call and turned back around.

"Okay," he said to Abriella. "It's done. Somebody had a connection. I'll write down the combination to the keypad at the front gate."

"Thank you, Peter," she said softly.

"All I ask is that you keep a very low profile," Peter begged her. "You'll probably be one of the only guests they have. You'll stand out."

At that moment, the sun doused behind the mountain and Nate no longer felt the heat and light of it on his face.

And she suddenly looked up. For a brief second, before ducking his head under the balustrade, he looked into her eyes and felt an icy chill deep within his guts.

They were the dead black eyes of a raven. He'd seen them before.

"What?" the tall man asked. He'd obviously noticed that she was looking up toward the top of the pharmacy. "Did you see something?"

"Maybe," she whispered.

Nate remained still and out of view.

"Maybe not," she said. Then: "Give me those numbers. I want a hot shower and a cool drink. You know where to find me when everything is ready."

"It might be sooner than you think," he said. "We have the address."

CHAPTER THIRTEEN

RYLE HAMM ANSWERED the telephone when Joe called Katelyn's house in Shell. It was after dinner and Joe had repaired to his garage.

"Hey, Ryle. This is Joe Pickett. Sorry to call you at home, but could I talk to your wife?"

"Hey, Joe. How are things on the other side of the mountain?"

"Odd," he said, still stinging from the encounter he'd had with Bill Hill. "That's what I wanted to talk to Katelyn about. I've been trying to get in touch with her all day."

"Just a second."

Because Joe was calling the Hamm landline, the reception was much clearer than when he and Katelyn conversed via cell phones from bouncing pickups in the mountains. Therefore, he could distinctly hear her whisper, "Tell him I'm not home."

Joe frowned and wondered for a moment what he'd interrupted.

It took twenty seconds for Ryle to come back on the line. He cleared his throat, and said, "I guess she's not back yet. When I see her, I'll give her the message to call you."

"I thought I just heard her."

Ryle paused a long time, and Joe could envision him imploring Katelyn to take the handset from him or at least give him more direction.

Finally, Ryle said, "You must have heard one of the boys from the back rooms. Or maybe the TV. Anyway, I'll let her know you called."

Joe was certain the voice he'd heard was Katelyn's.

Joe said, "I've left a bunch of messages on her phone. Do you know if her phone is working?"

"I think it is."

Another long pause. Then: "She might have been out of cell range. You know how that goes sometimes. But I'll let her know."

Joe said, "Tell her it's about that POI we've been investigating. She said she wanted in on that."

"POI?"

"Person of interest."

There was more whispering in the background, but it was muffled. Joe guessed that Ryle had covered the handset microphone with his hand.

But why? Joe got an odd sense of déjà vu that harkened back to his college years, when he was pursuing a girl for a date to the football game who'd decided she didn't want to go with him but couldn't make herself tell him outright. Instead, she made herself unavailable and had a roommate run interference.

In this scenario, Ryle was the roommate. The girl had been

Marybeth. Fortunately for Joe, he'd been too dense and determined at the time to pick up on the nuance.

"I'll pass that along when I see her," Ryle finally said. Then: "Gotta go."

Ryle couldn't have sounded any more uncomfortable with being put in the middle, Joe thought.

He placed his phone on the workbench and stared at it for a moment as if it might give him an explanation for why Katelyn Hamm was suddenly avoiding him.

Had something happened Joe didn't know about? Had he interrupted an argument between the Hamms, or date night? Was she flaky all along and he just hadn't picked up on it?

Or had somebody scared her off?

He vowed to drive over the Bighorns the next day and find out for himself.

JOE REALIZED THAT Lucy was standing near the garage door. She'd come in so quietly during his conversation with Ryle that he hadn't heard her enter. She was looking around as if seeing the interior of the structure for the first time.

"I didn't mean to eavesdrop," she said.

"You didn't."

"But it sounded like a strange conversation."

"It was. I was trying to talk with another game warden, but her husband claimed she wasn't there."

He didn't want to explain what the conversation was going to be about, given the circumstances.

"A lady game warden?" Lucy asked.

"Yup. There's a few of them around."

"I could see Sheridan doing that someday. I could see Sheridan arresting April for poaching, couldn't you?"

Joe chuckled.

"So this is your secret cave," she said.

"It's not exactly a secret."

"Do I have permission to come inside?" she asked with a sly grin.

"It doesn't look like you need it."

"So what are you doing out here?"

"Making some calls. Thinking. Plus, I still have to organize all my tools from the old house."

Most of Joe's everyday tools had been damaged in the fire at their previous state house. Those he'd been able to rescue were black with soot and he'd been cleaning them up when he got the chance. The plastic handles of his screwdrivers had melted into strange shapes that were not ergonomic.

She pointed toward a soot-covered urn on a shelf on the side wall of the garage. "Is that Grandpa?"

"Yup."

"Where are you going to spread his ashes?"

He thought that if he was being true to the man, the ashes would be dusted on barroom floors throughout northwestern Wyoming. But he said, "Probably Yellowstone Park. He loved that place."

"They'll let you do that?" she asked.

"Not officially."

"Is that why his ashes are still in the garage?"

"Yup."

She looked at him. "When you go to do that, I'd like to go along. I didn't really know Grandpa all that well, but it might be nice to have somebody along for company."

"Maybe you can distract the rangers while I do it," Joe said with a smile.

Of all his daughters, Lucy clung the tightest to family relationships and traditions. Even though she'd seen Joe's father only once when she was four or five, it was enough to form a connection in her. If anyone were to ever write a biography on the Pickett family, Joe thought, it would be Lucy.

"I'd like that," she said, meaning accompanying Joe.

"I would, too."

"I'm sorry I was such a brat this afternoon out at Justin's place," she said. "I know you were doing your job. I shouldn't have said anything."

"It's okay."

"No, it isn't. I was just really uncomfortable and a little scared. I thought that big man might try to fight you."

"I was a little scared myself," he confessed. "And I didn't like knowing you were there watching it develop like that. You *or* Justin."

She nodded. "Everything's cool with him. He's just really embarrassed that his dad acted like that to you. Justin said to tell you he's really sorry it happened."

"Tell him thank you for me."

"I will."

Joe leaned back against his workbench and crossed his arms over his chest. "Justin seems like a good kid. And you know how much I hate to say that about anyone going out with any of my daughters."

She laughed. "Believe me, he knows that about you. I warned him."

Just as Lucy had taken on the role of peacemaker between her two sisters over the years to cultivate harmony within the family, she also carefully observed the interactions between Joe and various boys who showed interest in Sheridan and April. She'd seen him bristle instantly if the boy was too cocksure, too obsequious, or too overfamiliar. Justin didn't seem to be any of those things.

"So what do you know about Justin's dad?" Joe asked. "I'm not asking you to spill secrets, but I'm sure Justin has talked about him."

She shrugged. "Not really that much. I think you've heard everything I know. Mr. Hill is kind of a mystery and Justin just doesn't want to talk about him. Justin kind of turns off when the subject comes up, in fact."

She said, "I sort of wonder if his dad wasn't in the CIA or something like that. Maybe the NSA or one of those supersecret agencies. Like he had a job he either can't talk about or he just doesn't want to. That's the vibe I get from him—that he left his past behind, you know?"

"What's the deal with the two guys living at that place, Tom Kinnison and Jeff Wallace? Doesn't that seem odd?" Joe asked.

"Yes."

"And that Justin gets chauffeured to school every day?"

"Yes. He's totally embarrassed by that."

"I may have to go out there and take his dad into custody if he doesn't turn himself in," Joe said. "Will you and Justin be able to get through that?"

She winced. "That would be awful, all right. I texted Justin and asked him that question."

"What did he say?"

She sighed. "He said his dad told him there was no chance in hell that would ever happen and that Justin shouldn't even worry about it."

"He said *that*?"

Lucy nodded her head.

"What does Mr. Hill mean? How can he be so sure, I wonder?"

"I don't know, Dad."

"Hmmm."

WHEN JOE'S CELL PHONE lit up and skittered across the workbench, he expected the call to be from Katelyn Hamm. But the caller ID read UNKNOWN and that it was originating from Cheyenne.

He assumed it was a solicitation or someone had misdialed so he held up his finger for Lucy to wait for a moment.

"Joe Pickett."

"Joe, this is Chuck Coon. Do you have a minute to talk about something in confidence?"

Coon was the special agent in charge of the FBI office in Cheyenne. Joe had worked with him several times in the past, and despite territorial disputes and the FBI's difficult relationship with Nate Romanowski, they got along well. Joe had found Coon trustworthy and professional, if also harried and overly bureaucratic.

Coon looked like an FBI agent who'd gone to seed. He was fleshy with a crew cut turned silver and he wore suits that needed to be taken out at the waist or replaced with larger versions. He had two boys the ages of Sheridan and Lucy, and one of his good qualities in Joe's mind was that he wasn't just passing through the Wyoming office en route to somewhere bigger or more glamorous. He genuinely seemed to like Wyoming, and he ran a tight and clean operation. He'd told Joe it was his intention to retire in the state. That in itself was unusual.

Joe covered the phone mic and said, "I need to take this" to Lucy, who gestured that she'd see him later inside the house.

When she was gone, Joe said, "What's up? It's been a long time."

"It has, and I'm okay with that."

Joe smiled to himself. Coon had stuck his neck out on Joe's behalf, and Joe had helped insulate Coon from his superiors as well. Neither owed the other a favor anymore, which made the call intriguing to Joe.

"I've been following your exploits over the years," Coon said. "I heard you got your old job back."

"It was governor versus governor, and mine won," Joe said. Then: "Did you get a new cell phone? I didn't recognize the number and I almost didn't answer."

"This isn't an official call, Joe."

Which meant Coon was calling him from an alternative cell phone or even a prepaid burner. That made it even *more* intriguing.

"What can I do for you, Chuck?"

"Consider this a helpful call between a couple of old pals."

"Helpful to whom?"

"Both of us," Coon said with a sigh.

"I'm listening."

"Look, I have breakfast with a couple other feds here in Cheyenne nearly every morning. One of them happens to be the state manager for the FAA. He said your county attorney called him asking questions about licensing requirements for private drones . . ."

"That would be Dulcie Schalk," Joe said. "Go on."

"My friend was interested because it sounded like this prosecutor was building a case against someone in your area. When he checked the name against his database, it didn't come up that the man had a license."

"Bill Hill," Joe said.

Coon paused. "Yes. That's the name."

"I'm familiar with him."

"You are?" Coon sounded surprised.

"It's a small county, Chuck. Plus, my daughter is going out with his son."

"Ah. We know of him as well, but only because of an HQ directive."

Joe recalled the Cheyenne license plates on Hill's vehicles.

"I'm kind of surprised you'd call me about something so . . . small."

"It's not just that," Coon said. "There's something else. I can't give you any names or specifics, but as you know we've got a lot of procedures here in the bureau. One of them is that if agents from outside the area are coming to Wyoming to follow up on a lead or investigation, they're obligated as a courtesy to inform our office. That way, we don't get cross-ways with our own people."

"That's as clear as mud," Joe said.

"Look, I'm trying to do this without leaking any inside business," Coon said defensively.

"That's why you're in Wyoming," Joe said, laughing. "You don't know how to leak like your bosses in Washington."

"Not funny."

"I thought it was. But go on."

"Okay," Coon said. "Well, a courtesy notification came across my desk this morning that a couple of high-level special agents from our New York office are here. Specifically, they're up in your area right now."

"Okay," Joe said tentatively. He wasn't getting the connection.

"They're involved with a very sensitive case, Joe. A matter of domestic security. Very big."

"*Okay*," Joe said as he rolled his eyes. The self-importance of so many feds—even Coon, unfortunately—was often grating to him.

"Do your people have names?" Joe asked.

"Yes, but this is absolutely confidential between you and me. Special Agents Jeremiah Sandburg and Donald Pollock."

Joe committed the two names to memory. He knew he could

remember them because he knew an ex–game warden in Saratoga named *Steve* Pollock.

Coon said, "The word is out on Sandburg and Pollock within the bureau. They're kind of . . . abrasive. They operate with their own set of rules, and they get away with things that would hang the rest of us out to dry. There's even been speculation that they've got some kind of dirt on the director or AG, so they're pretty much given free rein out in the field. But don't quote me on that. Anyway—they're following up on the disappearance of a certain asset in the Southwest. For reasons I don't know and can't explain, the trail leads to your neck of the woods."

" 'The Southwest' is a big area," Joe said. "Texas?"

"Arizona. But that's all I'll say about it."

"What can you tell me about their case?" Joe asked.

"Not much, but it might have to do with the earlier subject," Coon said.

"What are you saying, Chuck? Are you asking me to tell Dulcie to back off with the FAA?"

"Exactly," Coon said with palpable relief in his voice. "And you, too. Just stay away from this."

"You know I'm not good at that," Joe said. "Is Bill Hill a confidential informant? Is that what this is about?"

"Maybe something like that."

"Is he your CI or not?"

"I can't say it outright," Coon explained. "But if you blow his cover, we both might be in the shit since it happened in my state. Is that clear enough for you?"

Joe shook his head, even though Coon couldn't see him doing so. "The guy we're talking about is a chronic violator of wildlife laws. I take that seriously."

"There are charges?" Coon moaned. "This keeps getting worse."

"You want him to walk?"

"That's exactly what I'm saying, Joe."

Things clicked together. Maybe Katelyn had already been warned off by Sandburg and Pollock and that was the reason she refused to talk with Joe. Bill Hill *was* untouchable. Or so he thought.

"I'll give it some thought," Joe said.

"You can do better than that. Please, Joe. This thing has enormous implications. Bigger than you could wrap your mind around. You have to trust me on that."

"I said I'd think about it."

"Do the right thing here, Joe," Coon said.

"That was exactly the wrong thing to say," Joe said as he disconnected the call and angrily tossed his phone aside on the workbench.

AFTER HE'D COLLECTED himself, Joe turned off the garage lights and went out into the night. There was an ancient river cottonwood between the garage and his new house that was getting ready to bud.

But because there was no foliage on it yet, the large figure perched on a lower branch stood out against the sky awash with stars.

Nate said, "I thought you might want to hear about some visitors in town."

"Did they look like FBI agents from New York?" Joe asked. He was astonished that he hadn't even reacted with alarm to Nate's sudden appearance. That it seemed like a somehow logical extension of the day and night he'd had so far.

"No," Nate said. "They looked like something else entirely."

"Are you going to come down here and tell me about it? Because I'm not going to climb up there in that tree."

CHAPTER FOURTEEN

KATELYN HAMM FELT like hell.

When she had a big problem to work out, she did what she always did: she spread out old newspapers on the kitchen table and fastidiously cleaned her gear and weapons. The acrid odor of Hoppe's Elite Gun Oil filled the room and it smelled of dilemma.

The boys were watching a bullriders-only competition on television in the other room and only occasionally slugging each other, and her husband had stormed out to his workshop after the telephone call from Joe Pickett. She knew she'd need to talk with Joe and smooth things over, but first she had to figure out what she would say and how she would say it.

And what she would do about it.

As she ran the .40 caliber bore snake through the stubby barrel of her dismantled Glock, Ryle stuck his head in through the garage door and crooked his finger at her. He wanted her to come to him.

Which meant they were going to have an argument. The garage was the place they'd agreed to fight things out—away from the boys.

She sighed and tried not to be bristle at Ryle's command. Then she wiped the gun oil off her hands with a spare rag.

"I DON'T LIKE being put in that position," Ryle said as she shut the door behind her. His face was red and he was pacing, which meant he was very angry. "I don't like being your receptionist and I don't like lying for you."

"I'm sorry," she said.

"You hardly say two words the entire night, but when the phone rings, all of the sudden you're telling *me* what to say."

"Please keep your voice down," she said.

"What the hell is going on?" he asked. "Are you having some kind of *thing* with Joe Pickett?"

"Lord, no," she said with a surprised laugh.

Of course that would be where he went, she thought.

"Then what is it?" he asked. "Why would you ask me to lie to him for you? He knew I was lying. He knew you were here."

"Ryle, calm down."

"I *won't* calm down. You made me feel like a fool. *A goddamn fool.*"

She cocked her head to hear if the boys had turned down the television so they could eavesdrop. Instead, she heard Tyler yelp because Brody had done something to him in the family room. Bullriding brought that out in them, and they were likely wrestling on the floor. For once, she was grateful they were tussling with each other.

She said, "You know those two men who were here this morning?"

"What about them?"

"They're FBI agents," she said. And she told Ryle everything, from first encountering the drone in the mountains, to working with Joe Pickett and Nate Romanowski, and what had happened that morning.

HE LEANED BACK against some shelving and listened attentively, but his face got redder. She misread his reaction as being angry at Sandburg and Pollock's methods and for putting her and their family in legal peril.

But when she was done, he said, "So this is all my fault."

"No."

She thought she should have known Ryle well enough by now to know how he'd twist her words to make it all about him. That in his mind she was accusing him *once again* of trying to blow up the family because of his past misbehavior.

"Ryle, I'm not saying that at all. I'm just telling you what happened. Those men threatened me, and that's why I couldn't talk to Joe. They set me up and asked what sounded like innocent questions, then they claimed they caught me in a lie. I looked up that statute—18 U.S.C. 1001—and it really exists. They can federally prosecute me for lying, even if it isn't material to anything else. It's insane.

"And they didn't record the conversation because they don't have to. It's my word against theirs, and I don't like my chances."

She checked herself because she could feel tears welling in her eyes. "I feel awful not telling Joe Pickett what's going on, but I can't because he'll be implicated as well. And I can't go to my supervisor either until I figure things out. Even though I didn't do anything wrong, it looks like I'm guilty, you know?"

Katelyn shook her head. "I'm not sure I know what to do."

She meant it, but he didn't take it that way.

"Your life would be just a hell of a lot easier if you were with someone like him rather than a fucking loser like me, wouldn't it?" he asked. "If you were with somebody you didn't feel like you had to lie about because you're so fucking ashamed? Or maybe if you were on your own?"

"That has nothing to do with it, Ryle."

"It has everything to do with it. You feel so stuck with me you have to lie about it."

"Please, let's not do this."

Ryle wheeled around and swept the shelf clean with a violent backhand. A dozen empty mason jars crashed on the concrete floor.

For a second, she thought that he might come for her next, and she rocked on the balls of her feet, ready to run back inside the house. Ryle seemed to catch himself, though, and he stood at full height and glowered down at her.

"I'm sure the boys heard that," she said.

In fact, she heard Tyler calling her name.

"Mom—what broke?"

Ryle appeared instantly ashamed—but he was still emotional. She wanted to hug him and tell him not to overreact, but she was afraid he'd misinterpret her gesture as pity.

He looked around and said, "I'm going out."

"Please don't."

This is how it had started before. She didn't want to remind him of that because he'd see it as hectoring. When Ryle hit a wall of frustration during an argument, his way of dealing with it was to not deal with it at all. Rather than talk it out, he fled the scene.

"Don't go to town, Ryle. Stay here and help me figure a way out of this."

He didn't even look back as he lumbered toward his pickup parked outside. He slammed the door behind him and she heard the engine roar to life.

KATELYN WAS RETRIEVING the broom and dust-pan to clean up the broken glass when Tyler and Brody cracked the door open to the garage.

"Is everything okay?" Tyler asked. When he saw the amount of glass on the floor, his eyes got big.

"Fine. Just cleaning up."

From behind Tyler, Brody asked, "Did Dad to that?" His tone was accusatory.

"No," Katelyn lied. "Not at all. Just an accident."

"I thought I heard him yelling," Brody said. "He didn't hit you, did he?"

"He's *never* hit me," she said. And it was true, but the question from her son hurt her more than anything Ryle had ever done.

"For sure?"

"Of course not," she said, trying to put a lilt in her voice. "Everything's just fine."

Brody said, "He needs to grow the fuck up."

"*Language,*" Katelyn warned. Then: "Don't talk about your dad like that. It's time to get ready for bed, boys. And really— everything is just fine."

CHAPTER FIFTEEN

AN HOUR LATER, Nate sat in the passenger seat of Joe's Game and Fish Department pickup as the two of them cruised by the parking lot of the Bighorn Motor Court. There were three vehicles parked in front of individual rooms, all with out-of-state plates. There were fourteen units in the court, but no white van from Arizona.

For Joe, Nate's retelling of what he'd witnessed earlier that evening was compelling. Equally, Coon's admonishing him to back off the Bill Hill case had done exactly the opposite. Joe had no idea if the four visitors connected in any way to what Chuck Coon had called about, but the coincidence had piqued his interest, so he'd asked Nate if he wanted to accompany him on a ride into town.

Even if the arrival of the four people was entirely unrelated, he thought, the fact that they had split up on arrival and that they were transporting what sounded like a small armory at least warranted a look.

He parked under the low-hanging branches of an ancient cottonwood on a side street across from the motel. He deliberately
faced away from the building, but he could see it clearly in his
large side mirrors. It was nearly eleven at night. The lights were
dimmed in the small motel lobby, which adjoined a living quar-
ters for the manager, and a red neon OPEN sign turned the sheer
curtains pink from the glow of it.

Joe observed that there were lights on in the three occupied
rooms in front of where the overnight guests were parked. One
room had the drapes wide open and he saw a fat man without a
shirt emerge shamelessly from the bathroom brushing his teeth
with one hand while gripping a long-necked bottle of beer with
the other. The second occupied-room window had the curtains
closed but danced with colors from the television inside. The
third was beige with muted light from a bedside lamp.

"Look at those two rooms down at the end," Joe said.

The curtains were drawn in each, but were lit up from strong
lights inside. Every few seconds, figures would pass and their
shadows would move across the fabric. The guests were in units
ten and twelve.

He said, "It looks like they're busy in there doing something."

Nate grunted his agreement.

"But no cars," Joe said.

"They only had two. The van and the Mercedes."

"I'd guess those two are waiting for someone to pick them
up," Joe said.

"So what do you want to do?" Nate asked.

"We wait."

A minute later, a door opened inside the office from the living area into the lobby. The manager of the motel was an obese free spirit in his thirties with an Afro and a full beard. Joe had seen him as he passed by the business in the past. The manager wore enormous cargo shorts no matter what the weather. His calves were the size of twin jugs of white milk.

Joe and Nate watched as the man cranked open all the windows in the lobby, looked around the courtyard and onto the street, then stepped behind the counter and fired up a huge blunt. Blue marijuana smoke wafted out through the now-open windows.

"There's my opportunity," Joe said.

"Need help?" Nate asked, knowing the answer.

"Not your kind of help," Joe said. "Not yet, anyway."

"Suit yourself, Dudley."

Nate's approach to interrogating witnesses was to rip their ears or limbs off or whack them with blunt objects until they told him what he wanted to hear. Although effective, Joe thought, it was much too early for that. He didn't even know if Nate's suspicions were valid.

Joe clicked the toggle switch under the dashboard that prevented the interior lights from coming on when he opened the door. He climbed out and crossed the empty street and walked directly toward the office. Because the manager had lights on inside and it was completely dark out on the street, Joe knew he wouldn't be seen until he was literally inside the lobby.

A ribbon of bear bells—used by hikers to alert bears of their presence—rang out when Joe threw the door open and stepped inside. He did it so quickly the manager leaped back from behind the counter and the blunt fell out of his mouth into a shower of sparks on the tile floor.

"Howdy," Joe said. "Clever use of bear bells, I have to say."

"Bear bells? Is that what they are? Some hikers left them in a room."

"Ah."

"I didn't see you coming, man," the manager said as he scrambled to retrieve the smoke. When he stood back up, he stubbed out the joint in an ashtray as if he were punishing it for being there.

Joe reached out and retrieved a business card from a holder on the counter.

"You're the manager?"

"Yes, sir."

"And your name is Ranger?"

"Yes, sir."

"Just Ranger?"

"I had it legally changed. I'm kind of a Tolkien nerd."

"I get that."

"I thought you were a cop," the manager said.

"I am, sort of."

"Not really. We used to call you guys 'fish cops' back in Michigan."

"But here we are in Wyoming," Joe said. "I guess you know why I'm here."

"To bust me?"

"Nope," Joe said. "I don't bust guys for smoking weed unless they're hunting, fishing, or driving while they do it and they're impaired. But there's nothing that says I can't give the sheriff a call."

"Man," Ranger said, shaking his head. "That would be a really, really lame thing to do."

"Let's make this easy," Joe said, placing both of his palms on the counter. "I want to know the names of the two guests in the rooms at the end of the court. Room numbers ten and twelve."

"You know I can't give you that information," the manager huffed. "It's against the law."

"So is smoking a joint."

"Man . . ."

"I can call the sheriff to come meet us here if you'd like."

The manager did an epic sigh. He ran his big hands through his big hair. Then he reached out and rotated the monitor of his computer so Joe could see it, and he tapped a few keys on his keyboard.

Room ten was occupied by John Blumenthal, and Jimmy Orr was listed for room twelve.

Joe looked up and recalled Nate's description of the men. He said all three of the men appeared Hispanic.

"Did they look like a John Blumenthal and a Jimmy Orr to you?"

Ranger replied, "How would I know? I didn't look that close."

"Did they show you ID?"

The man hesitated long enough that Joe guessed he was attempting to put together the least incriminating story that he could.

"I didn't look at their IDs because they didn't rent the rooms directly. Another guy did."

That also checked out with Nate's story.

"Did you look at *his* ID?"

"I didn't. He paid cash for both rooms."

"But he's not staying here," Joe said.

"He drove away."

"What did his vehicle look like?"

"It was a white panel van."

"Did he write in his license plate number?"

"He didn't need to," the man said. "He wasn't staying here, so I didn't need that information." Then: "He gave me a one-hundred-dollar tip for taking care of his friends."

"I see." Joe now knew why the manager hadn't looked that closely at his two customers or hadn't pressed for additional check-in information.

"Did your guests have a lot of luggage with them?"

The manager said, "Wouldn't know."

Joe tried to remain calm. "What else can you tell me about them?"

The manager said, "It was kind of weird. After the guy checked in his buddies, he left with one of them in the van. When the van came back, the boss guy wasn't in it, but the other guy—"

"Would this be John or Jimmy?" Joe asked.

"Whatever. I don't know which is which. But let's just say John came back and Jimmy got in with him and the two left here for about two hours. When it came back, all three of them were inside, so I guess they picked up the boss man. Then the boss left John and Jimmy here and he hasn't been back."

"How long ago was that?"

The manager shrugged. "Maybe fifteen minutes?"

Joe drummed his fingers on the counter. "Thank you for your time, Ranger," he said.

"So we're cool?" the manager said with palpable relief.

"For now."

WHEN HE SLID into the cab next to Nate, Joe said, "I don't know what's going on exactly, but there's a lot of activity going on with these folks."

Nate nodded. "I've been watching the two rooms while you were in there. Those two guys open the curtains every few minutes to look outside. They're obviously waiting for someone to come back."

"Where they're off to at this time of night is the question," Joe said.

All of Saddlestring, except for the Stockman's Bar, was closed.

"The van is either at the Holiday Inn or the Eagle Mountain Club," Nate said.

"Let's check one and then the other. Then I may have to wake up Mike Reed and let him know we're doing his job for him."

"Fine," Nate said. "Then I need to get home."

Joe looked over, puzzled.

"Liv's at home, as you know. She texted me to bring her some peach-flavored frozen yogurt." Then he sighed. "As far as I know, she's never eaten frozen yogurt before."

Joe laughed. "Soon it'll be Pampers and formula."

Nate winced.

TEN MINUTES EARLIER, Infante had punched in the key code to enter the Eagle Mountain Club, and he'd idled the van while the gate rose.

He drove up a long sweeping drive over manicured lawns and through thick pine trees. Magnificent empty homes were situated along the drive with the road on one side and a golf course on the other. The view of Saddlestring below in the river valley was all-encompassing; strings of streetlights and homes, the S-curves of the Twelve Sleep River reflecting silver in the moon- and starlight. Beyond the edges of the small community it was dark all the way to the Bighorn Mountains.

The road curved up toward a main compound. He passed by hotel-looking buildings until he saw a sign indicating THE COT-TAGES. There were no cars out in front of either the main lodge or the condos until he saw the white Mercedes parked along the side of cottage number one. Next to the SUV was a golf cart with a white roof parked rakishly half on and half off the front lawn.

Did Abriella have a guest?

He cursed under his breath after he killed the engine and got out. She seemed put on earth to devil him and further compli-cate an already complicated assignment.

He looked around and saw no one about, then he knocked softly on the heavy front door. He could hear no sounds from inside, but there was a dull band of light framing the curtained window and a strip of it on the bottom of the door.

When several locks were thrown from the inside, Infante took a step back on the porch and reached behind him for the pistol grip of the 9mm that was tucked into his waistband.

The door inched open, revealing a young brown-eyed man with high cheekbones and tousled black hair. He wore a white terry-cloth robe with *Eagle Mountain Club* embroidered on the breast. His ankles and feet were bare beneath the hem of the robe.

He looked scared at first, but when he saw Infante his expression changed to confusion.

"I'm here to see Abriella," Infante said softly.

The young man turned his head to where she was inside, and when he did, Infante leaped forward in a Superman MMA maneuver and shoved at the open door with both hands. The force of it sent the young man sprawling.

Infante stepped into the cottage and closed the door behind him while the man landed unceremoniously on his back with his feet in the air. The robe flew up and exposed his naked legs and genitals. Infante looked away and took in the interior quickly: an empty champagne bottle on the table next to a silver room service tray, half-eaten tulip-shaped orders of shrimp cocktail, fresh flowers in a vase.

A pile of clothes consisting of black trousers, a white shirt, and a white jacket were on the floor near the foot of the bed.

And on top of the bed wearing a sheer lavender negligee, her long brown legs crossed over each other and a glass of champagne raised near her lips, was Abriella.

"That was mean," she said.

"Sorry," Infante said. "I didn't want to be seen standing outside."

"Pedro, meet Fidel," she said while the room service waiter scrambled to his feet and smoothed the robe over his thighs. "He's from home. From Baja—a little fishing village called La Ventana. Have you ever been there?"

"No."

"Me, either. But it sounds cute."

Fidel backed away from Infante and raised one of his hands to ward off the man. "I'm sorry," he said. "I didn't know."

Infante looked at Fidel for a moment before he realized that the waiter assumed he was a jealous husband or lover there to break up the tryst. The waiter's eyes flashed over to Abriella in the bed as if to say, *She invited me in.*

But of course she did, Infante thought.

He told Fidel to go into the bathroom, close the door, and turn all the faucets on full. Infante didn't want Fidel to overhear his conversation with Abriella.

"Don't come out until I tell you," Infante ordered.

Fidel nodded briskly and nearly sprinted across the room. Infante waited until he heard the white noise of open spigots before turning to her.

"Really?" he asked her. "On our first night here, you risk everything by bringing a stranger in?"

She sipped at her glass and then placed it on the bedside table. As she did, the camisole tightened over her breasts and her nipples poked through the fabric like buttons. She knew *exactly* what she was doing, he thought.

"I get lonely when I spend my days with you and your goons," she said. "Don't worry, he knows nothing."

"He doesn't have to. All he has to do is place you and me here. We already stand out like sore thumbs."

"Not my fault," she said with a flip of her hair. "This is your operation. You're in charge of everything. I'm just along for the ride until I'm called. So I'm making the best of a bad situation."

Infante knew—and Abriella knew as well—that he'd strayed a few times on operations himself. He couldn't help himself, because he loved and needed women, and when the tension was high he needed them even more. But he'd always bedded them on the side, during downtime or in a location other than one where they were working.

This was different and they both knew it. She was literally the only guest in the entire private club. Every staffer there would know about her. And that she'd invited a waiter into her room . . .

Infante breathed deeply to calm himself and he rubbed his temples with the balls of his hands. He didn't want to provoke her into turning on him with her particular kind of twisted black rage. He could tell by her expression that she was pleased with herself and calm enough, but a harder push from him might end it.

"He's a sweet boy and he's a long way from home," she said, as if it were about Fidel and not her. "He'll keep quiet about this because he doesn't want to lose his job."

"You're sure about that?" Infante asked.

"I'm absolutely sure," she purred. "He may want to see me again."

Infante conceded her point. He said, "Cesar and Adelmo have located the target. They're getting ready now and they're waiting for us to pick them up at the motel. We need to move on our subject tonight."

"Tonight?" she said, her eyes flashing. "I just got unpacked."

"They said they could see luggage stacked up on the porch of Mecca's house. That says to me he's preparing to leave in the morning."

"Did someone tip him off?" she asked.

"I don't know. Maybe. But we can't risk him hitting the road. We might never find him again."

She frowned, which to Infante was frighteningly attractive.

"*I'd* be able to find him again," she said.

"And that means we'd stay out in the open even longer," he said. "I thought you wanted to go home and get paid."

"I do," she said as she stole a glance at the closed bathroom door as if reconsidering.

"Please pack your clothes," he said. "I'll stay here until you're done and keep an eye on Fidel. When you're gone, I'll have a talk with him."

She nodded, then swung her legs off the bed and stood up. He was always amazed how small she was next to him. On the bed she'd seemed longer, all limbs and warm brown skin.

She nodded toward the bathroom door. "Don't be too cruel to him," she said.

215

"Of course not. But he'll understand. I'll tell him we can locate his family in La Ventana within hours if he talks."

He watched as she dressed in front of him without embarrassment and expertly rolled up her remaining clothing and jammed it into her bag. She was experienced at clearing a room out under pressure.

As she zipped up her bag, she paused and her eyes turned dark.

"This better go well," she said.

"It will."

With that, she pushed past him and went out the door.

HE WAITED UNTIL her taillights vanished into the trees before he went about wiping the door handles, the surfaces of the small kitchen, the champagne and shrimp cocktail glasses. He double-checked to make sure she hadn't left anything behind. He even looked under the bed for stray panties. Then he stripped the bedsheets off and balled them up. He'd take her DNA with him.

Meanwhile, the water flowed in the bathroom.

When he was satisfied that he'd missed nothing, he knocked on the bathroom door. It was good that Fidel couldn't hear him because it meant he hadn't heard their conversation. When there was no response, he rapped harder.

"Yes?" Fidel sounded terrified.

"You can come out."

Infante stood aside while Fidel turned the water off and

opened the door. Inside the bathroom it was a cloud of steam from the hot-water taps. The waiter beaded with sweat from both the steam and the situation.

He took in the room as he came out, looking for her.

"She's gone," Infante said.

"I swear on the head of my mother that she invited me in."

"I believe you."

Fidel nodded. "I want to get dressed and leave now," he said.

"Soon."

Fidel looked at him, his lower lip trembling. "I won't say nothing. Ever."

"That has to be the case. If you do, we'll know. And it will be the worst thing you've ever done in your life. We have people in La Ventana."

Fidel nodded. He knew it to be true.

"Tonight never happened," Infante said. "You never saw me, and you never met *her*."

"*Si*, of course."

"Is there a closed-circuit camera at the front gate?"

Fidel nodded. "There is, but they don't turn it on until the club opens up in the summer."

"Good. I hope you're telling me the truth about that."

"I am. I swear it."

Nevertheless, Infante chinned toward the pile of clothing at the foot of the bed. "Gather up your belongings and step outside with me. I know there has to be another way to drive out of here without going through the front gate."

"There is the service road."

"Good. Come point it out to me."

Infante followed Fidel out the door until the waiter paused between his room service cart and the white van. Fidel clamped his clothing in a ball under his left arm while he pointed through the trees to the southwest. The lights of Saddlestring twinkled across the river.

"There is a road over there," Fidel said. "It will take you over an old bridge and into the town."

"Is there a security gate?"

"Not that way. No one will see you."

"Thank you, Fidel. I know it's been a crazy night," Infante said. "Remember what we talked about."

"There are some crazy nights here in the summer when the members show up," Fidel said with a smile that revealed white teeth in the starlight. "But nothing like this."

As Fidel turned away toward his golf cart with his clothes in his arms, Infante pulled out his semiauto with the suppressor and fired two quick rounds into the base of the waiter's skull.

Pop-pop.

He dropped like a sack of rocks.

Infante opened the back doors of the panel van and dragged the body over and grunted as he lifted it and rolled it inside. He threw the clothes as well as the bedding on top of Fidel and closed the door.

Then he pointed the golf cart downhill toward a small lake and weighted the accelerator with a large rock from the landscaping. He watched as the vehicle whined down the hill on the grass and entered the lake with a splash.

Since Abriella had been registered after hours under a false name and she was now gone, it would take the local cops a while to piece anything together. Maybe the strange beautiful woman left with the Mexican national? Maybe she'd been kidnapped by him?

Who knew? Who would ever know?

Of course, now there was a body to take care of. But later tonight, there would be more.

And Cesar was good at that.

TEN MINUTES LATER, Joe and Nate drove through the dark and empty second homes and rental cottages at the Eagle Mountain Club looking for either the white van or the Mercedes SUV.

The resort was deserted.

TUESDAY, MAY 1

He's mad that trusts in the tameness of a wolf,
a horse's health, a boy's love, or a whore's oath.

SHAKESPEARE,
KING LEAR

CHAPTER SIXTEEN

THE NEXT MORNING, Joe drove his pickup through a cold hard rain to Winchester with dark storm clouds pressing down on him and obscuring the mountains. The temperature hovered at thirty-eight degrees and he knew that the moisture could morph into heavy spring snow at any time as he climbed in elevation.

"April showers bring May flowers" was a maxim that applied to other places. In the Northern Rocky Mountains, it was: *May showers bring blizzards, muds, and bad flash floods.*

Before turning around and heading to Winchester, he'd been on his way into town first thing that morning to meet with Sheriff Reed and let him know about the four visitors to Saddlestring whom Nate had seen—who now seemed to have vanished. Ranger at the Bighorn Motor Court said he hadn't seen his guests leave, only that they'd left their keys in the rooms and cleared out sometime during the early-morning hours.

But when Joe called Reed to set up the meeting, the sheriff

was en route north to Winchester with a small convoy of department vehicles.

"It looks like a murder/suicide," he told Joe.

"You're kidding."

"I wish I was. Meet me there."

He gave Joe the address.

Joe said, "Oh, no."

"You know them?"

"I know where they live."

"Better use the past tense from now on."

Joe disconnected and frowned to himself. He couldn't recall a murder/suicide happening in the county since he'd been on the job.

Daisy looked over from where she'd curled up on the passenger seat and cocked one eye.

ELKHORN DRIVE WAS darker and seemed closer than usual. The gloom fooled the automatic headlights into thinking it was night. Moisture dripped from the overhanging branches and his windshield wipers could hardly keep up with the deluge. Potholes in the old surface of the road were filled with mocha-colored runoff.

Joe squinted at his GPS unit as he made the sharp turn from Elkhorn Drive onto the ancient muddy two-track that led to a semicircle of three Twelve Sleep County Sheriff's Department SUVs and Reed's wheelchair-accessible van. The vehicles were all pointed at the old single-wide trailer set back in the trees that

Joe had noted before. The one marked by the hand-lettered sign tacked to a tree trunk that said *Behrman*.

Deputy Ryan Steck stood in the front yard in a yellow cowboy slicker with a spool of crime scene tape he was preparing to unwind. Justin Woods, the other deputy rumored to be running for Sheriff Reed's job, paced on the rickety covered front porch with his phone pressed to his face.

Joe parked his truck behind the county vehicles and climbed out. The ground was soft and the heels of his boots sunk into the mud. He pulled on a Simms rain jacket he used for flyfishing trips and splashed through the yard toward the trailer.

Rain was an unusual occurrence in Wyoming, where precipitation was largely made up of snow. Joe was reminded once again that locals became discombobulated when it rained because few people had raincoats and fewer yet had umbrellas. He wondered if the weather conditions had somehow been a factor in the tragedy at hand.

"Sheriff around?" Joe asked Steck.

"He's inside where it's warm and dry," the deputy said as he gestured toward the trailer. His slicker was beaded with rain and his beige cowboy hat was brown from being soaked.

Joe thanked him as he passed by. "Murder/suicide, huh?"

"That's what it looks like."

"Who called it in?"

"Mrs. Behrman's cousin," Steck said. "She showed up early this morning to give them a ride to the Billings airport."

Joe noted that there were old-style suitcases without wheels lined up on the wooden porch. Deputy Woods was weaving around them as he gave directions to the evidence tech and the coroner about how to find the place.

"That's odd," Joe said. "They were going somewhere this morning, but they died last night?"

"Apparently. But you'll need to talk to the boss man."

SHERIFF REED SAT slumped to the side in his wheelchair with his elbow on one of the arms as he rubbed his chin and studied the scene inside.

Joe was careful not to leave more muddy tracks in the house as he approached his friend. He looked everywhere except at the two bodies in the small living room, but he'd seen just enough when he stepped inside that he thought there was a good possibility he might lose his breakfast.

Although he didn't stare directly at the bodies or the crime scene, what he glimpsed he couldn't unsee: two overweight and elderly victims seated in chairs that looked to be afloat in pools of coagulating blood. Both bodies were collapsed into the chairs, their legs and arms askew, displaying the casual immodesty of the dead.

Instead of looking over, Joe found himself facing a shelf of framed photographs. There were black-and-whites of a couple holding a baby in front of a sixties-era Pontiac, and later shots in color of a husband and wife dressed up for a wedding or graduation, camping with a tent, and standing next to a dark-haired boy who stood a head taller than both of them. They seemed to Joe to be a sweet couple. The man was jug-eared and squat and obviously uncomfortable smiling for the camera, and the woman was stout with tight curls of hair and cat-eye glasses.

Reed was describing the crime scene to himself as he observed it, using a recording app on his iPhone. It was standard procedure with the sheriff since his days as a patrolman and he'd told Joe it helped him recall all the details when he sat down later to write his report.

"Rex Behrman, age seventy-two, is sprawled out in his lounge chair. His pant legs are hiked up revealing his ankles as if he's in the process of sliding forward out of his chair. His legs are straight and he's wearing slippers. Both of his hands are hanging palms-out on the sides of the chair. There is a revolver that looks like a Smith and Wesson .357 in a pool of blood on the floor next to Rex just beneath his right hand.

"Rex's head is thrown back and it looks like he's staring at the ceiling. There's an entry wound with powder burns beneath his chin and a large exit wound on the crown of his skull. Blood spatter on the walls and ceiling, including the light covering."

The dank metallic smell of blood inside the trailer was unmistakable, and Joe turned to go back outside for fresh air.

But he paused as Reed continued.

"The blood under both bodies is separating on the floor, leaving a two-inch outside ring of viscous fluid, which indicates the victims died at least six hours ago. Long enough for the blood cells to clot up, but not long enough to dry.

"Rex's wife, Fran, also seventy-two, is slumped over to the side in her lounge chair not five feet from Rex. She's wearing a housedress and slippers as if she was getting ready to go to bed.

It appears she was shot in the heart at close range. There's singe-ing around the hole in the fabric of her dress from what looks like a point-blank shot. The round exited the back of her chair and I can see a hole in the refrigerator door where we'll likely find it.

"From the look of things it appears obvious that she was shot first before Rex turned the gun on himself.

"Poor old gal," Reed said.

"The note on the kitchen table appears to be written by Rex because he signed it. It says, 'We've had it. There ain't nothing good for us left in this world.'"

Which rendered Joe incredibly sad as well as nauseous.

"LOOKS PRETTY CLEAR-CUT from what I can see," Reed said after he rolled his chair out onto the porch to join Joe and await the evidence tech.

They both huddled on the south end of the covered porch to avoid slashes of icy rain being driven by wind on the north end.

Reed said, "From the look of the scene, they'd had it with everything and decided to end it last night. I think they both had pretty serious health issues, judging by the shoe box full of pills on the counter. We'll know a lot more after the autopsies."

Joe nodded.

"I talked to Fran's cousin Marge," Reed said. "She was the one who showed up to take them to the Billings airport this morning. The Behrmans were on the way to Wichita, apparently, because their son is in critical condition after a head-on collision yesterday morning."

"Good Lord," Joe said.

"Yeah, I know. He's their only kid and his prognosis isn't good. They obviously booked their tickets before they decided there wasn't anything to live for. It's a damned shame, though."

"That it is," Joe said. "But why do you suppose they packed and got ready to leave and *then* decided to kill themselves?"

Reed said, "It puzzles me, too. But sometimes people do things that don't make logical sense. Maybe uprooting their lives was more than they could stand. Maybe Fran was still planning to go, but Rex made the decision to end it for both of them. We shouldn't assume it was a suicide pact until we know more."

Joe asked, "Any signs at all of anyone else in the trailer?"

"Not that I could see."

"No forced entry?"

"Nada."

"No tracks on the road in?"

Reed said, "I'm having my guys check all of that out. But with this rain, I'd be pretty surprised if we find evidence of any vehicles besides ours on that road. Or I should say, I'd be surprised if we found tracks we hadn't already driven over the top of."

Joe agreed. The five vehicles that had come to the Behrmans' place had cut ruts into the dirt road that were swirling with muddy rainwater.

"Did you know them?" Joe asked Reed.

"Not really. Rex was a custodian at Winchester High School.

Fran worked in the cafeteria and they both retired seven or eight years ago. They kept to themselves, and about the only thing they did in public was go to church. They liked their privacy."

"I can see that. So they kept a pretty low profile around here."

"I'd say that," Reed said with a sad shake of his head. "They were the kind of couple you might notice in the grocery store or pharmacy and not think another thing about them. We've got lots of folks like that around here we never really think about, because we're too busy going after miscreants and bad actors.

"They pay their taxes, they keep to themselves, and they don't complain or cause trouble," he lamented. "We never pay any attention to them unless something like this happens."

"What were they doing in there before it happened?" Joe asked. "Was the television on? They look like they sat in those chairs to watch TV."

"Nope, it wasn't on when I got here," the sheriff said. "Who knows—maybe they were having an argument or something."

Joe thought of the photos on the shelf. "How long were they married?"

"I saw a couple of cards on their refrigerator from friends congratulating them on forty-eight years. That's a long time."

Joe turned to Reed. "How long have you been married?"

"Married or happily married?"

"Come on, Mike."

The sheriff chuckled. "We've been married thirty-three years."

"Twenty-seven for us," Joe said. "So tell me: Even if your medical or emotional situation was really bad, could you shoot your wife point-blank in the heart?"

Reed seemed to think it over. Finally, he said, "If things were really bad, I think I'd choose another way. Poison or something. Or maybe we'd both sit in the garage with the doors closed and the windows locked and the car running and listen to the *Grease* soundtrack until we couldn't hear it anymore. But no, I couldn't shoot her first like that. What about you?"

"Never," Joe said. "I get chills even thinking about it."

"There are days when Janice would probably like to put me out of my misery," Reed said. "But I doubt she'd really ever do it, and Janice is a mean, mean woman."

"She's not that bad," Joe said.

"Naw, she isn't really," Reed said with a grin.

"This crime scene doesn't sit well with me," Joe said. "It's too weird."

"I agree. But who would want to hurt that old couple and make it look like something else? There's obviously nothing worth taking from the place, which rules out a home invasion or a robbery. Maybe we'll find out they were the kind that hoarded cash or gold and somebody found out about it. But I doubt that.

"And if someone was casing the place, I'd think they'd see that luggage out front and wait a day to sack the place when no one was home."

"I wonder if they had enemies," Joe said, doubting it even as he said it.

Reed said, "It won't take long for us to find out if they did. Winchester is full of gossips. But I can't imagine that's the case."

"Me neither, although it's interesting that their nearest neighbor is Bill Hill."

The sheriff looked at Joe and closed one eye. "Are you suggesting maybe they had a dispute of some kind?"

"I'm not suggesting anything," Joe said. "Just pointing out the obvious. Have you sent anyone to talk to him to find out if he knew them or saw anything last night?"

"Do you think I've forgotten how to do my job?"

"Not at all."

"I suppose you're volunteering to do that interview?"

"Not necessarily," Joe said. "We kind of got off on the wrong foot."

"That's what I heard," Reed said. "I think I'll send Woods or Steck over, just to cover all our bases. But at this point it seems more like CYA than actual investigating."

Reed rolled his chair a few feet farther to the south to avoid a wet gust. He said, "Maybe it is just what it looks like and we'll never know the motivation that went into the decision, Joe. I mean, they left a suicide note. It won't be hard to match up the handwriting with samples from Rex or Fran. All we can do is follow the evidence where it leads us."

"Yup."

"It's a hell of a way to start off the morning," Reed said.

"It is."

Joe shook the rain off his jacket and prepared to go.

"What did you want to talk to me about earlier?" Reed asked.

Joe gave the sheriff a brief version of what Nate had seen and heard the night before and a description of the vehicles.

"But they're gone now," Reed said.

"As far as I can tell."

"Interesting," the sheriff said. "I'll keep them in mind if something happens."

"You mean, like this?" Joe asked, nodding toward the Behrman home.

Reed said, "Hard to connect those dots."

"I agree at this point."

"And here's another thing to add into the mix," Reed said. "The club called this morning to report a missing staffer. They think he might have run off with a guest."

THEY KICKED IT around for a few minutes: the four visitors, the missing vehicles, the fact that an Eagle Club employee was nowhere to be found, as well as a cottage guest no one at the office saw or met.

They got nowhere.

As Joe turned toward his pickup, Reed said, "How did you know this place if you'd never met Rex and Fran Behrman?"

"This is where my GPS stops on the way to 2204 Elkhorn Drive," Joe said.

"What do you mean your GPS stops?"

Joe shrugged. "Apparently, the Bill Hill place isn't on the map. I've noticed it a couple of times. The first time it happened, I looked up here in the trees and saw this place."

"Well, that's strange."

"It is."

"It's a morning filled with strangeness," Reed said philosophically.

Joe was halfway to his pickup before he stopped. When he turned around he said to Sheriff Reed: "Maybe I wasn't the only one to be fooled by my GPS."

"What's that?" the sheriff asked, puzzled.

"Never mind," Joe said. "Let me think about it a little and I'll get back to you."

JOE DID WHAT Joe did whenever he was flummoxed, which was often: he called Marybeth.

She was on her way to work at the library and she'd already heard about the Behrman deaths via Facebook.

"It's terrible," she said. "I knew both Fran and Rex—they were patrons of mine. They were gentle people and wonderful with each other. Rex read every Dick Francis novel we have and I was able to get all the rest on interlibrary loan. He was so grateful he brought me rhubarb jam he made himself."

"So that's where that came from," Joe said.

"Yes, and Fran liked romances and thrillers. I have the new Sandra Brown on hold for her. It's just . . . unbelievable, really."

"In more ways than one," Joe speculated.

He told her he was driving over the mountains to Katelyn Hamm's district in the hope of tracking her down, since she wouldn't answer her phone or return his calls.

Then: "I was hoping you could do some research for me if you have the time today."

"Of course. We have our staff meeting first thing, but I'm pretty free after that."

Joe told her about the two instances where his GPS had failed him on the way to the Hill compound.

"What I'm wondering," Joe said, "is how it can be that a legitimate physical address won't show up on GPS navigation software. This can't be the only time something like this ever happened."

"I'll look into it," she said. "I'll give you a call if I find any answers."

"Thank you once again."

She was quiet for a few beats. "Why are you asking me to do this? What does it have to do with the Behrmans?"

"I'm not sure," Joe said. "But what I know is that on the two instances I plugged in Bill Hill and Tom Kinnison's physical address, my GPS took me as far as the Behrman place and stopped. So of course I wonder . . ."

"If the same thing happened to someone else," Marybeth said, finishing the thought for him. "Interesting."

"Let's keep this between us," Joe said.

"As always," she signed off.

CHAPTER SEVENTEEN

AS THE NORTH FORK of the Tongue River raged with snowmelt through the snow-encrusted willows out his passenger window on U.S. Highway 14 into the Bighorn Mountains, Joe noticed there was a car behind him keeping a respectful distance.

The road was lonely even in the summer, so it was notable to see another vehicle on it in the spring.

The route switchbacked up the incline, and he caught glimpses of the new-model black Ford Expedition behind him every time the road straightened out. He noted it, but gave the vehicle no further thought as he waited for Marybeth to call him back and he tried to puzzle out the discrepancies of the Behrman deaths.

The snow on the sides of the road got deeper the higher he climbed. U.S. 14 paralleled the turns of the river to its source high in the mountains and it offered spectacular views of the breaklands to the east and eventually the Powder River Basin to the west. It was the kind of road that terrified some flatlanders when they took it in the summer, and it wasn't unusual for state troopers to call for tow trucks to rescue motorists who became simply too frightened by the top-of-the-world feeling to keep driving.

Although the highway was closed during the winter, snow-plow drivers working from both sides had recently met on the summit in their own low-key annual version of Promontory, Utah, where the Central Pacific and Union Pacific construction crews had rendezvoused to complete the transcontinental rail-road. The high-elevation sun had melted the remaining snow and ice on the surface of the black asphalt, although it still steamed in some places.

When he emerged from a stand of spruce, the view opened up and he saw movement in the distance in a leafless aspen grove on the far mountainside. Joe instinctively slowed down. He was grateful that the snowplow had carved a pullout into the three-foot drifts on the right side of the road. Joe parked and shut off his truck.

He dug out his WOF and focused his binoculars on the trees.

What he witnessed was a chilling and remarkable sight: a mature cow moose high-stepping it through deep snow headed down the mountain. Behind her in pursuit were four wolves.

He recognized the lone black alpha male he'd seen on Herman Klein's ranch. The wolves had roamed a lot of miles in a short period of time.

The moose was built for deep snow with her long legs, but she was obviously struggling from fatigue. Meanwhile, the wolves with their large paddle-like paws were able to lope along on top of the surface and harass her. One even caught up with the moose and darted across her path before she could elevate on her hind legs and strike down at it.

What Joe saw, he thought, was a real-time example of Tennyson's line "Nature, red in tooth and claw."

The wolves displayed the killing acumen that had been honed through the ages. They followed the cow moose, darting in and nipping at her as she ran, taking chunks of hide and flesh. If one of the wolves was quick enough, it would get to her underbelly and rip open a small hole that others would target until ribbons of intestines trailed along behind her and stained the snow red.

Joe didn't see the denouement because the moose ran into the heavy timber of the other bank of the river and disappeared in a steep ravine with the predators on her heels. The wolves would either take her down and finish her off, or the cow could somehow escape to live another day.

Life was hard in the mountains. Wolves were wolves. They had to eat. The cow moose was handicapped by her exhaustion and the deep snow, but she was also capable of turning on her pursuers and injuring them or driving them away.

The growing number of wolves had done a serious number on the moose population in the last decade. Joe's agency had steadily reduced the number of available moose hunting permits to mirror the decline. He was reminded once again how well-intentioned actions, like the reintroduction of wolves into Yellowstone Park, had had unanticipated consequences.

He noted the location in his WOF log and vowed to come

back in the summer and walk the gulch. Maybe he'd find moose bones, maybe he wouldn't.

He yearned to know how it turned out.

AS HE STARTED his pickup and prepared to pull back out on the highway, he realized that the black SUV hadn't passed him. But when he came out of the next turn, it was back there again. Which meant that the driver had stopped for as long as Joe was stationary.

Maybe he, too, had seen the moose and the wolves? Joe doubted it. The viewing angle farther down the mountain toward the aspen grove would have been blocked by a dense wall of spruce trees. Joe had been afforded the only open look at the pullout.

So he drove on, checking his mirrors on every straight section of highway. Although the Expedition had put more distance between them, it was still back there.

And it stayed back there for the next fourteen miles.

AT BURGESS JUNCTION on top of the mountains, Joe slowed and pulled sharply off the road into the parking lot of a state-managed rest stop. Although the restrooms were still encased in snow and officially closed, the lot had been cleared.

He performed a quick three-point turn and backed his pickup into the four-foot wall of snow so the nose of his truck pointed out toward the entrance. That way, he could see the Expedition go by.

He hoped he could get a glimpse of the driver and any other occupants. If the vehicle contained a family on vacation, he'd stop worrying about it. But if the driver looked suspicious in any way, Joe planned to get back on the highway and reverse the game. He'd follow the Expedition to see where it was headed.

The black SUV drove past the entrance to the rest stop slower than Joe had anticipated. Although the window glass was darkened, he made out two men inside. The driver, and a passenger, who turned his head and made eye contact with Joe as the vehicle went by.

Joe heard a screech of braking tires. Then, before he could put his pickup into drive and get out of the parking lot, the Expedition reversed and filled the entrance so there was no way to get around it. The walls of snow were too deep to try to ram through.

"Uh-oh," Joe whispered aloud, realizing too late he'd trapped himself in the clearing.

He did a quick inventory of his weapons in case he needed to go into action. His Remington Wingmaster twelve-gauge shotgun was loaded but secured behind his seat. The M4 carbine was in the gun rack behind him. His .40 Glock was on his hip, but he'd need to get out of the cab to draw it and hope against hope that he could hit something with it.

The Expedition backed up a few more feet, then turned into the lot.

There was no doubt in Joe's mind now that he'd been followed. And that now he was going to find out who and why.

Although when the two men opened their doors and got out, he had a pretty good idea of who they were. Feds always had a fish-out-of-water look about them. Joe got out as well and left his door open in case he had to jump behind it. Daisy stayed put.

At more than eight thousand feet in elevation, the summit was treeless, snow-covered, and windswept. The sky was deep blue and cloudless, and although the temperature was below forty degrees, the high-altitude sun warmed his exposed skin instantly.

The two men approached him, but stopped about ten feet away. It was a law enforcement tactic: stay just outside a subject's personal space, but close enough to make a point—and close enough to draw and fire a weapon.

Also, stay separate so that the subject has to divide his attention between the two of them and can't observe them both at once. It was a luxury Joe rarely had, since he never had backup or a partner.

"Joe Pickett?" the driver asked. He was wearing a heavy parka that looked very new, and he displayed an open badge wallet.

"Yup."

"I'm Special Agent Jeremiah Sandburg of the FBI," the driver said. "This is Special Agent Don Pollock. We'd like to ask you a few questions in regard to a special matter on behalf of the Department of Justice."

Joe leaned back against the grille of his pickup. He could feel the warmth of the engine through his jacket. Joe saw no reason to tell the agents he'd been tipped off about them from Chuck Coon and possibly get his friend in trouble.

He said, "I've got an office and a telephone. I've also got a supervisor in Cheyenne who would have forwarded your request to meet. So I wonder why you tailed me up the mountain until you had me cornered."

Sandburg smiled and chuckled, as if Joe's question were pointless to answer. "We wanted to make sure it was you," he said.

"It's me. What can I help you with?"

Sandburg did a slow pirouette to theatrically take in the vast treeless vista on top of the mountain. He finished back where he started, face-to-face with Joe.

"It's real pretty, spectacular mountain country, but I'm more of a beach guy myself. This is like being on top of the North Pole, isn't it? You sort of feel like you can see forever up here."

Joe nodded. Sandburg was obviously the designated talker. Pollock's job was to glare and lend gravity to the encounter.

"You're not from the Cheyenne office," Joe said.

"No, you're right. We work out of Manhattan."

"You're a long way from home," Joe said. "You guys must have followed me for a reason."

"Are you in a big rush?" Pollock asked. "Where are you going, anyway?"

"To the other side of the mountains."

The two agents seemed to communicate with each other without looking. It demonstrated to Joe that they'd spent a lot of time together. Sandburg said, "We have a special interest in somebody you might know."

Joe thought, *Bill Hill.*

But Sandburg said, "I believe you're acquainted with Nate Romanowski."

Joe tried to stanch his surprise. He said, "He's a friend of mine."

"We're aware of that," Sandburg said. "Are you familiar with the fact that there are outstanding federal charges against him, including aggravated assault and conspiracy?"

"The charges were dropped," Joe said. "His record is expunged as far as I know."

"Did he tell you that?"

"I was there when the deal was made," Joe said. "I was in the room. Nate took on an assignment given to him by feds a lot like the two of you in an exchange for dropping the charges. A lot of people got hurt in the process, but Nate did what he was asked.

"Speaking of," Joe said, "were you two aware of or involved with the death of an old couple outside of Winchester last night? On Elkhorn Drive? It's being called a murder/suicide, but I have my doubts. And believe it or not, we don't have many crimes like that around here."

At the mention of *Elkhorn Drive*, Joe noted that Pollock's mouth twitched slightly. The location meant something to him.

"We're sorry to hear about that," Sandburg said. "But I think you've misunderstood something. *We* ask the questions."

Joe felt his neck get warm. As Coon had intimated, Sandburg and Pollock were of a rare breed of upper-echelon FBI agents who thought of themselves as superior to every other LEO— especially a lowly state game warden. He bristled at their condescension. While the mention of the address had broken Pollock's attitude for a moment, he'd now gone back to full-on cop look.

"We were asking you about your relationship with Mr. Romanowski," Sandburg said. "When is the last time you saw him?"

"Last night, in fact," Joe said.

"So he's around," Sandburg stated, as if surprised by the admission.

Joe said, "He's so around you can look him up on your phone and give him a call. He's a legitimate businessman now. You don't have to follow me up a mountain to find that out."

Sandburg rocked on his heels and thrust his hands into his parka pockets. He said, "I'm afraid we got off on the wrong foot, Mr. Pickett. We just need to get some information from you in a friendly way. We're not here to interrogate you or put you on the defensive."

Joe nodded. "Did you meet with my fellow game warden Katelyn Hamm already?"

Finally, the two exchanged a quick look.

"Thought so," Joe said. "This is all about Bill Hill and the case we're building against him, isn't it?"

This time, they didn't turn their heads toward each other. But they didn't need to.

"What is the deal with that guy that makes him so important and untouchable?" Joe asked. "Maybe if you guys came clean with me, we could get along a little easier."

"We're not here to ask about this Bill Hill," Sandburg said. His attempt to feign ignorance of the name came across as hollow, Joe thought. "We want to know about your relationship with Nate Romanowski."

"Ah. Back to that."

"Yes, back to that. Specifically, we want to know if you're aware of other crimes, particularly aggravated assault and murder, that might have been committed by Nate Romanowski over the years, but were never charged."

Joe crossed his arms over his chest. He knew of plenty. He also knew how dangerous it was to talk. This was not the environment to try and explain Nate's unique sense of justice and how he went about wreaking it.

"Maybe you should talk to him about it," Joe said.

"So you're admitting you have knowledge of additional crimes?" Sandburg asked.

"Nope. I'm suggesting you should talk to Nate."

Pollock turned his head toward Sandburg and raised his chin like a bulldog. "I think our man here is being less than candid with us."

Sandburg nodded as if contemplating that. Then to Joe: "Have you ever heard of 18 U.S.C. 1001?"

"Yup."

"If you have," Sandburg said, "you'd know that if we determine that you're lying to us or concealing material facts in a case under investigation, we can prosecute you and send you to federal prison. And it sounds to me like you're concealing crimes that your friend committed. Does it sound like that to you, Don?"

"It does," Pollock said.

"I haven't lied or concealed," Joe said. "I suggested you talk to the subject of your investigation. That is, if he's actually your target and if you've really opened a new file on him after your bosses already closed it. But I have a feeling your target is *me*. I have a feeling that you two have your own agenda and it has nothing to do with Nate. Am I right? You want me to drop the charges in regard to Bill Hill?

"So again," Joe asked, "what is the deal with Bill Hill? Why did you two come all the way out here?"

"We don't have to answer your questions," Sandburg said again. "But to be honest with you: Yes. We'd like to strongly urge you to drop any charges against Mr. Hill. If that happens, you might just see the 18 U.S.C. 1001 violation go away as well."

"Interesting how that works," Joe said, shaking his head. Then: "What is it with Bill Hill, anyway?"

"We can't give you specifics, because they involve several ongoing investigations," Sandburg said. "All I can tell you is that by showing some discretion here, you'll not only be doing your colleagues in the bureau a favor, you might be saving thousands of American lives. Maybe millions."

Joe arched an eyebrow. "Millions?"

"You have no idea how far-reaching the damage would be if you prosecute. And what for? Some deer and elk? Don't you see how ridiculous that sounds?"

"It does sound ridiculous," Joe admitted. "But I think you're telling me about thirty percent of the story."

"And that is more than we should," Sandburg said. "So I've appealed to your sense of duty and patriotism. That's the best I can do. What Don and I agree on is that, by your answers, you've violated 18 U.S.C. 1001. That's a very serious offense. Do you think your agency and governor will foot the bill for your lawyer?"

Nope, Joe thought but didn't say. That ship had sailed.

Sandburg continued. "Do you think a jury would believe your version of this interview against two highly placed and highly trained special agents who both testify to hearing you violate the statute right in front of us?"

"No," Joe said while patting the breast pocket of his uniform shirt where he'd activated his digital recorder while getting out of the truck. "But they might change their mind when they hear the actual record of this conversation."

Pollock took a step toward Joe with his fists dropped low and clenched. "That's bullshit."

"Keep talking," Joe said. "It's legal in Wyoming to record a conversation if one of the two parties is aware of it. And since the FBI makes it a practice *not* to record their interviews, it'll be your testimony versus your actual words."

Sandburg reached out. "You'll need to surrender that device."

"I won't be doing that," Joe said, gesturing behind him at his pickup cab. "And if you try to take it from me forcibly, you'll be recorded on video by my dash cam."

Sandburg froze for a few seconds, obviously trying to figure out his next move. Pollock simply glared at Joe, his face a darker shade than when he got out of his SUV.

Joe said, "I'll tell you what. I'll give you my card and be on my way. You can give me a call anytime and maybe we can work together on whatever important federal thing it is that brought you out here to my district. I'd like to help if I can—especially if we're saving lives as you claim. But you don't have to follow me around or try to intimidate me."

Joe drew two business cards from his pocket and handed them both to Sandburg, who reluctantly took them.

"Now, if you'll move your vehicle from the opening, I'll be on my way," Joe said.

AS HE CRUISED by the Expedition, Joe could see Sandburg and Pollock engaged in a heated discussion. He took a deep breath to calm himself as he did so.

He accelerated on the highway to put as much distance as he could between them before the two special agents decided to follow him again.

Joe said to Daisy, "Remind me to download that recording when I get home so I can send it to Dulcie and Chuck Coon."

He also made a mental note to send a copy of the digital file to ex-governor Spencer Rulon, in case he needed a lawyer in the future.

Then: "No, we don't have a dash cam. You know that as well as I do. But they don't."

JOE WAS SEVEN miles from Shell when Marybeth called. He transferred her voice to the Bluetooth audio system his new pickup had available but he was just figuring out how to operate.

"I've learned more about GPS technology than I ever wanted to know," she said with a weary laugh. "So your question was why your device said there was no 2204 Elkhorn Drive on the map, right?"

"Correct."

"Well, it's not an easy answer," she said.

"That figures."

"Apparently, there's an error in the mapping software in the device itself. It needs to be corrected or updated. But in order to report a mistake, you have to send a request to whatever developer created the software you're using, meaning you have to contact Google Maps, Apple, MapQuest, and all the other companies that provide the technology. It could take weeks or months for them to respond and add the address to their software."

"There's no quicker way?" Joe asked.

"Well, I saw some references to other companies that specialize in what they call 'business location data management.' That means they specialize in a one-stop service to notify all the software mapping firms about an error or omission. So if someone opens a pizza shop that doesn't show up on customers' devices, the data management firm can literally help put them on the map."

Joe frowned. He wondered if all the companies were missing Bill Hill's address or if it was only his device. Finding that out might be crucial information.

Marybeth said, "Joe, do you think that somebody was using the same software, which took them to the Behrmans instead of the Hills?"

"That's what I wonder," he said. Marybeth was sharp.

"God, that would be horrible."

"Yup," he said.

"But it also means it wasn't a murder/suicide and that Bill Hill might have dodged a bullet. Literally."

"That's what it could mean," Joe said. "But we're completely speculating at this point."

"Of course. But that's what we do."

He chuckled.

He said, "I appreciate the info, but I'm still a little puzzled. What you're saying is that the mapping software might be different depending on your device. That an address might come up on your phone but not on your GPS in your car if they have different software?"

"I think so, yes."

"So there's not one master map out there? It's every company for themselves when it comes to navigation?"

"Basically, yes. But they all use the same satellites."

He thought about that. "How can that be?"

She said, "The official Global Positioning System is operated by an agency called GPS-dot-gov. From what I could find online, the GPS satellites are more like beacons. GPS-dot-gov also refers to them as being like lighthouses. They send radio signals down to earth that bounce from your device to at least four other GPS satellites, and your device does the calculation to determine where you are. That's what I understand, at least. Each mapping company uses those signals in their own way."

Joe sat up. He said, "GPS-dot-gov?"

"Yes."

"It's a federal authority?"

"From what I can figure out. I think it's part of the air force."

"So if a specific address was somehow jammed up or withheld from the official GPS network, none of the platforms would have it?"

"It's beyond my pay grade to know the answer to that question," she said. "But I'd guess that if the guy at the address that couldn't be found didn't make an issue of it to all those individual companies and he completely bypassed the government system, he'd just stay lost."

Joe said, "Or if there was an official government request to the air force, like a directive from the Department of Justice . . ."

"I don't know," Marybeth said. "But I'm sure you or I couldn't get an address not to show up."

"*Bingo*," Joe said.

CHAPTER EIGHTEEN

EARLIER THAT MORNING, Peter Infante, Adelmo Cruz, and Cesar Reyes sat at a table in the corner of the rustic little restaurant on the outskirts of Shell and waited for their breakfast to arrive. A table occupied by local ranchers was located in the other corner, and Infante listened casually to complaints about cattle prices and farm equipment, and worries about whether the winter snowpack would carry them through the summer.

He was bone-tired and anxious at the same time. He observed that the customers at the rancher table rotated as new men came in and others left. How the waitress kept track of who ordered what and who got specific checks, he didn't know. The men had, to Infante's ear, humorous names like Ned, Les, Wyatt, Hank, Hoss, and Shorty. It was like waking up in an episode of *Bonanza*.

Deer antlers and complete heads of moose, deer, antelope,

and elk covered the walls of the place. They were dusty and he thought their glass eyes seemed to follow him and read his thoughts.

The waitress had introduced herself as "Sally—Sagebrush Sally," as if she were "Bond—James Bond."

The primary burner phone was on the table next to his silverware. He was waiting on confirmation from New York, and he was beginning to be concerned about how long it was taking. He checked to make sure he had a good cell signal—it was moderate, but good enough—and he wondered if this little town had some kind of stupid cell service that interfered with his ability to send and receive messages. He wouldn't doubt that.

Sally, Sagebrush Sally arrived carrying all three platters at once. She got the orders correct and slid a massive plate of huevos rancheros in front of Reyes and a breakfast burrito the size of a small log in front of Cruz. Infante had opted for what he thought would be the safe Anglo choice and had ordered pancakes. They resembled a stack of hubcaps.

"Jesus Christ," Reyes said with a delighted laugh. "Who can eat all of this?"

"Me," Cruz answered, stuffing a chunk of fried egg and green chile into his mouth. He chewed slowly and nodded his head. "I can't believe it. They know how to make green chile here. See the chunks of pork and tomato?"

"The cook is Mexican," Reyes said. "I seen him peek out of the kitchen a minute ago."

Infante slathered his pancakes with butter and soaked them

in fake maple syrup, which was unfortunately the best the restaurant could offer. He wished he'd ordered Mexican like his compadres.

The operation had taken all night to initiate and clean up, and none of them had slept. Afterward, they'd cleared out of Twelve Sleep County and driven over the mountains in the dark. The little town of Shell was the first village they'd encountered where the restaurants were open for the morning.

Infante was ravenous, like he always was after they'd completed their work. He attributed it to adrenaline burning through calories in his body. But he didn't know that to be a true scientific explanation. All he knew was that he was hungry.

As the three of them ate, shoving food into their faces as if their arms were pistons, he noticed that Adelmo and Cesar shot looks at his silent phone.

They knew how things worked and they were waiting for confirmation as well.

"SHE'S BEEN GONE a long time," Cruz said as he sopped up the last of his green chile with a flour tortilla.

"I hope she didn't leave us here," Reyes said. "My stuff is in her car."

He was only partially joking.

"She probably dumped it on a street corner," Cruz offered.

"There are no streets here, idiot."

"She said something about finding a place where she could get a Bloody Mary," Cruz said.

"Fine by me." Reyes shrugged.

Infante didn't mind that Abriella wasn't with them. She'd been smoldering with anger for hours, in a dark mood since he'd retrieved her from the Eagle Mountain Club. And he wasn't completely sure she didn't have a point. While she was often critical of him and questioned his methods and tactics, this time he'd had a kernel of doubt throughout the entire operation. Something felt off about it that he couldn't put his finger on.

So he couldn't wait until the all-clear came via the burner, so the four of them could go their separate ways.

He was as sick of all of them—especially Abriella—as they likely all were of each other and him. It was difficult living, traveling, and working twenty-four/seven with anybody. And what made it more difficult was that they were in the Mountain West where they didn't know their way around. Infante didn't like how the four of them stuck out in these tiny little towns, where everybody else seemed to know one another.

Abriella was the worst. She was destined to shine wherever she went, and she didn't seem to mind attracting attention. She was used to men looking at her and women glaring at their boyfriends and husbands as they did so. She could tone it down, he thought. She could wear looser clothing and adapt her hairstyle to the area. She could wear less makeup. She could respect their assignment and the safety of the team.

But she didn't.

"There she is," Cruz said, looking out the window toward the road.

"Uh-oh," he moaned. "She doesn't look happy."

———————

WHEN ABRIELLA BLEW into the restaurant, her eyes were black, and Infante felt a knot form in his stomach. The ranchers stopped talking as they watched her storm past them. She strode through the room with her head down and her arms pinned to her sides like a human missile.

She took the empty chair directly across from Infante and leaned across the table toward him, leading with her chin.

"You fucked up," she hissed. "We hit the wrong target."

"What are you talking about?" Infante asked. Cruz and Reyes looked up but said nothing. A dark cloud seemed to descend upon them all, Infante thought.

"It wasn't him," she said. "How many times did I tell you I thought he looked too old?"

She had, but then again she questioned everything.

"How do you know this?" he asked.

Infante was grateful she was keeping her voice low, but he feared it wasn't low enough. He welcomed the arrival of Sally, Sagebrush Sally at the ranchers' table to tell them about getting her Jeep stuck in the slush and mud on the way to work that morning. She had a loud voice, and demanded the ranchers' undivided attention.

"Where did you get your information?" Infante asked in a whisper.

"From someone who knew," she said. "Word travels fast in these small towns," she said. "Everybody knows that couple is dead. The *wrong* people."

She stated it calmly. For Infante, her calm was more terrifying than her black eyes.

His phone lit up on the table and he grabbed it. He could feel all of their eyes on him, trying to read his face.

The text read *Negative. It's not him.*

He knew his face gave them the answer they were looking for.

"*Fuck*," Cruz spat as he sat back and threw his napkin onto his empty plate.

"I fucking told you," Abriella said. "But you went ahead anyway."

"We know that was the address," Infante said.

"Too bad we didn't have a picture," Reyes said.

It was true. This was the only time they'd ever gone after someone when they didn't have photos of the target. They'd been flying blind. There were people back east who knew what their target looked like, but there wasn't a single photo to be found of him anywhere. Somehow, the Internet had been scrubbed of their target's likeness. Nothing like that had ever happened before.

Which is why Infante had photographed the old couple's dead faces from several angles and forwarded them on for confirmation. And why it must have taken them so long to respond in New York. He envisioned a phone being passed around to principals who had personally known the target.

"How is this possible?" he asked.

"It's possible because you're a fuckup," Abriella said.

"We had good intel," he said. "We had the address, and the address was confirmed. So what happened?"

"I'm not going back," Cruz said. "Now we don't know where he is, and we sure don't know what he looks like."

Reyes sat back and rubbed his temples. He wasn't as hotheaded as Cruz. And he knew that if they didn't finish the job, they not only wouldn't get paid but they'd become targets themselves.

Infante was at a loss for words as well as a plan. He needed to get away and think.

They'd made mistakes before—there had been unanticipated collateral damage—but the Wolf Pack had never failed to complete their contract.

"There's a way to find him," Abriella said, looking one by one at each man at the table. "But we've got bigger problems we've got to solve first."

"What?" Infante asked her. "What bigger problems?"

Abriella took a quick look around the room. Sagebrush Sally was still going on and on, and the ranchers were politely listening to her, although a couple were eyeing the exit door.

Abriella said, "I wound up at a little tavern up the road because I needed a drink. There was one other customer in there—your typical pathetic small-town loser. He was drinking his breakfast and he looked like he'd been out all fucking night.

"His name is *Ryle*," she said with a roll of her eyes. "Even though I was minding my own business, he came over and sat next to me. I was thinking about sticking a knife into his throat when he asked if I knew anything about that poor old couple who killed themselves over by Winchester last night.

"I said, 'I'm not from around here,' and he looked me over and said, 'You got *that* right.'

"Then, without any prompting, he starts telling me a sob story about him and his wife. She's a game warden, and the feds scared the living shit out of her yesterday because she's investigating some big shot from New Jersey they want her to leave alone. Ryle says this guy is named Bill Hill and he lives on—listen carefully here, boys—Elkhorn Drive."

She paused to let that sink in. Infante felt his eyes flutter.

"Bill Hill lives on a big estate with a couple of other guys who also happen to be from Jersey. They all showed up here a couple of years ago at the same time."

"Jesus Christ," Reyes said. "It's them. It has to be them."

She nodded. "So Ryle tells me all about this mystery case. Something about this Bill Hill using drones to harass animals. But Ryle is pissed at his wife because she seems more involved with this case and putting this guy away than she is in him. Ryle said his wife is working with four other people to close the net around Bill Hill."

Infante shook his head. "Do these people know who he really is?"

"It's not clear," Abriella said. "Ryle only knows what his wife told him before he wussed out and went on a bender."

"If the FBI is involved, they probably do," Infante said.

"Either way, we can't take the chance. We've got to take them all out before we go after Hill. We can't leave anyone standing who can link Hill to us or to our bosses. It has to be done quickly before information gets out beyond that circle of people. Simple as that."

Infante looked away. It seemed as if the room were spinning out of control.

Abriella's eyes sparkled. She looked directly at Infante and said, "What we've been doing isn't working. The methods we've used have exposed us. Maybe they haven't put it all together yet, but it's just a matter of time before they connect the dots. When they do, *we'll* become targets. This is about self-preservation. *This is about our survival.*"

Infante could see that Cruz and Reyes were really listening to her. That they were now on board with what she was saying. That he'd lost them.

"Who are these five people?" he asked her.

"I've got their names," she said. "I had him write them down on a cocktail napkin."

"And he just wrote them down for you?" Infante asked skeptically.

To demonstrate how she made it happen, she softened her face, tilted her head slightly to the side, and opened her eyes wide in apparent admiration. Infante had to confess to himself that if she showed that beautiful and sympathetic face to him he'd probably tell her anything she wanted to know as well.

Then her expression hardened and turned back into the devil face.

"Pretty easy," she said. "Back to business."

"Five targets before we go after Ernie Mecca?" Infante said, incredulous. "How can we even be sure it's him?"

"Oh, it's him," she said with a toss of her hair. "I'm sure of it. Jersey guy, brand-new property, showed up two years ago out of the blue, living with a couple of thugs on *Elkhorn Drive*."

She practically spat out the last two words, and they stung Infante.

"Not to mention that the feds are running interference for him," she said.

"But . . ."

"It has to be choreographed," she said. "It has to be done all at once so the killing ground is totally clear. We have to be creative for once. We need to split up and design this so all of our targets go down at the same time. Then we can regroup and go straight at Mecca."

Infante felt a surge of anger well up in him. He said, "Abriella, that's not how we operate. We're deliberate. There are good reasons for what we do as a team. What you're describing is sloppy and reckless."

"You mean like killing a couple of geezers for no reason at all?" she asked with another toss of her hair. "No, it's time to turn off the slow waltz. It's time to rock and roll."

She slapped the table and acted as if she were about to leap over the top of it. Infante had never seen her so passionate, so engaged.

She said, "We've got four very professional operators sitting right here at this table, and we've got a van filled with weapons and gear we never use because all we do is slink around and hide in the shadows. It's time to make a fucking statement about what we're capable of."

"What are you saying?" Infante asked her.

She stared at him with those black eyes until he had to look away.

"I'm saying you're out," she said. "I'm taking over."

Infante looked to Cruz and Reyes. Both averted their eyes.

"Give me the phone," she said to Infante. "I need to send those five names to the bosses so they can get their people to start digging into them."

He sighed and handed it over.

WITH ABRIELLA BEHIND the wheel of her Mercedes, Infante sat fuming silently in the passenger seat, but trying not to show it. He took the offer to ride with her as a kind of gesture of peace. It was the best she was capable of, he thought, because an actual apology was beyond her and she'd need him eventually. The only reasons he had stayed with the team after being deposed were money and pride.

He also knew that if he protested to the bosses or threatened to quit unless he was restored as top man, he wouldn't win. Abriella was a legend, and they'd choose her over him. And he'd probably go on a ride with a couple of their associates from which he'd never come back.

They'd gassed up in Shell and he'd paid for the fuel for both vehicles with cash, as always. Now they were headed back through the tiny town to link up to the highway and go back in the direction from which they'd come the night before.

Infante was patient. He bided his time. He knew that planning the kind of operation Abriella had proposed would be beyond her experience and level of skill. Pure ruthlessness was no substitute for careful planning. She had no idea how complex these things were, and she had no appreciation for all the preparation and strategy he employed to keep them all alive and successful. But she'd find out, he thought. And he'd be there to catch the ball when she dropped it or tossed it back.

At the same time, his biggest fear wasn't that she'd screw up and expose them all. His biggest fear was that she wouldn't.

"There he is," she said.

"Who?"

"My new best friend, Ryle."

Infante looked up to see a man lumbering along the side of the road with his back to them about a quarter of a mile ahead. Ryle looked dejected, and he seemed to have trouble putting one foot ahead of the other.

"Hold this," she said, handing Infante the phone back. He took it and dropped it in his lap.

He felt the SUV surge and he braced himself. She waited until the last possible instant—just as Ryle started to turn his head toward the source of the accelerating engine—to swerve off the asphalt.

There was a sickening *thump*, and Infante got a glimpse of Ryle's broken body as it was thrown to the side in a heap.

The rear end of the Mercedes fishtailed in the soft mud until she recovered the wheel and got it back on the highway. Infante could see ripples in the sheet metal of the right front quarter panel and he assumed the headlight was gone.

"Good thing it's a rental" was all she said as she drove and studied her rearview mirror. Then: "He's not moving."

Infante said nothing. He looked down at the phone and tilted it away from her so she wouldn't detect what he was doing.

He retrieved the last text she'd sent.

It read:

> We need everything we can get on:
> Katelyn Hamm (game warden)
> Joe Pickett (game warden)
> Dulcie Schalk (prosecutor)
> Mike Reed (sheriff)
> Nate Romanowski (falconer)

INFANTE SAT BACK and closed his eyes. He found it hard to breathe.

Two game wardens, a DA, and a sheriff on the list? Plus an unknown birdman? It was absolutely dangerous and completely audacious at the same time.

It was pure Abriella Guzman.

CHAPTER NINETEEN

TWO HOURS LATER, Joe arrived at the game warden station in Shell to find that Katelyn's work pickup was parked on the side of her house and there was a muddy white Chevrolet SUV in the driveway with SHELL COUNTY SHERIFF'S DEPARTMENT emblazoned on the door.

Joe parked across the street, told Daisy to stay, and got out. As he did, Sheriff Bob Marek walked out of the Hamms' house talking on his cell phone. He saw Joe approaching and nodded at him to stand by.

Marek was in his midforties with ginger hair and a red beard streaked with gray. The whiskers around his mouth were stained with tobacco juice from a big wad of it he always had in his cheek. To Joe, he resembled a baseball player or a squirrel. But he knew the sheriff to be quiet and competent, and he'd heard from Katelyn that he ran a good department and was easy to work with. That wasn't always the case, as Joe could attest. Mike Reed only had nice things to say about Marek.

"Okay," Marek said into his phone, "call me when you hear something."

He punched off and slid the phone into his waistband for easy retrieval.

"Hey, Joe."

"Bob," Joe said. "Is Katelyn around?"

Marek frowned. "You haven't heard?"

Joe felt a quick bolt of fear. "Heard what?"

"Ryle got hurt bad. Katelyn's with him. That was my dispatcher I was just talking to. She's waiting to hear something from the doctors."

"Hurt how?" Joe asked, recalling that he'd spoken to the man just the night before.

"Hit-and-run east of town on Highway 14. Ryle was walking home after a big night, I guess, and somebody nailed him and fled the scene."

"Any idea who did it?"

"Not yet," Marek said. "I've got my guys putting together a timeline from last night. Ryle left his house mad—that's according to Katelyn—about eight, and we've got witnesses saying he hit just about every bar in the area. We're trying to find out if maybe he got into an altercation with someone who was angry enough to track him down. Ryle's a pretty mild-mannered guy, but he used to get downright chippy when he drank."

Marek gestured to the west. "We found some busted headlight glass and tracks in the mud, but that's all. We searched the town for damaged vehicles and didn't locate the right one, so we'll put out an APB. There's only so many ways out of here."

Joe tried to remember if he'd seen any damaged vehicles driving east on the highway as he came down the mountains. He couldn't recall any. But there were plenty of forest service roads and two-tracks off the highway that cut into the heavy timber.

"Man, that's terrible," Joe said.

"Ryle's been airlifted to the Billings hospital," Marek said. "Katelyn's with him."

Which was why her empty pickup was parked alongside the house.

"Is he expected to live?"

"Can't say," Marek said. "I got a quick look at him on the gurney and I wouldn't give him much of a chance. It looked like both legs were broken and probably his pelvis. He was unconscious, so we couldn't ask him if he knew who hit him. I hope like hell he wakes up, but who knows what kinds of internal damage he's got."

"Why was he on foot?" Joe asked.

Marek shrugged. "My best guess is he forgot where he'd left his truck. We found it behind the Two-Bit Saloon with the keys in the ashtray."

Joe shook his head. He recalled Katelyn alluding to some tough times she'd had with Ryle in the past, but Joe thought they'd weathered the storm and moved on.

"How was Katelyn doing?" Joe asked. "I've been trying to talk with her for a couple of days."

"She was worried, of course," Marek said. "But she's one tough lady. She called Cindy and asked her to pick up her boys.

They'll be staying with us at our house tonight, and however long they need to be there."

Joe nodded. That's the way it was in small towns. The sheriff and his wife took care of their neighbors' kids.

"My boys will like that," Marek said. "They get along great with Tyler and Brody."

Marek agreed to let Joe know about Ryle's condition as soon as he heard something himself.

"I'll keep an eye out for dented vehicles on the way back home," Joe said.

"If you find 'em, I really don't care if there's an altercation and the driver winds up in the hospital or worse," Marek said. Then: "Don't quote me on that."

"I won't."

"It's quite a day, isn't it," Marek observed. "You've got a murder/suicide on your side of the mountain and we have a likely fatal hit-and-run on my side. What the hell is going on?"

"I wish I knew," Joe said.

"THAT'S JUST AWFUL," Marybeth said to Joe via the Bluetooth. "I'll text Katelyn our best wishes and ask her if there's anything we can do."

"Thank you."

Joe was doubling back on the route he had taken to Shell that morning, although this time he drove more slowly and took several detours on side routes to see if he could locate a newly damaged car.

At one point, he thought he'd hit pay dirt when he glimpsed the reflection of chrome and glass through a stand of trees ahead of him about ten minutes off the highway. With his shotgun out and pointed muzzle-down on the seat next to him, Joe eased down the road around a bend and drove up on a pair of naked high-school-age kids cavorting in the back seat of a sedan.

When they looked through the back window and saw him coming, their faces changed from pleasure to shock and embarrassment. They were so young, he thought. The same age as Lucy and Justin, but from Shell.

Joe was just as embarrassed. He plucked the mic from its cradle and said over the loudspeaker: *"Shouldn't you kids be in school?"*

THE TRIP BACK was uneventful—no damaged cars, no feds in Expeditions, no more spring trysts, no wolves on the hunt—until he received a call at the top of the summit, with the Twelve Sleep River Valley filling his entire windshield.

The caller ID said: CHEYENNE FBI OFFICE.

Joe thumbed the button on his steering wheel that connected with his cell phone.

"Hello, Special Agent Coon. You decided to use your work phone this time."

Which meant the call was official business now, Joe knew.

Coon had a chuckle in his voice when he asked, "What did you do to my New York brethren today to make them reach out to me?"

"Nothing major," Joe said. "They wanted to strong-arm me to drop the Bill Hill charges and I wouldn't let them."

"That's not the way they explained it to me," Coon said. "They said you got belligerent and you refused to cooperate."

"Did they tell you I got the entire exchange on tape?"

Coon paused for three beats. "They left that part out."

"Well, what do you know?"

"It's all water under the bridge anyway," Coon said. "My fellow agents have decided to come in from the cold, which is a good development. Apparently they've decided they have no choice but to do things by the book after all. So they notified me that they were in the state and they asked for my help to sort out the mess in your county."

"What mess?"

Coon chuckled again. "The way they tell it, the whole place is chock-full of intransigent locals who don't respect their authority."

"Probably just me," Joe said.

"Probably. But the fact is they reached out, and it fills my heart with joy."

Joe nodded. He was glad Chuck Coon's bureaucratic heart was filled with joy.

Coon's voice flattened and he took on a much more serious tone. "Joe, what they're doing out here really is a big deal. Not just to the bureau, but for the whole country."

"I keep hearing that. What's the nature of the case?"

"That I can't tell you," Coon said. "Not now, over the phone.

But I can tell you that this interests the government at its highest levels, and it's very, very important that we get this right."

Joe eased to the side of the road. Although he was talking hands-free, he wanted to be able to concentrate on the conversation without having to negotiate hairpin mountain turns at the same time.

"Okay," he said. "Go on."

"First they asked me to rein you in. I told them I couldn't do that."

"Good."

"I also told them that you aren't a lone wolf up there. That other local authorities were involved."

"Good."

"So we came up with a strategy, and I hope you'll consider it in good faith."

"Why wouldn't I?"

"That's what I told them," Coon said. "So what we agreed on was to have a meeting in Saddlestring. We want you there, as well as your sheriff and county attorney. Sandburg and Pollock will be there, along with someone else involved in the case from DC. Her name is Sunnie Magazine and she's number three in the bureau. That's how important this all is."

Joe said, "Sunnie Magazine? That's really her name?"

"I know, but yes it is. This will be her first trip out here. I met her at a conference in DC a couple of years ago and believe me when I tell you there's nothing sunny about her personality. She's hard as nails."

"Great," Joe said. "We all enjoy getting yelled at by hard-as-nails feds."

"I'll be in the room to broker the whole thing and serve as the liaison between the bureau and local law enforcement," Coon assured him.

Joe cocked an eyebrow. "This sounds a lot like transparency. I thought you people were against that."

"Please." Coon sighed. "Enough with the sarcasm."

"Chuck," Joe said, "your New York brothers followed me this morning like I was a suspect, then they tried to entrap me by saying I violated 18 U.S.C. 1001."

" 'Entrap' is a serious charge, Joe," Coon cautioned.

"And it's the right one. They tried to pretend to ask me about Nate Romanowski in the hope that I'd say something they could use against me later. And they did it without taking a single note or keeping a record of our interview."

"That's acceptable procedure," Coon said defensively.

"Well, it's something you people ought to change," Joe said. "The only thing that saved me was my recording of the whole thing. I suspect they did the same thing to a fellow game warden I've been working with, but they were more successful there. And these are the people you want me to meet with and trust anything they say?"

"As I said, they have another version of what happened," Coon said. "But be that as it may. I'll be in the room. Your people will be in the room. And it's important, Joe. It really is. I wouldn't bullshit you about a case of this magnitude."

Joe paused for a moment. "I trust you, Chuck."

"Thank you." Then: "So you're in?"

"Yup."

"Good. I'll be in touch with the others. We need to make this happen as quickly as we can before things get even more out of hand."

Joe thought of the murder/suicide and the hit-and-run. He said, "It's possible they already have."

JOE MOANED WHEN his phone went off again, and he put aside the thought that his days were much more pleasant when he couldn't get a cell signal.

This time, it was County Attorney Dulcie Schalk.

She asked, "Where are you?"

"Twenty minutes away from town."

"Good. Can you meet me at the Holiday Inn lounge in a few hours? Judge Hartsook-Carver is in town for a hearing and she agreed to meet me about that search warrant for Bill Hill's place."

Joe shot his sleeve out and looked at his watch. "I can do it."

"I'm glad to hear it," she said. "She's only in town for tonight, so this is our best shot. Have you heard anything about the forensics on the drone yet?"

"I haven't. Katelyn over in Shell was doing that, but I can call the lab in Laramie. Katelyn's husband, Ryle—"

"I heard," Dulcie said. "It's terrible. Do they have any idea who's responsible?"

He filled her in on what Sheriff Marek had told him.

"I hope they catch the bastard who did it," she said. "That's a case I'd love to prosecute."

"I'll let Marybeth know I might be late tonight," Joe said. "I'll make sure she knows to blame *you*."

"Have her come meet us," Dulcie said. "We can all go get dinner after we talk to Judge Hartsook-Carver. You can do things like this again, Joe. You can be spontaneous. Don't forget you're an empty nester."

"Not quite yet," Joe said. "Lucy's still around."

He felt a pang of guilt for saying it that way, as if he couldn't wait for her to go.

"I'll bet you dollars to donuts she won't be home for dinner tonight," Dulcie said. "Did you forget what it's like the last month as a senior in high school?"

"I see your point."

She was probably right, Joe conceded. But since his recent conversations with Lucy, he was already starting to miss having her around more. And he felt remorse about looking forward to the empty nest without her.

"I'll text Marybeth and we'll sort out the details," Dulcie said. Then: "Gotta go. I've got a call coming in from Agent Coon. I'll see you tonight."

Joe knew what the call was likely about. Coon and the FBI were performing at record speed to put the meeting together.

What, he wondered for the hundredth time, was so important about Bill Hill that sent an entire federal law enforcement agency into warp drive to save him from a minor charge?

CHAPTER TWENTY

LATER THAT AFTERNOON, Infante asked Abriella, "What is it that we're looking for?"

She said, "I'll know it when I see it."

He winced and turned away.

They'd been on mountain gravel roads ever since she'd turned off the highway that morning. He understood why she'd done it—to get off the main roads because they and their vehicles had become more recognizable every day they stayed in the area. Especially since the car they were riding in had been damaged from hitting Ryle in broad daylight. That made sense.

What didn't make sense to him was where they were going in high-elevation terrain with which none of them were familiar. Abriella seemed to have no actual destination in mind.

The all-wheel drive of the Mercedes allowed them to take roads that he wouldn't try in a sedan, but he was worried about the panel van keeping up behind them. More than once, after she'd driven up a treacherous incline or bumped their way over rocks where the road had washed out, he turned in his seat to make sure Adelmo and Cesar were still behind them.

It also didn't make sense that she drove so fast. Rather than pick their way on rough and narrow roads, she drove in a stop/start way; gunning the engine on short straightaways and stomping on the brakes at the last possible second for hazards or turns. She was, he thought, quite literally a fearless driver. The biggest problem with that was he was in the passenger seat.

They were traveling vaguely east. Few of the roads were marked with signs except for posted numbers designating U.S. Forest Service routes. They'd lucked upon an aging sign at one junction that indicated Shell was seventeen miles behind them and Saddlestring was twenty-one miles ahead. She took the road that meandered toward Saddlestring.

The gravel road cut through the timber on the side of a mountain. The drop out his window was precipitous, and there were places where the trees cleared and he could look down to see a thin creek of white water in the far distance below. Almost straight down. There was no shoulder to the road and no guardrails. And they kept climbing higher.

If Abriella—who was often distracted—ventured too far to the right, Infante could envision the SUV rolling and tumbling down the mountainside until it finally stopped down there in the water. He'd cautioned her several times to slow down, on the chance that an oncoming vehicle might suddenly appear around a corner, but she'd ignored him.

They'd climbed so high into the mountains that the air was thin and Infante felt himself becoming light-headed.

It was obvious that they'd finally reached the summit of the mountain by the treeless snowfield that covered a flat. The road disappeared under a long drift and emerged on the other side before it plunged over the top of the mountain and dropped down the other side.

He determined that there was no way to gauge how deep the snow was without getting out and assessing the route. She mumbled a curse as they got close and the Mercedes slowed down.

As Infante prepared to unbuckle his seat belt to get out, she said, "To hell with it," and stomped on the gas. His head snapped back.

"Abriella, please . . ." was all he could get out before the Mercedes plunged into the drift.

He held on as the car powered across the field, sending twin rooster tails of grainy snow up behind them. Although they foundered for a few seconds within sight of the exposed scree and grass on the other side of the drift, the tires gripped hard-packed snow beneath the crust and they made it across to dry ground.

Then she just kept going. Without them knowing what kind of drop was ahead of them or what the terrain was like, the front of the car plunged over the edge and they descended into heavy timber.

"What about the van?" Infante asked when the angle of the car was such that he could no longer see behind them over the summit.

"They have shovels if they need them," she said.

But somehow Adelmo and Cesar made it, probably using the

tracks through the snow Abriella had established. The van was behind them again within ten minutes.

When he looked over his shoulder, Infante could see Cruz make an angry and frustrated *What the hell?* gesture behind the wheel of the other vehicle.

THE PATH THEY were on spit them out to a better road, and they continued to switchback down the mountain. Infante used the navigation system on the Mercedes to zoom out as far as it would allow, until it showed the Twelve Sleep River at the top of the screen and then the town of Saddlestring.

What was the point of taking all of these bad mountain roads in the middle of nowhere to avoid being seen, he wondered, if they were going to lead them to another town?

She turned onto an even better unpaved route labeled Hazelton Road on the screen and she followed it for a few miles in a southeastern direction. Again, she drove too fast for him to read most of the signs and roadway markers as they shot past.

Abriella zoomed by a gap in the pine trees and hit the brakes so hard the SUV fishtailed and nearly slid off the gravel. Then she reversed the car a hundred feet and stopped again. Infante looked back to see Adelmo stomp on his brakes as well and nearly collide into the back of them.

An improved path led down into the timber with sparkling new PRIVATE ROAD and NO TRESPASSING signs mounted on poles on each side. A freshly varnished wooden sign read ARROWHEAD VALLEY LODGE.

Without hesitating, Abriella turned onto the road and sped up as if she had a vital appointment waiting on the other end of it.

THE PINE TREES eventually opened up to reveal a lush river valley and an assemblage of small structures below them. There were still pockets of snow in the shadows of the trees on both sides as they descended.

Infante asked, "What is this place?"

"We're soon gonna find out," she responded. "But I think I found what I was looking for."

The road finally leveled out and Abriella cruised through the parklike flat toward a large central building made of logs with a steeply pitched roof. The grounds were manicured and attractive, he thought. As they passed, Infante identified the rest of the structures and neatly appointed cabins with porches, decks, and individualized names on each door: BRIDGER CABIN, IN-DIAN PAINTBRUSH, WILD IRIS, RAINBOW LODGE.

She didn't stop at the main lodge, but drove right by it.

"The office was back there," Infante said.

"Fuck the office," she said as she gestured toward a huge home located on the far end of the property. "That's where we're going."

It was a three-story house facing away from the lodge compound toward the river, as if turning its shoulder away from it. He noticed several satellite dishes mounted under the eaves.

Abriella drove through a gate that said PRIVATE RESIDENCE, NO ADMITTANCE.

As she studied the exterior of the home, she said, "Satellite television, Internet, phone service. *This* is the place. I knew I'd find it."

"You were planning to come here all along?" Infante asked.

"No, I've never heard of the place. But I told you I'd know it when I saw it."

A metal building tucked nearly out of sight in the trees behind the house was filled with vehicles: a GMC Suburban, a maroon Yukon, a Range Rover, several ATVs with cabovers, and a tracked snowcat that hadn't yet been put away for the spring.

Abriella turned into the circular drive and parked across from the front door. The van pulled in behind them.

Infante got out cautiously while keeping an eye on the front windows and door. The place looked locked down and vacant. Closed storm shutters covered the windows and deck chairs were folded up and stacked under the covered porch.

Then he heard the sound of an approaching vehicle. A man riding a four-wheel ATV was coming fast up the road from the Arrowhead Valley Lodge. He looked angry. The rider had a dog covering his lap as if it were a blanket, and he wore a floppy cowboy hat with the front brim pinned straight back by the force of the wind. He looked to be in his sixties and he had a gray beard and thick horn-rimmed glasses.

"This looks like our host," Infante said. He reached behind his back and touched the grip of his weapon to assure himself it was there.

"No need for that," she said. "I'll handle it."

Abriella smiled in a cold-eyed way Infante had seen before. *Fearless.*

THE MAN ON the ATV passed through the gate and released the pressure on the accelerator so the machine decelerated and rolled to a silent stop on the side of the van. Both Adelmo and Cesar had remained in their vehicle.

"Are you folks lost?" he asked Infante with a lecherous side-eye toward Abriella. "We don't open to guests for another month, and even if we did, this is the owner's place. Didn't you see the damned signs on your way in?"

"Are you the caretaker?" Infante asked.

"That's what I am," the man said.

"What's your name?" Abriella asked.

"Name's Tom."

"What a cute dog, Tom," Abriella said with her most disarming grin. "Can I pet him?"

"It's a her," Tom said. "She don't like strangers."

"She'll like me," Abriella said, laughing. She approached the ATV and the dog. The animal looked to Infante to be a gray-and-black blue heeler mix. It raised its head and glared at her with piercing and unfriendly blue eyes. Then the dog growled.

"Maybe you're right," Abriella said, stepping back. "But give her a chance to get to know me and she'll change her tune. Everybody does—including grumpy old caretakers."

Tom didn't take offense. He looked her over from head to foot, and Infante could see that the man was taken with her.

Infante thought, *At least that dog has the right instincts.*

"Look," Tom said to Infante when he managed to tear

himself away from Abriella, "you'll need to get in your vehicle and drive on out of here. It's just me on the property right now, and as I said, we ain't open yet."

"So this is the owner's house?" Abriella asked Tom.

"Yep. As I said, it's off-limits to guests."

"And the owner is away right now?"

"He is," Tom said with impatience. "Mr. and Mrs. Baker won't be on property until July."

"We'd like to rent it from you," Abriella said. "Just for a night or two at the most. If you'd like, we could do it off the books for cash. The Bakers will never know, and you'll get a nice little bonus for your hard work. Does a thousand dollars a night sound fair to you, Tom?"

"A thousand a night?" Tom said. "That's a lot of money."

Abriella nodded to Infante. "Pay the man."

"Naw," Tom said while shaking his head. "That's not something I can do. The Bakers have been real good to me over the years and it wouldn't be right. So just keep your money and hit the road. There's motels in town that would gladly take it."

"But I like *this* place," Abriella said with a pout on her mouth.

Tom looked to Infante and shook his head, exasperated. "Maybe you folks aren't hearing me. The lodge ain't open, and even if it was, this is a private house. You're trespassing right now."

Tom took in both vehicles. "I see you're from Arizona, so you're a long way from home. I don't know how things work down there, but you can't just show up at the lodge here and say you want to rent the house."

"But we do," Abriella said.

"Then I got no choice but to call the sheriff," Tom said.

"You've got a choice," Abriella replied.

Tom looked at her for a moment, and Infante could see the man change his attitude from frustration to sudden fear of the unknown.

Abriella looked over to Cruz and Reyes and nodded her head.

The driver's-side window powered down and Cruz's arm stuck out with a cocked Colt 1911 .45 in his fist aimed at the side of Tom's head. It was less than five feet from the muzzle of the weapon to the caretaker's ear.

Tom saw it and his eyes got huge.

"Do you have the keys to the house on you?" Abriella asked.

"Yes, ma'am," Tom said.

"And you better keep that dog under control," she warned Tom.

Infante knew what that meant.

LATER, TOM WAS bound with duct tape and heaped on the floor of the mudroom next to the body of his late misbehaving dog. He had spent forty-five minutes opening up the owner's house for occupancy. He'd pulled the shutters off the windows, turned on the water, rebooted the electronics and modems, and he'd even gotten a fire going in the fireplace to warm it up until the central heat could catch up.

Abriella exalted at the amenities as she strolled from room to room. Infante had rarely seen her in a better mood.

She'd chosen the largest bedroom for herself and sweet-talked

Tom into turning on the propane fireplace, and she'd assigned other bedrooms to the other three men. Infante recognized that she'd chosen the second largest for him.

"What have we here?" she cooed as she pulled bottles out from behind the wet bar and placed them on the counter. "Johnnie Walker Blue, Gran Patrón Piedra, Casa Dragones . . . This is premium booze. I think we're going to have a little party. Cesar and Adelmo are going to love it here."

She found steaks and lobster tails in the freezer, a wine cellar with hundreds of bottles, and she was pleased that the satellite Internet was fast and reliable.

AFTER DIRECTING CRUZ and Reyes to walk Tom out to the river and throw him in—followed by the body of his dog—Abriella poured two glasses of Johnnie Walker Blue and gestured to Infante to sit down at the table with her.

"This is better than sneaking into a town and splitting up at a bunch of hotels," she said. "In those little places, we stick out and people notice us. Here, we've got a comfortable base of operations away from our targets where we can plan things and prepare in comfort. No more sneaking around waiting to get caught."

Infante didn't react to the criticism of his methods, but he seethed inside.

"I know you don't like it," she said, meaning her ascendancy. "But I think we'll be stronger together like this. In fact, I'm sure of it."

She patted the burner phone. "They've already sent the details on four of the five on our list. We've got addresses, photos—everything we need. The only target they can't find much on is this falconer, whatever that is, but I'm sure they'll come through by tomorrow. Then we move."

"Tomorrow?"

"Of course. We have to strike fast."

She paused and sipped and looked hard into his eyes.

"Are you on my team?" she asked.

He nodded.

"Say it," she said with a forced smile.

"I'm on your team."

"Good," she said, sitting back. She looked around and once again listed why the place was perfect for her.

"I don't get it, though," she said to Infante. "Why do these Anglos live in a place like this way up in the mountains where they freeze in the winter? Where there are bears and other animals that can eat you? I just don't get it. If you have as much money as these people do, why not live in the Bahamas or Florida?"

Infante shrugged. "They like it, I guess. I do have to admit that a couple of times I looked out of the car today, I thought it was beautiful. Very rugged, but beautiful in its own way."

She poured herself some more scotch. "I don't see it. All I see are trees, trees, trees. And rocks. Why look at trees and rocks when you can lay on a beach and see the ocean? It makes no sense to me."

Then she abruptly changed the subject. "I hope Cesar and Adelmo remember to take the tape off of Tom. We want him to look natural when he's found."

"I'm sure they will," Infante said. "They're professionals."

"Of course they are," she cooed.

At that moment, the burner chimed and she picked it up from the table and opened a new message.

"Good," she said. "Here's the skinny on our falconer. Our people are working late tonight and so will we.

"First, a nice dinner," she said. "I'll cook. Then we'll all sit down together and divide up assignments."

Infante felt light-headed again.

CHAPTER TWENTY-ONE

JUDGE CAROLINE HARTSOOK-CARVER sipped her second vodka and diet tonic and cocked her head a little to the side to better hear the playback of Joe's taped confrontation with Bill Hill. Then she picked up his recorder from the tabletop and held it to her ear. Joe watched her carefully to try to get a read on her reaction. Dulcie did the same.

They were at the center table in the Holiday Inn lounge, and the three of them were the only customers, except for a single man in a blazer who sat at the bar trying to strike up a conversation with the young redheaded bartender. He was a traveling bull semen salesman, he said to her, and he tried to make it sound interesting.

"Oh, the stories I could tell you," Joe had heard him tell the bartender.

Judge Hartsook-Carver was trim and severe and in her midsixties. She'd left her robes in her hotel room and she was wearing a dark pantsuit, a white shirt with a lace collar, and a single strand of pearls. Her hair was dyed dark red, which made her light complexion appear very pale. In Joe's opinion, she wore twice as much makeup as she needed to in order to appear younger. She'd been curt and businesslike from the minute he sat down and there was a definite edge to her manner.

She asked Joe to stop the playback and rewind an exchange she'd just heard. She placed the device on the table so they could all hear it.

Joe: *"Do you fly your drone around here or just over the mountain on the winter range?"*

Hill: *"More over there than here. I like to observe the wildlife up close."*

Joe: *"Observing is one thing. Running elk and deer to their death is another."*

Hill: *"I can't help it if they run. I don't make them panic. All I want to do is get good photos, and you should see some of them I've got in the house. Some people say I should enter some of those shots in the* Wyoming Wildlife *photography contest, they're so good."*

"So he just admits it outright," she said.

"Yup."

She continued to listen. She asked Joe, "Who is that speaking now?"

"His name is Jeff Wallace."

Wallace: "Not only that, you do it in front of his son. And you're too stupid to know nothing at all is going to come from this. I think maybe the best idea is for you to get back in your truck and get the hell off our place."

Joe: "I think maybe you're right."

Hill: "Spend a little time reflecting tonight. Reflect on the fact that you can quite easily make all of this just go away. That, my friend, will make it easier on everyone concerned."

"What exactly does that mean?" Judge Hartsook-Carver asked. "It sounded like a threat."

"That's how I took it," Joe said.

"So you think you've got probable cause to search his property for the controls to the drone, is that it?" she asked Dulcie.

"Yes, Your Honor," Dulcie said.

"Come clean," Hartsook-Carver said. "What else are you two expecting to find?"

"We don't know, Your Honor. But we do know the FBI would rather we stayed away from the Hill compound altogether."

"The FBI is involved with this?" Hartsook-Carver asked with arched eyebrows. "Why would they care about harassing wild animals in Wyoming?"

Joe recounted to her what agents Sandburg and Pollock had alluded to and that Coon was putting together a meeting with all the principals the very next day.

"So you suspect Bill Hill might be connected to the FBI in some way?" she asked.

"Possibly," Joe said.

"Probably," Dulcie added.

"Is he actively working with them on a case?"

Joe said, "I think he did back in New York and New Jersey, but I don't know the details."

"So it's conjecture at this point?" she asked Joe.

"Yes, ma'am."

She sniffed. "I don't allow conjecture in my courtroom and I'm not going to allow it here."

Chastened, Joe sat back in his chair.

"What about the forensics on the drone you recovered?" she asked.

"We're still waiting," Joe said. "The game warden in charge of that just had a personal tragedy—"

"I heard about that," the judge said, cutting him off. "But I've got the tape where he admits it.

"I need to think about this," Judge Hartsook-Carver said as she signaled for a fresh drink from the bartender. "I'll make my ruling on the search warrant tomorrow, after you've told me what happened in the meeting."

"But, Your Honor," Dulcie said, "the meeting has no bearing on these charges."

"I'll make that decision, Counselor," Hartsook-Carver said sharply.

Then she arched her eyebrows and looked from Joe to Dulcie to indicate they were dismissed. The judge went back to her vodka tonic.

She hissed at the bartender, who was in the process of returning to her station behind the bar.

"Miss, I ordered *diet* tonic."

"WHAT WAS *THAT* about?" Joe asked Dulcie as they made their way through the lobby of the hotel.

Dulcie walked with purpose. She was angry. "One of two things," she said. "Either she's thinking that defying the FBI might hurt her future political ambitions, or she's already talked to them and she was warned off of the case. Either way, I'm pretty sure we won't get that search warrant approved in time to seize any evidence. We'll have to wait for Judge Hewitt to get back from his stupid hunting trip, and by then I wouldn't be surprised if the Hill compound is as clean as a whistle."

Joe clucked his tongue.

"This case has 'loser' written all over it," Dulcie said. "Too many impediments."

"What do you mean?" he asked, although he kind of knew.

Dulcie said, "It's been hinky from the start, and as you know I like things clean and clear. The feds have taken a big interest in it and they keep throwing hand grenades. Your fellow game warden is out of the picture for the time being. Forensics is late. And now we've got a judge who doesn't seem to want me to prosecute."

He sighed.

"On a happier note, I got a text from your lovely wife," Dulcie said. "She's meeting us at the Stockman's Bar and we can figure out from there where we're going to dinner."

"Okay."

Apparently, Lucy wasn't going to be around for dinner, as Dulcie had correctly predicted.

Dulcie pushed her way through the front doors of the hotel and said, "Believe me when I tell you there will be some wine consumed tonight."

KATELYN HAMM STOOD up quickly from the uncomfortable couch in the waiting lounge of the hospital when the surgeon she'd met earlier pushed through the door. He was wearing green scrubs, and a white surgical mask dangled from one ear.

The surgeon was trailed by an earnest woman with a grim set to her face. She was carrying a clipboard, and the lanyard around her neck indicated she was a comfort consultant.

Katelyn's heart dropped. She knew the woman was only there for the purpose of consoling the surviving family members.

"I'm sorry," the surgeon said while meeting Katelyn's eyes. "Your husband has passed. To put it simply, there were too many internal injuries to fix all of them at once."

"He went peacefully," the comfort consultant said.

"Never regained consciousness," the surgeon added.

The woman—named Regina, according to her lanyard—placed her clipboard on the seat of a chair and approached Katelyn with open arms.

Katelyn recoiled. She didn't want a hug from a person she'd never met and whose job it was to hug.

Instead, Regina reached out and grasped Katelyn's hand with both of hers.

"It's hard," Regina said. "It'll take a while to process, but that's why I'm here. Grief is not something that you complete by yourself. We share in comfort knowing Ryle is no longer suffering."

Katelyn bristled and glared at Regina for a second, but then she realized they had two different interpretations of Ryle's suffering. Regina, of course, had no idea at all what Katelyn and Ryle had gone through and that her husband might say his misery was due to her occupation and where they had to live. Regina was referring to the injuries sustained in the hit-and-run.

"It just happened so fast," Katelyn said, as much to herself as to the surgeon and Regina. "He was there last night in the garage and now . . ."

She couldn't complete the sentence. She wondered if it was better to have a spouse die suddenly than after a long illness.

"The boys . . ." *Would no longer have a dad.*

The surgeon said, "If you'd like, we could get you something to help you sleep."

She shook her head. The news was overwhelming, but she couldn't help but think her way through it. She had two sons to raise. They'd need her to be strong. And if she was completely honest with herself, Ryle had made her life more difficult and complicated than it should have been. Without him—and she hated herself for even thinking of it now—her life might be happier.

But still.

She wanted to blame the two FBI agents who'd started the problem the day before, and she had to at least partially blame herself. There was probably something she could have said to Ryle that might have defused the situation so he wouldn't have left angry. Someday, she thought, she'd come up with the perfect sentence that might have worked to calm him down. But she couldn't think of it now.

And she had to blame Ryle himself. Going out on a bender, forgetting where he parked his truck, walking—no, likely *staggering*—down the side of the road.

There was plenty of blame to go around, she thought.

But the ultimate person responsible for Ryle's death was behind the wheel of a car somewhere.

And she made a vow at that moment to find him and take him down.

As if a prayer were answered, her phone lit up with a message from Sheriff Bob Marek.

Katelyn:
    Attached are two stills from a closed-circuit camera at the bank across from the gas station from this morning.

She tapped on the icons and the photographs downloaded and revealed a dark Mercedes SUV and a white panel van. The angle of the camera was such that she could see the hoods and roofs of the vehicles but no one inside.

We think whoever hit Ryle was driving one of these two vehicles. The gas station owner said they both had Arizona plates. Three male Hispanic subjects, one Hispanic female. They were seen at breakfast in town. A rancher saw both cars headed up the mountain this morning at about the time we think Ryle got hit. APB is issued nationwide. We'll find them.

Cindy says your boys are fine. We both hope Ryle is okay. Our thoughts and prayers are with you.

Bob

Katelyn knew she needed to talk with her boys. The next phone call she had to make was going to be the hardest one of her life.

She'd tell them that she was going after the people who killed their dad. Immediately. At least they'd have that to focus on.

NATE ROMANOWSKI WAVED his hand over the coals of his grill to make sure they were hot enough and then he laid a pronghorn antelope backstrap across the grate.

While brushing the meat with the Italian salad dressing he'd used to marinate it, he asked Liv, "Medium rare?"

"I usually want it rare, but I read where pregnant women should stay away from that," she said. "So medium instead."

He smiled to himself and flipped the backstrap. It cooked quickly because the coals were hot and there was no fat in the wild game.

Since Liv had become pregnant, her tastes had changed. She preferred her meat seared on the outside and red in the middle, and he'd observed her drinking dill pickle juice straight out of the jar, as if she were in a sixties sitcom.

She was seated at the backyard patio table wearing a light down coat and fleece winter moccasin slippers against the evening chill. She complained that her feet had swelled up and she couldn't wait to kick off her shoes at the end of the day.

He thought she looked lovely sitting there.

"Oh," she said. "I nearly forgot. You've got an estimate to do tomorrow."

"I do?" he asked.

"Yes, if you can."

"I can in the morning."

"She wants you there at two."

He shrugged. "I could do that. Why two?"

"She didn't say."

"Local?"

"Semi-local," Liv said. "A really nice young woman. Very friendly. She's having trouble with owls going after her chickens and she'd like you to go there and let her know when you can put your birds up to chase it off."

Nate had a thing about owls and he liked having his raptors go after them. It bothered him that so many people thought owls were wise simply because they had eyes facing forward like a human being. The fact was, owls weren't used by falconers because they were too dumb to be trained.

In the past year, he'd done a half-dozen owl abatement jobs.

Since it was becoming trendy for young families to raise chickens, he saw it as a growth area in the future.

"I know it sounds strange for me to say it," Liv said, "but she had a really sexy voice. I'm warning you now that you better get back here on time."

"You have nothing to worry about," Nate assured her with a smile.

She rubbed her hands over her belly and waggled her feet in the oversized slippers. "I guess I'm not exactly feeling real attractive at the moment."

"I disagree."

"Thank you for lying."

"Where am I going?" he asked.

The backstrap was cooked rare and he speared it with a fork and placed it on a platter to take inside.

"Do you know where the Arrowhead Valley Lodge is?" Liv asked.

"I do," he said.

"Do you mind if I tag along?" she asked. "I'd like to get out of the office and a little road trip sounds nice. We won't be able to spontaneously just pick up and go in a couple of months, so let's do it while we can."

Nate nodded. "I'd love the company."

"And it's not just because that woman had a sexy voice," Liv said as the struggled to her feet.

"Of course not."

"Well, maybe a little."

———————————

Justin: What R U doing tomorrow afternoon?

   Lucy: Going to class LOL

   Justin: The teachers have in-service training. We're free!

   Lucy: OMG—I forgot. I don't have plans.

   Justin: Want to come out here? We can catch a ride with Jeff and he can take you home later.

   Lucy: Sounds great ☺.

   Justin: That was weird the other day.

   Lucy: No kidding.

   Justin: My dad isn't usually such an A-Hole.

   Lucy: LOL

   Justin: I think he wants to show you he can be nice.

MARYBETH, DULCIE, AND JOE had dinner at a new restaurant that had just opened up on the first floor of the Saddlestring Hotel. The proprietors were a young couple from Cody and they were giving it their best, with white tablecloths and black-clad waiters and waitresses. Joe thought the menu had too many trendy items like beets and brussels sprouts, but he was willing to give it a try because Dulcie and Marybeth were excited about a sophisticated place in town and they wanted to support it.

"Oh, this building," Marybeth said as she looked around at the exposed beams and ductwork. "It brings back good and bad memories."

Before being hired by the library board, Marybeth had tried to modernize the old hotel on the corner of First and Main. It had once been the finest hotel in the county and *the* place where anyone of note stayed in the area. President Calvin Coolidge, Ernest Hemingway, Gary Cooper, and aviatrix Amelia Earhart had all stayed there.

She'd been stymied by an avalanche of regulations about historic buildings, as well as by an unsavory partner, and they'd been saved from financial ruin when the Bureau of Land Management bought it for expanded offices. The new restaurant was a nice addition to the property, she said.

Dulcie and Marybeth talked over their pasta dishes and Joe wolfed down a steak.

He was recounting the events of the long day in his head when he realized Dulcie was talking to him.

"What was that?" he asked her.

"He does that," Marybeth said to Dulcie.

"I know." Dulcie smiled. Then: "I said the feds have reserved the conference room in the county building for noon tomorrow," she repeated. "The FBI agents you met will be there as well as Chuck Coon from Cheyenne. And some big muckety-muck from Washington named Sunnie Magazine."

"Is that really her name?" Marybeth asked.

"It is," Dulcie said with a sly smile. "She's a deputy director of some sort. So they're bringing out the big guns. Sheriff Reed will be there as well. Joe?"

"I'll be there," he said. "I'm as curious as anyone to find out what the fuss is all about."

"I wish Katelyn Hamm could come. But of course I don't want to ask her right now. Oh," Dulcie said while snapping her fingers, "I forgot to tell you. Just before we went to the Holiday Inn, I got a call from Sheriff Marek over in Shell. They got a license plate number from one of the suspect vehicles."

"How did that happen?" Joe asked.

"Some rancher noted it as the car passed through town," she said. "I guess there isn't a lot going on in Shell in the morning.

"Anyway, they traced it to a rental agency in Arizona. It was rented on Monday, April 23, at Sky Harbor Airport in Phoenix by a guy named Peter Tork."

Marybeth said, "Peter Tork was in the Monkees."

"That's right," Dulcie said. "It was obviously a false name and driver's license. The credit card on file turns out to be stolen."

"Did he rent both vehicles?" Joe asked.

She nodded.

Joe shook his head. "So this guy rents two cars and drives them over a thousand miles all the way here? It sounds like the same vehicles Nate saw here in town."

"This is getting weirder by the hour," Marybeth said.

They kicked around the theory that the occupants of the two rental cars not only made a brief stop in Saddlestring, but were also the leading suspects in Ryle's hit-and-run.

"Does Katelyn know any of this?" Joe asked Dulcie.

"I assume the sheriff is keeping her up to speed," she said.

After ordering cheesecake for dessert and another glass of wine, Marybeth said, "I'm still working on that GPS mystery and I really haven't gotten anywhere, although I found a few interesting items this afternoon."

She explained to Joe and Dulcie that deep within several

obscure national defense websites and on the fringes of the intel-
ligence community in DC, there was speculation that the CIA
and NSA possessed the ability to alter location data emanating
from government satellites. The ability to do that had allegedly
confused hostile foreign forces and fighters in the Middle East
who used GPS devices for navigation. Nowhere, though, did the
U.S. government confirm that they had the technological know-
how to manipulate the service.

"It sounds plausible to me," Dulcie said. "And if it helped us
kill bad guys, all the better."

Joe agreed. He was grateful to have Marybeth and Dulcie—
two very smart women—on his side. Without them, he knew,
he'd be stunningly ineffective.

He said, "Let's ask Sunnie Magazine tomorrow if the Department of Justice can do the same."

Dulcie laughed. "Do you think she'd really tell us if they
could?"

"Nope."

Dulcie raised her glass for a toast. She said, "Here's to knowing what the *hell* is going on around here by this time tomorrow
night."

"I'll toast to that," Marybeth said, clinking Dulcie's wineglass with her own.

Joe tipped the mouth of his beer bottle toward the both of
them and took a long pull.

WEDNESDAY, MAY 2

We surrounded by the fuckin' wolves.

KANYE WEST,
"WOLVES"

Chapter Twenty-two

||||||||||||||||||||||||||||||||||||||||||||||||||||||||||||||||||||||||||||||||||||||||||||||||||||||||

JOE PULLED HIS pickup into the Twelve Sleep County Building parking lot at 11:48 a.m., next to the black Expedition that had been driven by Sandburg and Pollock the day before. Then he thought better of it and swung around the building into the alley near the dumpsters. There was no reason, he thought, to let anyone know he was in town for the day and not in the field. Local poachers paid special attention to his location.

He entered the building through the delivery entrance and avoided Stovepipe and his malfunctioning security machine. As his boot heels echoed on the tiles in the hallway, he could hear a low rumble of talk coming from the open door of the conference room. The space was used for county commission meetings and vendor presentations, and Joe had never spent any time in it before.

He removed his hat as he entered the room and found metal tables pushed into an oblong arrangement so everyone could face one another. Dulcie and Sheriff Mike Reed sat on one side.

FBI agents Jeremiah Sandburg and Don Pollock were directly across from them. On the far end of the oblong was Chuck Coon next to an attractive but fidgety woman with dark brown hair and green eyes wearing a charcoal pantsuit that seemed designed to suggest casual, but not really.

Pollock and Sandburg were asking Reed about the Wyoming Cowboys football team since their former star quarterback had been drafted high by the Buffalo Bills. Joe recognized it for what it was: small talk to break the ice and take up some time until the meeting officially started.

"Could you please close the door behind you?" the woman asked Joe.

He did, and then took a chair next to Dulcie and placed his hat crown-down on the conference table. Dulcie's eyes were a little red, he noticed. She probably regretted that last glass of wine with Marybeth the night before. But she seemed as sharp as usual.

"Thank you all for coming," Coon said. "I think it goes without saying that what we talk about today needs to stay in this room. It's that important."

Coon shifted his gaze from participant to participant to ensure that everyone agreed.

"I'd like to start by introducing Sunnie Magazine, deputy director of the Federal Bureau of Investigation in Washington, D.C. She flew out here on a bureau jet last night just so she could be at this meeting."

Joe thought, *A bureau jet?*

"Thank you for being here," she said. "I assume everyone knows each other?"

"We just met," Dulcie said, indicating Pollock and Sandburg across the table. "We're glad your spies came in from the cold."

No one laughed, although Joe liked the line.

Sheriff Reed cleared his throat and turned his chair toward her. "I've got to say for the record that I have great admiration for the FBI and the work you do. But I don't take real kindly to agents lurking around in my county without some notification. We have a responsibility to our constituents to know what's going on."

"Noted," Magazine said with a curt nod.

Joe observed that Coon sat back and did a side-eye to the deputy as if he shared Reed's concern. But he kept quiet.

"Sheriff," Magazine said, looking from Reed to Dulcie to Joe, "we sometimes find that in a case that involves national security the best way to proceed is to limit the number of people who have knowledge of it. We exempt everyone—even law enforcement officers like the three of you—who aren't on a need-to-know level."

"Seems like that 'need to know' stuff is a matter of opinion," Reed said. "Maybe if you kept us in the loop we could actually help you, since we're on the ground here. Sneaking around here threatening people and following them up the mountain sounds a lot to me like you're doing more harm than good. And what's this about national security?"

"I'll get to that," Magazine said.

Joe observed that Sandburg and Pollock had responded to Reed's little speech with contemptuous glares at him.

Joe didn't like that.

Reed gestured to both Dulcie and Joe. "Maybe if there was a little more transparency from you folks, we wouldn't have to be in this room right now, is what I'm saying. These two professionals are out there doing their jobs, and you guys are acting like we're all out to interfere in some big case of yours. Problem is, your big case is in *my* county."

Magazine sighed as if she'd heard enough. She said, "How much do you know about fentanyl?"

Reed said, "I know about it, but why don't you tell us dumb rubes?"

She ignored the jab. "Fentanyl is the number one killer drug in America. It doesn't come directly from poppy plants or from cultivated fields somewhere. It's a man-made synthetic opioid that can be manufactured cheaply in a crude lab using easy-to-buy chemicals. It's fifty times more powerful than heroin and the profit margin is astronomical. A bad-guy chemist can very easily turn a few thousand dollars' worth of chemicals into millions in a matter of months."

Magazine continued. "Compared to other drugs, it's a breeze to make, transport, and sell. Especially compared to weed or natural opiates. Over seventy thousand Americans died from fentanyl overdoses last year in thirty-five states, and this year it may hit ninety thousand. The rock star Prince died of it, for example.

"It's a national epidemic of staggering proportions," she said. "I'm in charge of trying to shut it down."

"Got it," Reed said. "I hope you're successful."

"We've had some wins," she said. "Not that long ago, we busted a young couple in the Bronx who were transporting a hundred and forty pounds of the stuff in a couple of suitcases. That much fentanyl could kill thirty-two million people. Think about it."

Joe took a breath.

"We've confiscated over three hundred and fifty pounds of pure fentanyl in the last year in New York. The city is the hub of fentanyl distribution for the Eastern Seaboard and heartland. What we've got in evidence storage could have killed sixty to seventy million people."

Magazine leaned forward and clasped her hands together on the table. "It gets into our country a number of ways, including the U.S. Mail. But the vast majority of it is transported by people. And believe me, these drug mules don't look like bad guys. Most of them are young couples with valid U.S. addresses. The majority of them don't even have records, and when we catch them they look like they're here for a *Star Trek* convention, not a massive criminal enterprise. They hide it in panel vans and cross the border, or they ship it to themselves. When it arrives in bulk form at a distribution center, it's sold to domestic gangs, most of them Dominican.

"That's right," she said, "*distribution centers*. We've busted four of them."

"Where is it coming from?" Joe asked.

"Guess," she said.

"Mexico," Reed answered. "Some from China."

Magazine nodded and said, "Correct. When some of our states decided to legalize weed, the cartels needed a new revenue stream, so they put their resources into labs that manufacture fentanyl. Eighty percent of all of the drugs seized in this country can be traced back to the Sinaloa cartel. They keep a tight grip on it so other cartels don't muscle in on their business. The Sinaloans are absolutely ruthless. They've killed thousands of Mexican rivals and hundreds of politicians and cops who've tried to stop them. Collateral damage in Mexico is into the tens of thousands of victims.

"Right now, as we speak," she continued, "the Department of Justice has indicted four of five Sinaloan-affiliated gangsters in New York and New Jersey. The indictments are the result of our efforts to identify them. The fifth one got away and we presume he's in Mexico. But we're on the brink of breaking up this major outreach by the cartel in our own country.

"So you see," she said, "why this is considered a matter of national security."

"SO WHAT DOES this have to do with us?" Dulcie asked. "And more important, what does it have to do with Bill Hill?"

"I'll get there," Magazine said. "But first I wanted to lay the groundwork. It's imperative you realize where we're coming from and why we place such importance on the issue."

Reed sniffed and said, "And here I thought you guys in DC spent all of your time rigging presidential elections."

"That's fucking bullshit," Pollock snapped.

Joe winced. He doubted Mike Reed would have said such a thing if he was running for reelection.

"Please," Coon said. "Sheriff, you know that was a low blow."

Reed nodded and suppressed a smile.

"Can I continue?" Magazine asked archly.

"Please do," Dulcie said.

Magazine said, "Thank you. What we've found is that the cartels have really upped their level of sophistication when it comes to drug distribution. They don't even try to control the retail operation anymore—they farm it out. That means they have less exposure, and vastly fewer associates selling on the street. By doing this, they've virtually eliminated strategies we've used in the past for arresting low-level dealers and rolling them up the hierarchy until we can go after the big shots. So we've had to employ . . . new methods."

For Joe, it suddenly clicked.

He said, "Bill Hill worked high up for the Sinaloan cartel and you flipped him. That's how you got your wins. He identified and testified against those five gangsters. And I'd guess that isn't even his real name."

The room went silent. Coon, Pollock, and Sandburg looked to Magazine for some kind of direction.

Joe knew he'd scored a direct hit. He felt a soft supporting jab in his ribs from Dulcie.

"We can't discuss the particulars," Magazine said after a long pause. "But we can say he aided us in our efforts."

"He's in the damned witness protection program, isn't he?" Reed followed up. He glared at Magazine. "You people have dropped a criminal kingpin right on top of us without a word of caution or warning."

"And you're doing all you can to make him untouchable to local law enforcement so we won't blow his cover," Dulcie added. "This is starting to make sense in a really twisted way."

Coon intervened in an attempt to cool down the invective.

He said, "The federal witness protection program is a very valuable tool in our arsenal. Without it, we wouldn't have the degree of success that we have when it comes to breaking up major criminal conspiracies. These people won't talk to us or turn state's evidence unless we can provide new identities and cover for them and their relatives. Without those kinds of guarantees, the witness usually knows that the people he's fingering will kill him and everyone he's related to."

Joe whistled and shook his head. It made sense now. The reason Marybeth couldn't find anything on Bill Hill that was more than two years old was because Bill Hill hadn't existed until then. The feds had to invent him.

He said to Magazine, "So you gave this witness a new name, a phony Social Security card, a few brand-new vehicles with Wyoming plates, and shipped him out here to start a whole new life? Do you also have people who plant false items on the Internet about him—and remove every reference to his prior life so no one can find a photo of what he looks like?"

"I'm admitting nothing here," Magazine said, her face flushing. "But theoretically, yes. We do everything we can to protect the life of a critical witness and his family. It's negotiated on a case-by-case basis who gets to come along with him when he relocates. We might give him a stipend and job training, but it's understood that the witness has to play by the rules and not commit other crimes while enrolled in WITSEC."

Reed said, "That must have been a hell of a 'stipend' you gave Bill Hill in order for him to afford his compound and bring along his personal thugs. Are they in the program as well?"

"Theoretically, they likely are," Magazine said in a well-practiced, lawyerly obfuscation.

"Just admit it," Reed said heatedly. "We all know what's going on here now. Bill Hill is a fake identity. So is Tom Kinnison and Jeff Wallace. You people gave them new names and backgrounds so they'd look legitimate. You spent hundreds of thousands of federal taxpayer dollars—maybe millions—to buy this guy property and vehicles and you pay him enough every month so that he can afford expensive toys like drones. Even his dad and his boy—they're all in your program, aren't they?"

Magazine said, "Theoretically, yes."

Joe felt a tremor wash through him. Had Justin misled Lucy all along, or was he even aware of the details for why he'd moved and was given a new identity?

"Why do you keep playing that theoretical game when we all know what the truth is, finally?" Reed asked.

Dulcie said, "Because the rules for the WITSEC program don't allow the government to admit who is in it or where they are. Right?"

"That's right," Magazine said. "We're advised to deny enrollment in WITSEC even if we're asked directly by local authorities. I'm sure you can understand why if you think about it. The only time we're required to disclose is if a judge orders us to in a closed hearing."

Dulcie said, "Even if someone in the program goes out and murders someone, the feds are prohibited from admitting that they know the actual identity of the witness."

"Is that true?" Reed demanded.

Magazine nodded that it was.

Joe squinted at her. "You just said that someone in WITSEC has to play by the rules or they're cut loose. But Bill Hill *hasn't* played by the rules. That's why we were investigating him."

From across the table, Sandburg scoffed. "Flying a drone around Bambi isn't exactly a big deal, is it? Taking a few photos of a lady game warden squatting in the bushes isn't something that would queer the deal, given the circumstances."

Joe turned on him. *"You've got photos of Katelyn?"*

Sandburg rolled his eyes and looked away.

"Hill must have sent them to you," Joe said. "You've been serving as his bodyguards. That's why he told me he was untouchable."

"Oh, just calm down," Sandburg said.

"That's the reason you're here, isn't it?" Joe asked Sandburg and Pollock, his ears getting hot. "You're here to protect him and shield him and his thugs. And they know it, which is why they're so arrogant. Hill and his pals know if we look at him, all he has to do is let you know about it and you'll swoop in here and start intimidating people."

"The WITSEC program is a hell of a lot more important than your minor violations," Sandburg said. "Convicting four cartel goons is a hell of a lot bigger than you and your little piss-ant tickets."

For a second, Joe saw only red. He felt the urgent need to leap across the table and pummel Sandburg's smug face. The only thing that stopped him was Dulcie's firm grip on his forearm.

"*Please*," Magazine implored. "Please calm down, everyone." Then sharply: "Agent Sandburg, stand down and for once keep your mouth shut."

Sandburg started to respond, but apparently thought better of it. He suddenly found that his hands on the table were very interesting. Coon's eyes shot daggers at the man.

"I think we've heard enough," Reed said, pushing his chair back and glaring at Magazine. "I don't like this game you're playing and I want no part of it. As far as I'm concerned, you can do your job and we'll do ours. And if that means we raid Bill Hill's place and arrest him for wildlife violations and what-ever else we find, that's just too damned bad."

Dulcie began to gather her papers and Joe reached for his hat.

SUNNIE MAGAZINE APPARENTLY concluded that she'd lost the meeting. She stood up and closed her eyes and took a deep breath.

"Sheriff," she said, "I didn't want to do this, but you give me no choice. Now, please listen to me before you leave the room."

Reed paused. "This better be good."

"If Bill Hill's face appears in a news article or mug shot, it's a death sentence for him and everyone associated with him."

Joe immediately thought again of Justin. He let go of the brim of his hat and left it on the table.

"It's not just about our federal case," Magazine said. "I can all but guarantee you those people out there will be tortured in the worst possible way and assassinated. That's how the cartel deals with snitches."

She took another deep breath, as if to weigh how much she could say. Then: "Our witness had a close associate who also qualified for WITSEC. He relocated in the Southwest. That's where most of our witnesses wind up. They're usually from the Northeast, so they like the idea of a warm weather destination. Very few decide they want to play cowboys and Indians and choose a place like this."

"Go on," Reed said.

"The close associate has vanished, along with his wife," she said. "Although their home was staged to look like they packed up and left on their own, we have reason to believe that a hit team from the cartel known as the Wolf Pack murdered them and covered it up. What we don't know is whether the associate revealed the whereabouts of our *theoretical* WITSEC in your county."

"Jesus," Reed said.

Then it hit Joe like a thunderclap. "Did this happen in Arizona?"

"I really can't say."

"So it did," Joe said. "And does the Wolf Pack consist of three Hispanic men and one very attractive woman?"

Her face twitched. It was a tell. He noted that both Sandburg and Pollock suddenly sat up.

"We used to think the Wolf Pack was mythical," Magazine said. "We thought their existence was a legend like the chupacabra that was made up to scare people who might want to defy the cartel. But we've concluded that the Wolf Pack actually exists. They've never been arrested."

"They're here," Joe said, standing and clamping on his hat. "They were seen here in town two nights ago."

In response, Magazine's eyes got big and Sandburg's face drained of color.

Before throwing open the door and striding out into the hallway, Joe turned to Magazine. "They've likely already murdered a bunch of innocent people around here in the last couple of days. It would have been good to know who they were and why they were here. Thanks to your program, you've got blood on your hands."

"What are you talking about?" Magazine asked, clearly shaken.

He said, "We've got a missing man at the Eagle Mountain Club where one of your Wolf Pack stayed, a hit-and-run over in Shell County, and a nice old couple out on Elkhorn Drive whose bad luck was having the address that showed up because you people fiddled with the GPS system so no one could find your Bill Hill."

"You're just blowing smoke," Sandburg said angrily.

"Maybe," Joe said. "But do you want to bet on it?"

Sandburg looked away.

"Where do you think you're going?" Magazine asked Joe.

"To go get my daughter," he said.

HE NEARLY RAN into Katelyn Hamm when he stormed out the delivery door. She was in uniform.

"Follow me," he said.

"Where are we going?"

"Bill Hill's place, where we might just find the people who hit Ryle."

Her eyes got wide and she nodded with determination. "That's why I'm here. Who are they?"

"I'll give you a call on the way there and tell you everything I know," he said. "But first I've got to call Nate. I think we might need some help."

Both of their cell phones lit up at once with a message. Someone had called the 1-800-STOP-POACHING hotline to report two dead elk near the highway on the top of the Bighorns. The text message was issued automatically from the dispatch center in Cheyenne.

"That'll have to wait," Joe said.

CHAPTER TWENTY-THREE

AT 1:45 P.M., Adelmo Cruz descended the steep granite steps of the Twelve Sleep County Building. At the curb, he looked both ways before crossing the street. He strolled across the asphalt and opened the door and slid inside the driver's seat of the maroon Yukon XL that was parked on the opposite curb.

Once inside behind the smoked windows, Cruz reached up and removed the light brown wig and false mustache and dropped them both on the seat next to him. He looked up at the rearview mirror and into the dead calm eyes of Cesar Reyes in the back seat.

"It's on," Cruz said to Reyes in Spanish.

In response, Reyes crossed himself.

Cruz lifted the burner phone and speed-dialed Peter Infante, who had stayed with Abriella at the Arrowhead Valley Lodge.

"I talked to a very friendly cowboy who was running the metal detector," he said in English to Infante. "Your intel about the meeting was correct. This guy must have been bored because he just kept talking. And here's the situation: three of the five targets are all together right now inside that building. It's a stroke of luck, I guess. They're having some kind of meeting in a conference room at the moment. I'm looking at a couple of them through the window."

"Three of them in one place?" Infante asked. Cruz assumed he was repeating it so Abriella could hear. "Not two, but three?"

"Correct," Infante said. "The sheriff, the prosecutor, and the male game warden. They're all in there. It means we can get all three of them at once. But there's more."

"More?"

"The cowboy said they're meeting with the FBI agents who oversee Mecca."

"Hold on."

Cruz waited until Infante and Abriella discussed the new information. Then Infante came back on.

"Do they have a clue you're outside?"

"I don't think so."

"Son of a bitch," Infante said. "Do you have a clear shot at them through the window?"

"No. I've seen them pass by when they go get a cup of coffee or something. And I seen that sheriff roll by once, but I could only see the top of his head."

"Did this cowboy tell you when the meeting will be over?"

"He said he thought it would be pretty soon on account of the yelling he could hear from down the hall."

"Stand by," Infante said. The phone went silent and Cruz

assumed Infante was covering the mic with his hand. He was no doubt getting further instructions from Abriella.

Infante's voice was hollow when he came back on.

"Abriella says kill them all."

"What?" Cruz said. "Even the *federales*?"

"Yes. She says this way we won't have to come back for them."

"Sweet Jesus," Cruz whispered.

CRUZ AND REYES each had a Heckler & Koch UMP submachine gun within reach. It was a stubby but lethal weapon chambered in Smith & Wesson .40 with a thirty-round magazine. At full automatic, the H&K fired at a rate of six hundred rounds per minute.

Before leaving on the mission, they'd trained with the pieces by sawing watermelons in half from twenty-five yards away.

They'd never used automatic weapons—much less two of them—on a target in any previous missions in this country. Cruz wasn't sure he welcomed the new wrinkle, and he knew Infante didn't. He'd talked about the escalation of weaponry with Reyes, and Reyes just shrugged. He had no strong feelings about it.

There was nothing more attention-getting and splashy than gunning down several law enforcement targets in broad daylight on the steps of their courthouse. This was the kind of thing that happened in Mexico, not in the U.S. It was audacious and risky, and it would bring down the wrath of LEOs across the entire nation on their heads.

Which was why the afternoon was perfectly arranged to produce maximum violence and chaos on a strict timetable of destruction. Even if the surviving cops could comprehend that three of their own had gone down simultaneously, the other planned actions at exactly the same time would create fog-of-war confusion.

By the time it was all sorted out, the Wolf Pack would be several counties away in cars belonging to the Arrowhead Valley Lodge—vehicles that were not mentioned in the APB about the white van and the Mercedes SUV.

The plan was even more outrageous than several of the drive-bys they'd accomplished on Mexican politicians and police chiefs in the past.

And it was pure Abriella.

INFANTE CAME BACK ON. "Leave no witnesses," he said. "Then get to the meeting place as fast as you can. Call me with the results."

"Okay," Cruz said and punched off.

Reyes said, "We're not going to get out of this alive, are we?"

"I'd be surprised if we did."

Reyes whispered a prayer to himself in the back seat.

Cruz saw commotion through the window in the conference room. The game warden stood up and then moved away from the window.

"Get ready," Cruz said. "I think the meeting is breaking up."

―――――――

INFANTE PLACED the phone on the countertop in the kitchen and rubbed his face hard with the heels of his hands. His stomach was in knots and he hoped he wouldn't have to run to the bathroom to void his insides.

Abriella, on the other hand, was ecstatic at the news. As the day went on, Infante could see her gain confidence and validation. Now that she was in charge and her plan was taking shape, she was a different person. Gone was the sulky woman with the bad attitude.

Abriella Guzman had been replaced by ABRIELLA GUZMAN, the alpha female of the Wolf Pack.

She wore a tight black top and camo tactical pants with lace-up boots. The grip of a 9mm semiauto stuck out of the side pocket on her right thigh and the left pocket bulged with extra magazines.

Her eyes sparkled.

He could see this image before him eventually appear on T-shirts and bandanas in Sinaloa. He could imagine her as the inspiration for *narcocorridos* sung throughout Mexico and beyond.

"Let me know when it's done," she said. "They know where to regroup with us, right?"

He felt a flash of anger. *Of course* they knew where to go afterward. She either thought Cruz and Reyes were dense and hadn't listened the night before, or she was tweaking him for taking them all to the wrong address two nights before. Or maybe both.

"They know," he said.

On the table were two additional H&K UMPs and a Benelli M4 H20 Tactical twelve-gauge semiauto with a pistol grip.

She grasped one of the submachine guns by the strap and threw it over her shoulder.

Then she looked at her watch.

"The falconer dude should be here any minute," she said. "Let's get into position."

Infante nodded. He picked up the H&K by the strap and the shotgun by the pistol grip in the other hand and followed her out of the house through the back door, where two of the ranch vehicles were positioned and waiting for them.

His eyes were on her buttocks in the tight trousers the whole time.

After all, he thought, even though he felt sick inside and a sense of doom hovered over his head and shoulders, he was still a man.

"HERE THEY COME," Cruz growled to Reyes in Spanish.

He heard the sharp snap of the bolt of the submachine gun being armed behind him and the *snick* of the safety being thumbed off. Cruz armed his weapon as well.

He knew they couldn't be seen clearly from the outside with the windows up due to the dark tint of the glass. He'd made sure that was the case when he crossed the street earlier.

"Don't open the window until you're ready," he said.

"I know," Reyes snapped.

The double doors of the county building opened at once, each side swinging out. The doorway was suddenly filled with people.

Cruz reached down and touched the toggle switch to power down the driver's-side window. But he didn't depress it yet.

There were five of them. Two bulky men who held the doors open, two women in business suits, and the sheriff in his wheelchair. They were intermingled at first and it was impossible to separate out the targets.

Then they did him a favor. The sheriff rolled to the left toward a handicap ramp on the side of the stairs. One of the women, who was young, fit, and attractive, went with him.

The other three knotted up and started to descend the stairs on the right side. The older woman led, coming down a step ahead of the two burly men behind her. Cruz got the distinct impression that the two sets of people couldn't get away from each other fast enough.

"We're missing the game warden," Reyes said. "Maybe he's coming out behind them."

"We can't worry about that now," Cruz whispered to Reyes. "I've got the ones on the right. You take the targets on the left."

"Got it."

Simultaneously, both driver's-side windows whirred down.

Reyes fired first, a high-pitched staccato ripping sound that tore open the afternoon and was even louder inside the SUV. In his peripheral vision, Cruz saw plumes of granite dust explode from the front of the building on all sides of the young woman and the sheriff. The woman went down in a heap and the sheriff's chair rolled down the ramp on its own with the sheriff's head flopped back and his arms limp at his sides.

Cruz locked eyes with one of the burly men, who instinctively reached into his jacket. Too late. Cruz pulled the trigger and didn't let go until the entire magazine was empty and three bodies lay sprawled on three different levels of the steps.

"*Ándale, ándale, ándale!*" Reyes shouted from the back seat.

Cruz tossed the weapon aside to the passenger seat and rolled up his window. It smelled of acrid burnt gunpowder inside the cab, and expended brass shell casings had pooled in his lap between his thighs and were burning through the fabric of his pants.

He cursed and swatted at them as he started the engine and peeled away from the curb.

In his rearview mirror, he could see the lifeless body of the sheriff roll slowly out into the street.

As he cleared the town, he stopped the vehicle and left it running while he jumped out to peel the magnetic ARROWHEAD VALLEY LODGE decals off the two front doors. He sailed the signs into the trees on the side of the road and jumped back into the SUV.

INFANTE FELT THE vibration of the burner phone in his pocket as he followed Abriella across the lawn toward the two ranch vehicles. He planned to take the four-wheeler the caretaker had used and Abriella had the keys for a Ford F-350 flatbed pickup.

She noticed that he'd stopped to answer the phone and she paused before mounting the sidestep to climb into the cab. She cocked her head expectantly to hear the news.

Over the hum of road sound, Cruz said to Infante, "It's done."

Infante whistled his relief. He noted that Abriella was watching him intently.

He nodded to her and she beamed.

"You got them all?" Infante asked.

"All but the game warden. He must have cut out early or gone out a different door."

Infante nodded to himself.

"What?" Abriella asked.

"They got them all except the game warden."

"Did they miss him?" she snapped.

"He wasn't there."

She pouted for a few seconds, then shrugged. "So no big deal. We keep to the original plan."

Infante nodded. Before learning from Cruz that the game warden was in the meeting, they'd already set that phase of the operation into motion by shooting two cow elk that were grazing near the highway that morning and calling it in to the authorities so the game warden would respond. Infante had found himself more bothered by the slaughter of two wild animals than he'd ever been by the death of a target, and the afterimage of the two big bodies steaming in the grass in the early-morning chill had stayed with him.

She glanced at her wristwatch and then signaled for Infante to wrap it up.

He said to Cruz, "Good work, my friend. Abriella is staying here to meet the falconer and I'm going up to the road to take care of the game wardens. Maybe both of them will show up. Then we meet."

Cruz grunted and terminated the call. He was apparently in no mood to chat.

As Infante swung one leg over the saddle of the ATV, Abriella called out to him.

"Peter."

He looked up at her. Her smile was radiant.

"I know you didn't like splitting up," she said. "I get that. But this way we can do it all at once. It's all coming together perfectly."

"Yes, it is," he said, trying to keep the cynicism he felt out of his voice.

"We'll leave our rentals here and take this truck to the meeting point."

He nodded. He didn't know if she was repeating the plan she'd devised for him or to remind herself. And he didn't care.

"I'll meet you back here when you've taken out the game wardens," she said. "I'm not too worried about doing the falconer by myself.

"After all," she said with a mischievous wink, "he's some dude who flies birds around, I guess. What could go wrong?"

Chapter Twenty-four

||||||||||||||||||||||||||||||||||||||||||||||||||||||||||||||||||||||||||||||||||||||||||||||||||||||||||||||||||||||||

AT 2:05 P.M., Nate and Liv drove the Yarak, Inc. van up the mountain highway into the Bighorns. They were running late because Liv had asked him to pull over twice so she could get out and throw up.

"It's been bad most days," she said about her morning sickness when she climbed into the van the last time, "but today it's especially bad. Maybe I should have stayed home."

"Not to worry," Nate told her.

But that wasn't completely true. Liv was a vibrant personality. He wasn't used to her being sick and it unnerved him. He found himself becoming more and more aware of the other presence in their lives: the baby.

The baby would change . . . everything.

"Still, I hate to be late," she said. "It's not professional."

"It isn't like there is another commercial falconry operation in the phone book."

Nate had loaded one of his peregrines into the van before they left and the hooded bird leaned deftly into every turn on its perch on the way up. He brought the bird along for demonstration purposes in case the client wanted to see a raptor in action.

His weapon was holstered and under his seat.

As they climbed, he noted how much snow was still on the ground inside the timber. He enjoyed the fresh spring smells of the thawing mountains.

"I hope we don't need to stop again," Liv said while delicately wiping her mouth with her sleeve.

"Again, don't worry about it. The turnoff isn't much farther up the road."

"If this client is as hot as she sounded on the phone, I'm glad I'm along," Liv said with a grin. "I'm sick, but I could still fight her."

To demonstrate, she threw a weak punch into the air.

Nate's cell phone lit up on the dashboard and he picked it up. "It's Joe," he said. "I'll call him back later."

"Why not take it?" Liv asked. "We might be out of cell range at this lodge we're going to."

"Because I hate cell phones and he knows it."

She rolled her eyes and said, "Take it."

THREE MILES FARTHER up the highway near Burgess Junction and the summit, Infante stood in crusty snow that went up to his knees behind the trunk of a massive ponderosa pine. He'd parked the ATV in a stand of buckbrush so it couldn't be seen from the highway, and he'd taken his position.

The two dead cow elk were thirty yards from where he hid. He'd watched as a pair of ravens landed on the carcasses and picked at the soft tissue around the eyes. If nothing else, he thought, the big ravens would draw the attention of the game wardens to the exact location of the bodies.

He was well within shotgun range of the dead elk.

Infante checked his watch. He was surprised the game wardens hadn't yet arrived. *What else did they have to do?* Infante asked himself.

His feet were cold and the snow he stood in had begun to melt into the fabric of his trouser legs.

A few minutes earlier, he'd observed silently as a car slowed down on the highway and came to a stop near the elk. One of the ravens had flown away, but the other stayed. The remaining bird was defiant toward the intruders and continued eating.

The car had been driven by two middle-aged tourists with green Colorado plates and a COEXIST bumper sticker. The driver, who wore a windbreaker and a Tilley hat, had left his car running as he got out and approached the dead elk in the snow. His wife did the same. They both stood and stared at the dead animals with their hands on their hips.

"That's just terrible," the man said. "Look how close they are to the highway. I could have hit them on the road."

"Do you think that's what happened?" the woman asked. "Someone hit them?"

She wore black yoga pants, Ugg boots, and a puffy down vest.

"Naw," he said. "When you hit an elk, it really messes up

your car. If a car hit them, it would probably still be here on the side of the road."

"Then what killed them, do you suppose?"

"Probably bears," the man said. "Or wolves. Or maybe some idiot shot them."

"Everybody around here has guns," she said. "I bet that's what happened."

"Oh well," the man said, turning back to his car.

"Shouldn't we call someone?" the woman pleaded.

"Who?"

"Well, *someone.*"

"Just forget it, honey."

"We can't just leave them here like this."

"What do you want to do? Bury them?"

"Someone should do something."

"Maybe we could call the Wyoming Fish and Game people," the man said. He was obviously unenthusiastic.

Infante hoped they did. Maybe a second call would light a fire under the game warden.

"Where do we find them?" the woman asked her partner.

"I don't know," he said. "Maybe you can look them up on your phone."

"I barely have a signal."

"Then wait until you do."

"This has really ruined my afternoon, Ted."

"Just get in, please."

Infante heard her sob, then two car doors closing.

They were the only people who had come by since Infante

had hidden himself. He looked at his watch again and wondered why the game warden hadn't responded.

He couldn't just stand there in the snow all day waiting to ambush the target. That would foul up Abriella's well-tuned agenda.

But that was the flaw with her plan, he thought. She didn't account for something going wrong—and something *always* went wrong. The unexpected always shouldered its way in.

His patient and deliberative approach to their contract work was designed to eliminate as many unanticipated variables as possible, like the game warden not showing up. But Abriella thought the world should operate according to her preconceived notions—that people should do and say what she thought they should do or say.

That was the problem with millennials, he thought.

DOWN IN the valley, Abriella heard the crunch of gravel up in the trees and she knew the falconer was coming. She glanced at her watch. He was a few minutes late.

She stepped out from behind the main lodge where she'd been waiting and walked out into the yard. She swung the H&K behind her on its shoulder strap and pinned it there with her elbow so it wouldn't be visible from the front.

A light-colored vehicle emerged from the timber across the grounds of the resort. It drove into the lodge compound tentatively, as if the driver were trying to figure out which way to turn.

Abriella stood up on her tiptoes and waved. She smiled radiantly to get his attention. She knew she looked good.

The car was near the main lodge building where the office was located when it turned toward her. The falconer had seen her. She waved again and walked out so she straddled the two-track path that led to the owner's home behind her.

She tried to maintain her smile even though it was obvious he wasn't alone. There was a woman with him in the passenger seat.

It struck her as odd, but she dismissed it because she had no idea what a falconer did. Maybe the passenger was his employee, or maybe his wife. She couldn't see either one very clearly because the afternoon sun reflected off the windshield glass.

When the car slowed to a stop twenty feet in front of her, she lifted her right arm and let the weapon swing around her body.

There was no hesitation. Abriella lifted it and pointed the muzzle toward the windshield and squeezed the trigger.

INFANTE SAW it all.

He'd given up on the game wardens coming and was riding the ATV back on a snow-clogged service road when the trees opened up and he could view the grounds of the Arrowhead Valley Lodge laid out just below him.

Abriella braced herself and lifted the weapon and it jumped around in her hands for a silent split second before the high-pitched *brrrrrrr* of the H&K reached him. He saw the front and back glass of the SUV explode, and the vehicle rocked with the impact of the .40 rounds. He could hear the echo of the submachine gun fire bounce back and forth across the valley.

Infante squeezed the throttle and accelerated down the mountainside.

When he got to the lawn of the owner's house, Abriella was approaching the damaged vehicle with her 9mm in her hand. The empty H&K hung from her shoulder by its strap. He looked the vehicle over. The front windshield was completely gone. He could see holes in the grille of the SUV and he could hear a punctured tire hissing air.

Through the opening where the glass should have been, he could see the bloody and dead faces of the couple from Colorado who had stopped at the dead elk. They must have decided to tell the lodge owners of their discovery, he thought.

"The falconer dude is older than I thought he'd be," Abriella said to Infante. "But he's deader than hell. So's the lady he brought with him."

"He's not the falconer," Infante said.

Abriella's eyes showed alarm and confusion.

NATE SAW it, too.

He'd parked the van on the side of the entrance road and walked down through the drifts in the trees until he could see the grounds of the Arrowhead Valley Lodge. He watched as the SUV from Colorado poked across the collection of buildings and diverted to meet a woman in the distance near a well-appointed house.

He recognized her as the same woman who'd had the argument

in the parking lot of the Saddlestring motel. Only this time she had an automatic weapon.

Nate winced at the sound of gunfire and he instinctively reached up to grasp the grip of his .454 Casull in its shoulder holster. He drew the revolver and steadied it against a tree trunk. It was a long distance, but he could make the shot, he knew. He'd done it before.

But she walked forward until the shot-up vehicle was between her and the crosshairs of Nate's scope.

Then a man riding an ATV appeared.

Nate studied him through his scope. He recognized the man as well. The crosshairs sat steady on his forehead.

It was obvious the man had just said something to the woman that made her angry. He looked like he enjoyed doing it.

"Nate? What was that sound?"

It was Liv. She'd gotten out of their van and she was following his tracks.

"It sounded like a gun," she said.

He turned and there she was, lurching clumsily from tree to tree through the deep snow. She had her hand out to rest on tree trunks for balance so she wouldn't fall. She was being overly cautious.

"*Shhhhhhh*," Nate hissed, holding his index finger to his lips.

She stopped and cocked her head to the side. She was out of breath from the hike.

Then Nate realized something.

Based on what Joe had told him on the phone, the man and

the woman down below on the grounds of the lodge were part of an assassination team. That meant there were two others out there . . . somewhere.

The woman had mistaken the couple from Colorado for Nate and Liv. And they'd slaughtered them in cold blood.

Liv—and their child—could have been down there.

He was suddenly flooded with a cold rage unlike anything he'd ever felt before.

When he turned back to his scope, they were gone. The man and the woman killers had either gone into the house or into another building.

He stood up and slid his weapon into its holster.

"Nate, what's going on?" Liv asked. "Who were those people down there ahead of us?"

"Tourists who took the wrong road at the wrong time," Nate said. "But it could have been us."

INFANTE TRIED to stifle his grin as he followed Abriella into the owner's house. She was waving her arms and cursing in both English and Spanish.

"So how was I supposed to know?" she asked him. "That car showed up when the falconer said he'd be here."

"I know," he said. "I think they came down to report those elk we shot. There was no way to warn you because you'd blown their heads off before I could tell you."

"So where is the falconer?" she asked.

"I don't know. He could still be on his way."

"Did you get the game warden?"

"He never showed up," Infante said.

She stood completely still for a moment, but he could see the blackness take over her eyes.

"How could this happen?" she asked. "Why didn't they come?" There was a hint of panic in her question.

He pounced. "Remember what you said to me when we went after the wrong old couple? You said, 'It's time to turn off the slow waltz. It's time to rock and roll.' Well, this is what happens. We all fuck up—even you."

It felt good to get it out, to confront her with her own words.

"So what do we do now?" she asked.

"You're the team leader," he said. "I've been replaced, re-member?"

And he saw a sight that astonished him. There were tears brimming in her eyes. He'd hurt her.

"Abriella," he began to say, but she was quick. She raised the pistol and aimed it at his face.

"I could shoot you nine times before you hit the ground."

He didn't respond. He'd left the shotgun and H&K on the ATV. If he reached behind his back for his pistol or bent over to grasp his boot knife, it would all be over. He stayed still and calm.

She said, "You remind me of the men who held me for six months. You're like them: overconfident assholes who are full of themselves. They raped me every day, but even worse, they denigrated me while they did it. They told me I was a whore, that I was trash. They tried to destroy me as a person. I'm not going to let you do that, either."

He didn't know whether to speak or stay silent. He hoped his eyes conveyed sympathy. Infante said, "I may be like them, but I wasn't there, Abriella. Let's not relive that time in your life now."

Her mouth twitched. He waited for the gun to fire.

He said, "My guess is that because of what happened in front of the courthouse, everything is chaos right now. No one is looking for us at the moment. We have a window of time to act and get out of here. I think we should take advantage of it."

Then she lowered the pistol. "You're right. Fuck the falconer," she said. "Fuck the game wardens. What can they do to us? We'll get them later.

"Let's go meet up with Adelmo and Cesar," she said. "It's time to get Mecca."

She turned on her heel and marched out toward the ranch truck. There was no acknowledgment of his strategy or leadership, and no apology. As far as she was concerned, she was still very much in charge.

Infante closed his eyes and let out a trembling breath of relief.

Abriella was so impulsive, so mercurial. He'd fully expected her to kill him. That he'd talked himself out of it was a miracle of sorts.

But that didn't mean that everything would ever be the same between them. He knew that she could turn on him again in a heartbeat.

She was too damaged and dangerous to remain alive, he concluded. He'd need her ruthlessness for the operation in front of them, but after it was over, he'd put a bullet into her brain when she least expected it.

But he'd rape her and humiliate her first for how she'd treated him in front of their crew. He needed to see her tears again.

He was at least owed *that*.

CHAPTER TWENTY-FIVE

‖‖

TWENTY MINUTES LATER, Joe's pickup nearly fishtailed off the road into a stand of old growth spruce when he rounded a corner too fast on Elkhorn Drive on the way to the Hill compound.

He forced himself to slow down and he checked to make sure Katelyn was still behind him. She was.

As he groped for the Bluetooth button to call ahead to Lucy, Marybeth's name appeared on his cell phone screen. He accepted the call.

"Hey," Joe said. "Can I call you right back?"

"*Thank God* you're all right," she said.

"I'm fine. What's going on?"

"Something happened outside the county building," she said in a rush of words. "There are sirens everywhere . . . One of my patrons came running in here and said a bunch of people are lying dead on the stairs outside. I knew you were there for that meeting . . ."

"I left early," Joe said as his chest tightened and his vision blurred.

A bunch of people.

"I tried to call Dulcie," Marybeth cried. "It went straight to message."

"Oh no," he said. "No, no, no."

"Somebody said it was a drive-by shooting," Marybeth said. "A bunch of people got shot coming out of the building together."

As she spoke, he passed the entrance to the Behrman place. The entrance was still blocked by sheriff's department sawhorses linked with yellow crime scene tape.

"I'm going to get Lucy," he said. "Then I'll come straight back."

"Do you think Dulcie was shot?" Marybeth asked. "And what about Mike Reed?"

"I don't know. I don't know. They were both in the meeting."

"It sounds like all hell is breaking loose out on the street right now."

He could hear the sirens in the background.

She said, "Bring Lucy home safe, Joe."

"I will." Then: "Close the library. Go home, lock the doors, and get your shotgun out and ready. There are at least four killers on the street right now."

"Four killers?"

"Yes. I just learned about them. They're the ones Nate saw the other night."

"They're here? Are they the people who did this?"

"I don't know. I think so."

"What about Dulcie?"

"I don't know," Joe said. "I hope she's okay. Right now, I'm just worried about Lucy and you. I think the killers are on the way to the Hill place."

He punched off and immediately called Lucy's name over the Bluetooth system. He hoped she would answer her phone right away because often she didn't.

"Dad?"

"Lucy, I'm on my way there right now. Have them open the gate."

"What's going on?"

"I can't explain it all right now," he said, "but believe me. Tell Bill Hill to open the gate for two Game and Fish pickups. Nate is on the way as well in his van with Liv."

He could hear her ask someone about opening the gate. When she came back on she said, "Mr. Hill says he'll open the gate, but only if you'll be civil."

Joe heard Hill laugh in the background. It enraged him.

"Tell him," Joe said, "that the Wolf Pack knows where he lives and they're on their way."

"What does that mean?" Lucy asked.

"Never mind. Just tell him."

He heard Lucy repeat the words. Hill stopped laughing.

"Dad, Mr. Hill says he's ready to open the gate right now."

"Good. Tell him to close the gate tight as soon as we're through it."

"Dad, is this about the shooting in town?"

Joe said, "What do you know about that?"

"I saw it on Instagram," she said. "Somebody said five people got shot."

Joe struggled for breath. Dulcie, Mike, Magazine, Sandburg, Pollock, Coon. That was six. Someone must have gone unharmed or the count was off. He could barely wrap his mind around it either way.

"You know more than I know," Joe said. "Just make sure that gate is open. And tell Hill and Justin to get ready to run."

"You're scaring me," she said.

"I'm scared myself," he said.

After they disconnected, he reached down beneath the dashboard and changed the channel of his radio from the Game and Fish frequency to the mutual aid band open to all law enforcement.

It was absolute chaos.

Through choking sobs, he heard the dispatcher say, "Sheriff Reed is dead and so is our county attorney . . ."

Then something about three FBI agents also gunned down.

When he saw Nate's Yarak, Inc. van fold in behind Katelyn's pickup in the rearview mirror, he thumped the steering wheel with the heel of his hand and said: "*Yes!*"

THE HEAVY STEEL gates were swinging inward when Joe rounded the last corner through the trees. He didn't slow down. The panels weren't yet fully open, but there was enough of a gap that he could fit his pickup through them into the compound yard.

The scene in the yard of the compound was unnervingly familiar: Bill Hill, Papa Hill, and Jeff Wallace standing around the smoking Big Green Egg.

Only this time there was a marked difference: Jeff Wallace had a Bushmaster ACR semiautomatic rifle with a thirty-round magazine over his shoulder, as well as a sidearm in a shoulder holster. Papa Hill sat in his lawn chair smoking a cigarette with his short double-barreled shotgun across his lap. Bill Hill appeared unarmed.

Lucy and Justin huddled together on the covered porch of the main house.

Joe skidded to a stop and bolted out of the cab of his pickup with his shotgun. Katelyn was right behind him, but she stayed inside her truck. Nate swung his van around the two Game and Fish vehicles and parked next to Joe's unit.

"We've got ribs smoking this time," Wallace said with bravado. "Pull up a chair."

"No time for that," Joe said.

He looked squarely at Bill Hill. "The jig is up. It's time to evacuate before they get here. I'm taking Lucy with me."

Hill smiled slightly and disagreed. He said, "Not to worry. I've got it handled." He nodded toward Wallace and Papa Hill with their weapons and said, "This is just for backup."

"What do you mean you've got it handled?" Joe asked. Hill was much too cocky for the situation at hand, he thought.

"I made a call," Hill said. "The cavalry is on the way."

Joe thought about it for a moment, then said: "Who did you call? Sandburg and Pollock?"

The mention of the names made Hill's mouth twitch. It was as if he said, *How do you know about them?*

"They didn't answer their phones, did they?" Joe asked.

"I left a message," Hill responded. "When I leave them a message, they jump."

"Not this time," Joe said. "My information is that the Wolf Pack got them in town. The same with their boss."

Hill's eyes got big and his face drained of color.

"No way," Wallace said dismissively.

"Jeff, shut up!" Hill barked. Then to Joe: "When did this happen?"

"Within the hour," Joe said. "My info is that all of them were gunned down in front of the courthouse in a drive-by. The sheriff and county prosecutor got hit as well."

Hill slowly shook his head, absorbing the news. When he looked back to Joe, his expression was wary. "Are you sure it's the Wolf Pack?"

"I'm not sure of anything," Joe said. "Everything is speculation right now. But from what I heard from Magazine and your protector agents this morning, it stands to reason that the killers are probably on their way here right now to finish their job."

Hill stepped back and almost stumbled. He seemed temporarily confused.

Joe realized that Nate was now standing next to him. He glanced over to the van and saw Liv in the passenger seat.

"Is there another way in or out of here besides going through the front gate?" Nate asked Hill.

"No," Hill said, shaking his head. "We made sure there was

only one so people couldn't sneak up on us. The feds helped us design it."

Joe confirmed that with a quick sweep of his gaze in every direction. The Hill compound was a clearing in the tight forest surrounded by walls of trees. There were no openings between the trunks of the lodgepole pines wide enough for a vehicle to get in or out.

"Amateurs," Nate hissed, indicating the Hill compound and everyone in it.

Then to Joe: "But those four people coming are professionals. The drive-by in town was step one. They tried to ambush Liv and me at the same time. It's all designed to clear the deck and confuse everyone as to what is really going on. We're trapped if we don't get out of here fast."

Joe nodded. He agreed with Nate. To Bill Hill, he said, "This discussion is over. You can get your guys and clear out or stay— I'm not going to argue with you or beg you to come. But I'm taking my daughter out, and Justin, if he wants to go."

As Joe shouldered his way around Hill toward the main house and Lucy, Hill said, "Hold it. Just hold it. I know how we can find out if they're close."

Joe hesitated.

Hill said, "There is only one road from the gate to the highway. If we all drive out of here and turn the wrong way, we might run right into them."

It made sense. Joe waited for more.

"Follow me," Hill said. He strode quickly toward the out-building where his vehicles were parked. Joe was on his heels.

Nate followed while Katelyn got out and went to escort Lucy and Justin into the vehicles.

"I hope this doesn't take long," Joe said to Hill.

"Mere seconds," Hill said over his shoulder. "I'm going to put a drone up so we can see what's out there."

"You've got a replacement?" Joe asked.

"Yes. As you know, someone wrecked my first one," Hill said with bite.

He raised the hatchback of his SUV to reveal a second DJI Phantom 4 Pro as well as a computer tablet and controls. Nate and Joe stood aside.

"We'll be able to see everything in the area," Hill said as he went about his work.

Joe looked to Nate. Nate didn't object.

Joe plucked the handheld radio from his belt and turned it on. There was a cacophony of desperate voices and the dispatcher was still sobbing. Protocol had gone out the window, and cops were talking over each other. There was no point trying to break through, trying to somehow get a response team organized and en route to the Hill compound.

"We're on our own," he said.

"As it should be," Nate said with a wolfish smile that made Joe uneasy. He placed his big hand on Joe's shoulder. "As someone once said, things are about to get Western."

Joe was afraid he was right.

He turned to Bill Hill. "So, you're in the witness protection program."

"I'm not supposed to talk about it."

"The secret is out," Joe said. "How were you able to get your family and your thugs into the program with you?"

"It wasn't that hard," Bill said. "The feds do that kind of thing all the time. I was surprised myself when they asked me to make a list of my closest associates who should come with me."

"Jeff Wallace is one of them," Joe said. "But what about Tom Kinnison? Where is he really?"

He shrugged. "Swole went on vacation in Arizona and never came back."

"Swole?"

"That's what we called him."

"What is *your* real name?"

"Ernie Mecca," the man said as he carried the drone out and placed it on its stand in the gravel. Joe was unfamiliar with the name, but he didn't expect to know it. Mecca quickly pushed buttons on the aircraft so it would power up.

"What was your job in the Sinaloa cartel?" Joe asked. "Were you the New York boss?"

"Nothing like that," Mecca said while untangling the cords for the controls. "I was the CFO. As such, I made all the payments. I was the only guy who knew the names and travel plans for each and every fentanyl mule. It's a very complicated system, as you might imagine. I was the only man who knew the details."

"And you still do," Joe said. "Which is why the feds still protect you."

Mecca gave Joe a *What can I say?* look.

Nate interrupted. "Are you two going to stand here and chat for a long time?"

"There are things I need to know," Joe said to him. "With the way things are going, I may not get another chance."

Nate rolled his eyes and crossed his arms over his chest.

Joe turned back to Mecca. "How do you live with yourself knowing what you've done?"

"It's surprisingly easy," Mecca said.

"How many people died because of you?"

Mecca didn't flinch. "We didn't put guns to drug addicts' heads and force them to take fentanyl, much less misuse the product. Those kinds of people are determined to kill themselves anyway. And if not us, it would have been somebody else."

"That's really cold."

"That's business, Mr. Game Warden."

"Why did you turn?" Joe asked.

"Do you mean why did I become a rat?"

"Yes."

"Please, guys," Nate said, "we're wasting time here."

Mecca ignored him and nodded toward the main house. "I didn't want my son to join the family business."

Mecca turned his back to Joe and grasped the tablet with both hands. After opening up the application, the drone came alive and rose straight up.

Joe and Nate watched as it shot up and cleared the tops of the trees.

Joe moved closer to Mecca so he could see the image on the tablet from the drone camera. The image was remarkably sharp. Mecca deftly guided the device as its lens point of view swept

Elkhorn Drive to the south. He noted the Behrman crime scene as the drone zoomed by.

"Does Justin know?" Joe asked Mecca.

"He knows nothing," Mecca said. "I'd appreciate it if you kept the secret. It's not his fault his old man fell in with the wrong businessmen."

"I'll do that," Joe said. "But tell me: Who is the Wolf Pack?"

"The road is clear all the way to Winchester," Mecca said. "I'll take a look the other way."

Joe watched the screen as the drone reversed direction with remarkable agility.

"I used to think the Wolf Pack was a myth made up to keep the soldiers and mules in line," Mecca said. "But I learned they were real. In fact, I was the one who paid them for services rendered.

"Pedro Infante, Adelmo Cruz, Cesar Reyes, and a young woman named Abriella Guzman. Together they're the Wolf Pack, but I didn't know it at the time. I just placed the deposits in four separate accounts."

Joe looked to Nate, and Nate nodded his confirmation. Three men, one attractive woman.

"From the stories I've heard," Mecca said, "Guzman is the most violent and ruthless of them all."

Elkhorn Drive was a tan ribbon with heavy timber on both sides. The drone kept far above it, surveying the road to the north. Joe saw the Behrman place again, then a glimpse of buildings that comprised the Hill compound. After the drone had passed, he heard a wisp of the propellers from far above them.

"What was that?" Nate asked. He reached out and tapped the tablet screen with his index finger.

"What?" Mecca said.

"I thought I saw something."

"The road is clear," Mecca said. "There are no cars on it at all in either direction."

"Bring that thing back," Nate said. "And this time, take it off Elkhorn Drive. Let's see the road into *this* place."

Joe felt his throat get tight. He watched as the drone did a rollover, which provided a full screen of blue sky, and then it shot back toward the two-track path to the compound itself . . .

Just in time to see a maroon Yukon smash through the gate and wedge itself between the rock columns. Outside, Joe heard the heavy crash.

"Oh shit," Mecca said. His face was drained of color when he looked up. "*They're here.*"

As Mecca tossed the tablet aside and dropped to a crouch, Joe was left with the last image he'd seen on the screen: a three-quarter-ton ranch pickup sliding to a stop behind the Yukon and a man and a woman jumping out.

IT ALL HAPPENED too fast.

Katelyn heard the crash and looked up from the porch of the main house to see the Yukon hit the gate open and stop. There was a pickup behind it with ARROWHEAD VALLEY RANCH stenciled on the door. Before she could react, the front doors of the

SUV swung open and two men emerged with automatic weapons. They used the open doors as cover and raised their weapons.

She reached out and grasped the collars of Lucy and Justin and jerked them back.

"Get in the house and get down," she yelled.

The sound from the submachine guns was akin to two chain saws cutting through timber. Jeff Wallace instantly went down before he could even arm his own weapon, and the impact of the rounds tipped Papa Hill straight back in his chair with his arms flopped to his sides and his shotgun thrown aside. The Big Green Egg broke into halves and both coals and pork ribs spilled out.

Katelyn ushered Lucy and Justin past her and in through the open door of the house.

When she looked over her shoulder, the Yarak, Inc. van rocked with incoming gunfire and the glass blew out of the side windows and windshield.

Liv Brannon somehow managed to get her door open. She ran toward Katelyn with one hand over her belly and the other flared above her head to ward off bullets as if they were falling raindrops. There was a bloom of blood on her right side.

In her years of fieldwork, Katelyn had never drawn or fired her weapon on duty before, and she fumbled her first attempt to undo the safety strap of her Glock in its holster. Then it was out and in her hand while she galloped down the porch steps to meet Liv. She snapped off four wild shots in the general direction of the SUV.

A rooster tail of rounds tore across the dirt of the yard, missing Liv by inches but peppering Katelyn from her knee to her neck.

It didn't hurt as much as immediately make her numb and cold. Her weapon dropped from her hand and her eyes rolled back as she pitched to the left.

Her last sight was of Liv diving into the open door of the main house.

JOE SAW it happen, but could do nothing to stop it. He ran from the open outbuilding with his shotgun. His destination was a thick concrete abutment that supported the footbridge over the stream. Mecca was on his heels like a puppy as Katelyn stepped in front of Liv and fired her service weapon. Then she went down as if her legs had been kicked out from under her.

For Joe, it was an out-of-body experience. He felt as if he were observing himself run across the compound yard toward the main house from above, as if *he* were the drone, while the two men from the SUV raked bullets in every direction. He didn't like his odds for getting to cover before he became a target himself.

To his left, Papa Hill was laid out and Jeff Wallace was a heap of tangled limbs. In front of him, Katelyn Hamm was still and on her side in the spring grass.

He caught a glimpse of Lucy's blond hair as she reached out and helped Liv inside the main house.

He thanked God that she was okay.

In his peripheral vision, Joe saw the dark handsome man sneaking along the side of the house with his handgun drawn and a submachine gun hanging under his armpit by a shoulder strap. He was the one who had come in the ranch pickup with the woman, and he was peering into the windows along the exterior.

Where he would likely see Lucy, Justin, and Liv in there.

Joe stopped short of the abutment and racked the pump on his shotgun and dropped to one knee. Mecca slammed into him from behind and nearly fouled up his aim. He swatted back at Mecca to warn him off.

The man on the side of the house looked up and saw Joe at the same time the bead of the shotgun muzzle settled on his chest. For a split second, their eyes locked.

Boom.

The dark handsome man slumped against the house and slid down it, leaving smears of blood on the siding until he settled into a seated position with his back to the exterior wall, as if he were taking a nap.

Before Joe could rack in another shell, clumps of mud danced around him as one of the machine gunners homed in. He heard bullets smack flesh behind him and Mecca grunt *"Ooof"* with each round that hit him.

Then, with a wallop that felt like he'd been hit with the full swing of a baseball bat against his shoulder, Joe was thrown to the side and there was dirt and grass in his mouth.

He thought, *That's it, Marybeth.*

Then: *Where's Nate?*

AT THE SAME TIME, Nate duckwalked along the stone fence with his head down and his .454 Casull cocked. He could see the front end of the Yukon protruding from the bashed-down gate and the barrels of the automatic weapons as they bucked and fired. Sizzling spent casings rained through the air.

But he could not yet get a visual of the shooters.

He'd been out the side door of the outbuilding when they'd opened up. There were two men down near the grill and another body in a red shirt—Katelyn Hamm—near the porch of the main house. The Yarak, Inc. van was pockmarked by dozens of rounds and he could only pray that Liv and the baby were all right.

Out in the yard, he saw Joe drop to a knee and raise his shotgun and fire off to the side of the main house. Then a flurry of bullets hit all around his friend, but the primary target was Ernie Mecca. Mecca was hit multiple times and he lost his bearings and went down.

And so did Joe.

Nate screamed with rage and charged the Yukon just as both shooters paused to eject their magazines and reload.

Mistake.

Using the stone side column of the gate as cover, Nate peered around the rock with his weapon at his side. The closest shooter was two feet away and he looked up as Nate painted the side of the SUV with his head.

The second shooter dropped down so that he couldn't be seen on the other side of the vehicle.

Nate stepped back and fired three rounds into the side of the Yukon. The third bullet passed through both doors and took off the bottom jaw of the second gunner. As the man rose from the utter bloody shock of it, Nate finished him with another head shot.

Then *he* reloaded.

INFANTE HEARD the heavy barks from the direction of the front gate, but he couldn't get his limbs to move. The H&K was pinned behind him against the exterior wall of the house and his handgun was somewhere near his feet. Blood pumped out of a dozen buckshot holes in his chest and stomach from the shotgun blast. He had no doubt that pellets had torn through the soft tissue of his core and severed his spine. That's why he couldn't react.

He knew he was as good as dead.

That damned game warden. Why hadn't the man seen Abriella sneaking down the other side of the house first? Instead of *him*?

After all, it had all been Abriella's stupid plan to charge the compound like that. To send Cruz and Reyes to ram through the front gate and open up on every living being within sight.

Since there was no more submachine gun fire after the four booming shots, Infante was pretty sure that Cruz and Reyes had been taken out. They could no longer provide cover fire while he and Abriella hunted down Ernie Mecca once and for all.

He closed his eyes briefly and heard his own breath rattle within his lungs. It sounded like blowing air into a water glass through a straw. He'd seen men bleed out as well as drown in their own blood before. He didn't have long.

From the moment Abriella had taken over, he'd known deep in his heart this was how it would likely end for him and the others. She'd placed her own welfare over theirs. Her savage and youthful exuberance had guided her every move. Her plans had been conceived on the fly. Sometimes they worked. This one hadn't.

When she appeared from around the back of the house, she was ecstatic. She skipped to where Infante was and crouched down beside him. Her eyes took in the blood on the siding and settled on the pool of it forming in his lap.

"We got him," she said in a rush of happy words. "Ernie Mecca, the old man, the bodyguard, the two game wardens—we got them *all*."

"You got everyone killed," Infante said. "Including me."

"You'll be all right," she said, reaching down and tugging on his arm. "Come with me and we'll get you to a doctor."

"It's too late for that."

"Oh, come on," she said. "Don't be so gloomy all the time."

She pulled on his arm and he flopped to the grass near her feet. He couldn't move.

"You're crazy," Infante said. "You destroyed the Wolf Pack. You're fucking batshit insane and you got us all killed."

"Not me," she said as her eyes went black. "And don't talk to me like that. I *am* the fucking Wolf Pack."

At first he thought she was pressing her fingertip against his temple. Then he realized it was too cold. It was the muzzle of her weapon.

AFTER GLANCING INSIDE the house to confirm that Liv, Lucy, and Justin were alive, Nate turned and ran to check on Joe.

He heard the shot when he was a few steps from his friend's prone body.

He instinctively spun around toward the sound of it with his revolver cocked, in time to see the woman retreat toward the rear of the main house.

Nate fired a snap shot that took a chunk out of her right shoulder and spun her to the ground. She scrambled on all fours and crawled out of his sight behind the house before he could hit her again.

"Can you move?" he asked Joe.

"Don't know."

"You got hit in the shoulder," Nate said, clinically rolling him from side to side to look him over. "There's also blood on your neck. Were you hit anywhere else?"

"I don't think so," Joe said. His face was white and there was a smear of mud on his cheek. Nate rubbed it clean with his thumb.

"It looks like the bullet entered your left shoulder and exited the front," he said, touching an exposed shard of bone near Joe's throat. "I think you've got a broken collarbone."

Joe grunted and winced. The shock was wearing off.

"I can bind up that wound so you won't lose any more blood. Can you walk?" Nate asked.

"Maybe."

"Then come with me. We've got to go after the last one. She's on foot. The other three are deader than hell."

"Katelyn got hit bad," Joe said.

Were the tears in his eyes from the pain?

SUNDAY, JULY 8

Then everything includes itself in power,
Power into will, will into appetite;
And appetite, a universal wolf,
So doubly seconded with will and power,
Must make perforce a universal prey,
And last eat up himself.

SHAKESPEARE,
TROILUS AND CRESSIDA

CHAPTER TWENTY-SIX

THE WEDDING OF Nate Romanowski and Olivia Brannon took place on a too-hot afternoon on the grassy bank of the Twelve Sleep River near Joe Pickett's new warden station. Guests sat on metal folding chairs in the tall grass under the shade of the river cottonwoods, and bees zipped through the wildflowers so that the soundtrack for the ceremony was a low buzzing sound. On the surface of the river, trout rose for newly hatched caddis flies.

Joe wore his ill-fitting suit and best hat. He stood next to Nate and felt a thin stream of sweat sluice down his spine into his trousers. He'd left the sling for his arm in his bedroom, but he planned to don it again as soon as the reception began. His shoulder and neck still ached every morning.

The ceremony was performed by a dubious reverend from Cody named Mark Landerman, who was one of Nate's falconry buddies. Landerman had a long gray beard and he'd arrived

363

with two red-tailed hawks and a Bible. His birds were hooded and perched on a long stoop occupied by most of Nate's entire Air Force: nine hooded raptors who sat erect one by one on a dowel rod that had been hung from the branches of the trees. The birds were somber onlookers and they reminded Joe of a choir that refused to sing.

Liv looked luminous, he thought. She wore a shoulderless white gown that made her smooth mocha skin look even more striking than usual. The large bouquet of sunflowers she held in front of her did little to hide her swelled belly.

At the time, Joe had been surprised to learn that she'd been hit in the attack, that a bullet had broken the skin of her side and creased her ribs. Another few inches and both Liv and the baby might have been mortally wounded.

"Does the best man have the ring?" Landerman asked Joe.

"Yup."

Joe dug into his jacket pocket and then looked up at Nate, feigning alarm.

"You can't find the ring?" Landerman asked. Joe shook his head. There was a titter from the crowd.

Then Nate stepped back, pulled on a thick welder's glove, and raised his right arm. The peregrine that had been circling unnoticed above flew down and gently landed on it. Joe reached over and untied the ring from the falcon's leather jess and handed it to Nate.

The crowd applauded and Landerman smiled. Joe winked at Marybeth to acknowledge his role in the ruse.

The band was simple white gold and it would look good next

to Liv's diamond ring. The stone was mounted in the crux of two gold talons. Nate had designed it himself.

As he handed the band to Landerman, Joe took in the small crowd. He found himself instantly melancholy over who was there and who wasn't.

His entire family sat in the front row in their sundresses and sandaled feet: Marybeth, Sheridan up from Saratoga, April over from Powell, and Lucy. Just looking at them gave him a lump in his throat.

Justin Hill wore his Navy blues and sat directly behind Lucy.

Ex-governor Spencer Rulon sat behind Marybeth with a rakish grin on his face the entire time, like this wedding had been his plan all along. He'd come alone, but he'd spread his arms out along the top of two chairs on either side as if to discourage visitors.

Sheriff Bob Marek and his wife, Cindy, occupied the third row. The two Marek boys thankfully took after their mother, Joe thought. They stood with Tyler and Brody Hamm, who were now living with Katelyn's sister's family in Casper. Joe felt for them and couldn't even imagine what they were going through.

Liv's mother, a spitfire from Louisiana, wore steel-framed glasses and a hat so wide it provided shade for her *and* Liv's younger sister seated next to her.

But Joe also saw who wasn't there. On empty chairs in the back there was no Dulcie Schalk, no Katelyn Hamm, no Ryle Hamm, and no Sheriff Mike Reed.

Marybeth had started a campaign to rename the Wyoming

Game and Fish headquarters in Cheyenne the Katelyn Hamm Building in honor of the fallen game warden. Joe had asked his supervisor to let him make the case to the Game and Fish Commission at their next meeting.

Dulcie, who had said she'd try to make the wedding, was unable to. She was still at her family ranch near Laramie recovering from five gunshot wounds. She was on administrative leave—perhaps for good.

She'd been one of two survivors of the courthouse massacre, with Jeremiah Sandburg being the other. Sandburg had been flown back to the East Coast to recover.

Chuck Coon had retired almost immediately. His decision to stop and talk rodeo standings with Stovepipe instead of go outside with the others from the meeting had saved his life, but torpedoed his desire to remain with the bureau.

ALL OF THEM had been victims of the Wolf Pack. Not to mention Ernie Mecca, Papa Hill, Jeff Wallace, Tom Kinnison, Sunnie Magazine, Don Pollock, Tim and Karen Kelleher, Rex and Fran Behrman, Fidel from the Eagle Mountain Club, the unlucky couple from Colorado, and who knew how many others.

Joe still couldn't wrap his mind around what had happened. His mental recovery had been much more difficult than his physical recovery.

Nothing like the massacre or the gunfight at the Hill compound had ever happened before in Twelve Sleep County. Because three of the victims were FBI, the incident had made national news, but quickly faded away when other events superseded it.

That wasn't the case in Saddlestring, or for Joe.

He still had trouble sleeping through the night, and the events of that day played over and over in his mind. Marybeth had suggested he should go through trauma counseling, and he'd agreed to seek it.

What he wouldn't tell the counselor, though, was what had happened on the hunt for Abriella Guzman that day. Only Nate, Liv, and Marybeth knew.

And no one else.

THEY'D PURSUED HER through the lodgepole pines away from the Hill compound. Nate was swifter and more nimble. Joe stumbled from tree to tree, relying on a combination of adrenaline and vengeance to fuel him.

The bandage Nate and Lucy had wrapped around his shoulder was tight, and the bleeding hadn't yet seeped through the fabric and tape.

They caught glimpses of her a couple of times. Once when she ran unsteadily across a mountain meadow but too distant for a shot, and another time as she scrambled over a rocky ridge before plunging down into the thick timber on the other side.

"She's hit," Nate said. "She's bleeding out. She's got to slow down soon."

Joe noted splashes of blood on grass and rocks. It was no different than tracking a wounded animal.

"Damn," Nate said with something like admiration. "There's no quit in her. I don't think there's many full-grown men who could lose this much blood and keep going."

Joe knew that on the bottom of the next incline there was a logging road that was used by locals to access an area the forest service had designated for cutting firewood. He told Nate that if she got all the way down there, it was possible she could intercept a vehicle and get away.

"She won't get that far," Nate said.

And she didn't.

"Hey," she called out. "Listen to me."

She'd stopped behind a group of boulders on the other side of a clearing.

"I was their prisoner," she said. "I'm the real victim here."

Joe and Nate stood behind thick tree trunks, using them as cover. Joe looked over and Nate's reaction was a dismissive eye roll.

"They held me for months," she cried. "They put me in a cage. When they brought me out, it was to rape me. They got me to do what they wanted."

Joe was torn on what to do, so he followed procedure. He summoned enough strength to shout, "Abriella, throw down your weapons and walk toward us. Keep your hands on the top of your head."

"They took everything from me," she said. "I'm the victim. I'll tell you everything."

Joe almost believed her. He looked to Nate for his reaction.

Nate was looking elsewhere, to the right, into a thick belt of mountain juniper.

He said, "Here they come."

"Here who comes?" Joe asked.

Nate chinned to the direction he was fixed on. Joe followed his line of sight.

The black alpha male nosed out of the brush, his attention focused on the bleeding woman in the rocks. Behind him, the rest of the pack milled impatiently. Joe got glimpses of black, brown, and tan coats.

Abriella said, "I'm really hurt bad. I can't come to you. You need to help me."

"Throw the weapons out first," Joe said.

"I will. I'm really hurt."

The semiautomatic handgun slid over the top of one of the rocks and fell to the grass at its base. It was the weapon she'd used to dispatch the handsome man.

"There, I did it," she said. Her voice sounded weak and pain-filled. "I need a doctor, fast."

Joe felt a pang of sympathy for her.

Until Nate said, "She's a manipulative little minx, isn't she? She still has the submachine gun."

Then: "There's nothing we can do for her now."

Following the lead of the black alpha male, the wolf pack broke into a sprint across the clearing toward Abriella's location. Joe could hear the heavy padding of oversized dog feet.

Apparently, Abriella couldn't until it was too late. They were on her before she could swing the weapon in their direction. She didn't know about Nate's special relationship with animals.

What Joe knew he would never forget for the rest of his life were the sounds of the attack while it was going on. Snarling, barking, breaking bones, and the inhuman cries of a woman being torn apart by sharp teeth . . .

"YOU MAY KISS the bride," Landerman said to Nate with a lopsided grin.

Acknowledgments

The author would like to thank the people who provided help, expertise, and information for this novel. Robert Anglen, investigative reporter for the *Arizona Republic*, provided valuable insights into the workings of the federal witness protection program (WITSEC) in a case gone wrong. Wyoming game warden Kim Olson provided her time, perspectives, and observations.

Jeremy Barnes, to whom this book is dedicated, is a law enforcement officer from Utah who risked his life and thwarted an armed robbery while on vacation in Montana. He said he was inspired by Joe Pickett.

Special kudos to my first readers, Laurie Box, Molly Box, Becky Reif, and Roxanne Woods.

A tip of the hat to Molly Box and Prairie Sage Creative for cjbox .net and social media assistance.

It's a sincere pleasure to work with professionals at Putnam, including Mark Tavani, the legendary Neil Nyren, Ivan Held, Alexis Welby, Ashley McClay, and Katie Grinch.

And thanks once again to my terrific agent and friend, Ann Rittenberg.